GARRISON GIRL

an ATTACK on TITAN novel

 BY
RACHEL AARON

ATTACK ON TITAN
CREATED BY
HAJIME ISAYAMA

 QUIRK BOOKS
PHILADELPHIA

Copyright © 2018 Kodansha Ltd., Tokyo. All rights reserved. Publication
rights for this novelization edition aranged through Kodansha Ltd., Tokyo.

Attack on Titan © 2009–2018 Hajime Isayama. All rights reserved.

Library of Congress Cataloging in Publication Number: 2017961225

ISBN: 978-1-68369-061-0
Printed in the United States of America
Typeset in Bembo, Meltow Sans, and Klang MT

Designed by Andie Reid
Production management by John J. McGurk

Quirk Books
215 Church Street
Philadelphia, PA 19106
quirkbooks.com

10 9 8 7 6 5 4 3 2 1

For Brian and Carmen Rivers,

Matt Braun, and Travis Bach,

the original X-Force.

Let's go beyond the walls!

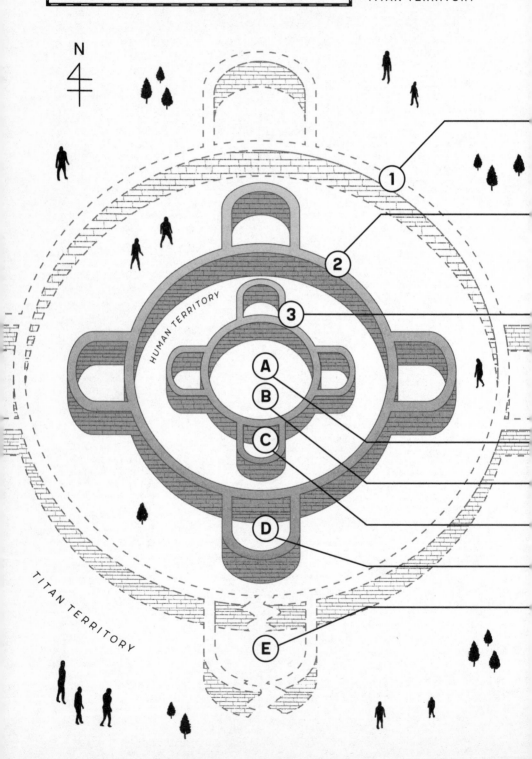

OCCUPATION MAP

N

HUMAN TERRITORY

TITAN TERRITORY

1

2

3

A

B

C

D

E

HISTORY: *After Wall Maria was breached, humanity was forced to retreat behind Wall Rose. The royal government and nobility occupy the territory within the innermost barrier, Wall Sina. Outside of these walls, titans roam the land.*

→ **1.** WALL MARIA

→ **2.** WALL ROSE

→ **3.** WALL SINA

→ **A.** Royal Capital

→ **B.** Dumarque Estate

→ **C.** Ehrmich

→ **D.** Trost

→ **E.** Shiganshina

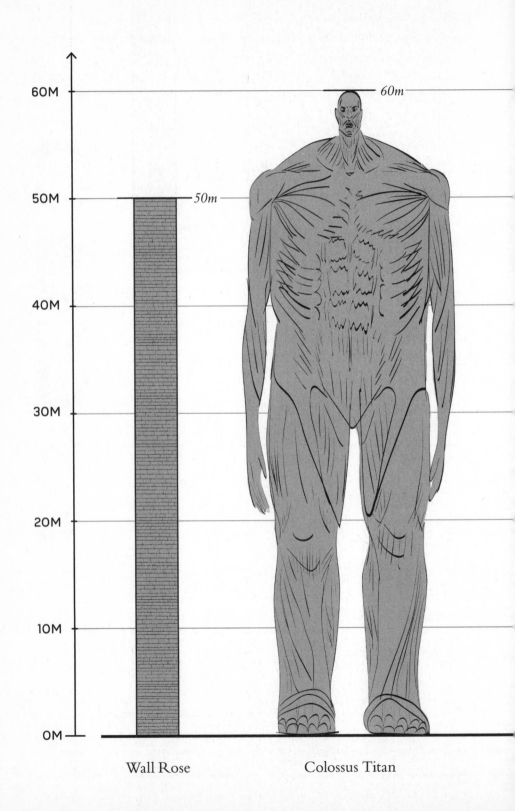

60M — ---- 60m

50M — 50m

40M —

30M —

20M —

10M —

0M —

Wall Rose   Colossus Titan

TITAN
SIZE COMPARISON
CHART

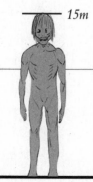

15m

7m

1.7m

15m Titan   7m Titan   Average Human

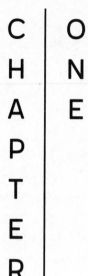

CHAPTER ONE

On a clear day, from the top of her house, Rosalie Dumarque could see all that was left of the human world.

Standing on the peaked roof of the colossal Dumarque Manor, which was itself perched atop one of the tallest hills in the district, she could look right over the fifty-meter-high circle of Wall Sina into the terrain beyond. This early in the morning, the towns and fields of the Rose Zone were still hazy with the autumn fog, but if she squinted, Rosalie could just make out the white ribbon of Wall Rose running along the horizon, 130 kilometers away.

The sight never failed to make her stomach tighten. More than a marvel of engineering, Wall Rose was a boundary. The fifty-meter-tall circle of stone marked the edge of human civilization, the end of the world.

It hadn't always been this way. For most of

her childhood, the end of the world had been at Wall Maria, nearly twice as far away. Growing up, Rosalie had considered the walls a default component of reality, like the sky or the ground. They were always there, the unbreakable barrier that shielded everything she knew from the monsters that stalked the wilderness beyond.

Then, five years ago, the monsters had broken through.

In a single day, the land left to humanity was diminished by a third. With Wall Maria broken, all territory between it and Wall Rose—all the cities and farms and forests in the Maria Zone—was now the domain of titans, not humans.

Rosalie's personal world was even smaller. She'd never been allowed outside Wall Sina, the heavily fortified inner ring that protected the king and all the noble families. She failed to see much difference; big or small, a prison was a prison. So long as titans existed, the world would always be walled in. And humans were no better than cattle in a pen, patiently waiting for the day the wolves broke through to finish them off.

As always, that bitter realization ruined the view. Clenching her fists, Rosalie pushed off the chimney she'd been leaning against and started down the steep roof. A few of the clay tiles shifted under her feet, reminding her sharply of the long fall to the ground below, but Rosalie wasn't afraid. She'd never been as graceful as her elegant older sisters, but her time in the Royal Military Academy had toned her muscles, honed her sense of balance, and erased any fear of heights. Also, she'd been climbing up here since she was tall enough to push open her bedroom window. She knew every wobbly tile by heart.

When she reached the edge of the slanted tiles, Rosalie lowered herself to sit back on her heels. Down below, her family's estate—extravagant even by noble standards—spread out like a perfect green carpet all the way to the base of Wall Sina. The army of groundskeepers was already hard at work pruning fruit trees, weeding flower beds, bringing in sheep to crop the grass, and all the other essentials necessary to keep the massive estate looking well kept.

She knew exactly how many essentials there were. Her mother had drilled her on proper land management for years, in preparation for the day when Rosalie would be lady of her own house. Soon, she'd be the one whose world revolved around making sure all the tedious little details of keeping up appearances were taken care of.

But not just yet.

Rosalie rose back to her feet. A wind blew up from the south as she stood, blowing a wisp of her blonde hair loose from its braid and into her face. Rosalie tucked the strand behind her ear impatiently as she turned to stare at Wall Rose again, its curved white line gleaming back at her like a mocking grin.

Rosalie grabbed the lip of the roof and lowered herself to her bedroom window to do what she'd come home to do.

Even with a maid to help fix her hair and lace her into the Royal Military Academy's fifteen-part dress uniform—sans swords, sheaths, spare blades, and vertical maneuvering gear—it still took Rosalie a good twenty minutes to dress. It took ten more to make her way down the stairs from the family wing, across the rose garden, through the grand ballroom, and up the stairs again to the thick carpeted hallway outside her father's office.

She knocked and stood at attention, holding herself as straight as possible while the ancient butler opened the door. As always, the old man gave Rosalie a sour look before shuffling sideways to reveal her father sitting at his desk.

Unlike Rosalie with her too-young face and highly unladylike habit of fidgeting, Charles Dumarque carried himself as every inch the noble lord he'd been bred to be. Even eating breakfast in his office at six in the morning, Lord Dumarque was impeccably dressed in the full officer's uniform of the Military Police. Every fold was pressed to a perfect crease, every medal on his chest polished to a mirror gleam. Even his hair—thinning now, but still the same golden color as Rosalie's—lay in rigid order, the short-clipped strands not daring to stir when he lifted his head to glare at his youngest daughter.

"I was wondering when you'd come," he said, reaching to turn down the oil lamp that was flickering on the shadowed side of his writing desk. Rosalie took that as evidence he'd started working before the sun rose. Her father didn't sleep through the night very often anymore. Not since the fall of Maria.

"Leave us," he told the butler.

The old servant bowed and left. When the door clicked softly behind him, Rosalie took a deep breath. "Father, I—"

"No."

She scowled. "But I haven't even told you—"

"You don't have to," he said sharply, moving the neat stack of papers to the side of his desk so he could focus the undivided force of his irritated attention on her. "There's only one reason you'd show up in my office wearing that uniform, and the answer is no. No, you may not enlist in the Military Police. No, you may not apply to the king's guard. No, you may not join the Garrison at Sina. And no, I will not allow you to re-enroll for another term at the academy." He arched a perfect eyebrow. "Did I miss anything?"

"With respect, sir," Rosalie said, fighting to keep her voice level, "I graduated from the Royal Military Academy at the top of my class. What was the point of all that training if I never get to use it?"

"A military education is never a waste," her father replied. "But you've had your fun, Rosalie. I let you play solider at the academy far longer than most fathers would, but it's time to grow up. You're sixteen now, a young lady, *and* you're engaged to be married."

"Not for six months," Rosalie reminded him. "The engagement contract clearly states that I can't be married until I turn seventeen."

"I am well aware of the contract *I* signed," he said, picking up a gold-rimmed teacup from the tray on his desk. "But that doesn't change the fact that by this time next year, you'll be a wife and running a household of your own. *That's* your future, Rosalie. That's the life you should be preparing for. I know Ferdinand Smythe isn't the best match, but he's rich, and given all the timberland we lost when Maria fell, money's what we need. This is your duty to the family. I won't ask you to be happy about it, but I do expect you to perform it as befits a lady of your station."

By the time he finished, Rosalie was imagining throwing his fancy teacup in his face. She clamped down on the urge at once. She'd spent the last week crafting a strategy for this conversation, one that even her harshest military science instructor would have approved of. But it was all for nothing if she let him make her too angry to use it.

"I'm not trying to get out of my responsibilities," she said with forced calm. "I'm holding you to yours. You promised when I got engaged that I could live as I wanted until my seventeenth birthday. Unless you're going back on your word, that means the next six months are still mine, and I intend to make the most of them."

"Doing what?" her father said, setting his cup down with a decisive *clink*. "Standing on top of Wall Sina with the Garrison and watching traffic come through the gate?"

"I don't want to go to Sina," she said, taking a deep breath. Here it went. "I want to join a Rose Garrison."

Lord Dumarque scoffed. "Don't be absurd. You know nothing about what it's really like out there. You've never even been beyond Wall Sina, much less seen a real titan."

"And I never *will* get beyond Sina if you have your way," Rosalie said. "If I'm to give the rest of my life for the glory of the Dumarque family, the least you can do is let me see what the rest of the world looks like first."

"There are plenty of places you can visit that aren't on the front line."

"I can handle the front," she said. "I've passed all the same exercises as the other recruits. I've mastered cannon tactics—standard *and* advanced—vertical maneuvering gear, swordwork, everything I need to fight."

"Vaulting around a training yard hacking at dummies is a far cry from the real thing," Lord Dumarque said crossly. "But if you're that determined to experience a soldier's life, I suppose I could arrange an internship for you in the Military Police."

That was more ground than she'd expected him to give this early, but Rosalie wasn't ready to compromise yet. "And what would I do in the Military Police?"

"Make useful contacts, hopefully," her father said. "Many noble families have children in the—"

"I know exactly where noble families send their children," Rosalie said. "They were my classmates. Every recruit in my graduating class applied to join the Military Police. They didn't care about the war. They just wanted their fancy officer's degree so they could wear a uniform and get a cushy, safe desk job as far from the titans as possible."

Lord Dumarque nodded. "A sensible way of thinking."

"It's a *cowardly* way," Rosalie said, her voice disgusted. "The Royal Academy is the best in the kingdom. We used the newest equipment, learned the most advanced tactics, no expense spared. But none of them want to put any part of that education to use. They just want to hide."

"And you think you're better if you don't?" her father snapped, back on the attack. "The Garrison has thousands of soldiers manning the walls. Do you think one more body, even a Dumarque, will make any difference?"

Rosalie stuck her chin out stubbornly. "It will make a difference to me."

Lord Dumarque leaned forward on his desk, rubbing his gloved hands against his temples. "Rosalie," he said, his voice exasperated. "I paid for you to go to school so you could learn some sense. Try to use it. You think you can go out there swords swinging like one of the heroes in those ridiculous books you read, but soldiering isn't some grand adventure. It's messy, ugly, and tediously brutal. It's not a game."

"I never thought it was," Rosalie said. "But I trained as a solider, so I want to *be* a soldier, like you are. Our family has always fought in the king's name. I only have six months left as a Dumarque. Let me use them to make sure our name remains associated with bravery and honor."

That was her big push, and for a moment, her father almost smiled. "You planned that well," he said, reaching again for his tea. "But the answer is still no."

"How can you say that?" Rosalie cried, her carefully maintained calm slipping at last. "You're always going on and on about our family pride, but you haven't visited the front lines once since Maria fell. I want to be the Dumarque who *doesn't* hide behind Wall Sina! If you really cared about our family's duty, you'd let me."

Lord Dumarque's jaw tightened dangerously. "That's enough, Rosalie."

"It is *not* enough!" she cried. "You want me to be like everyone else and spend my life hiding inside the walls where it's safe, but that's an illusion. So long as there are titans out there like the one that kicked down the gate at Shiganshina, no one is safe!"

"That's enough!" Lord Dumarque cried, rising to his feet. "You will not speak to me in that fashion!"

"I'll speak however I must to get you to listen for once," Rosalie said. "These next six months are mine, Father, and you know it. If I want to spend them on the front lines, I will."

"Want is for children," he said dismissively. "Adults live in the world of 'should' and 'must.' You are a noble lady. An engaged lady. You can't be running off to fight titans!"

"And you can't stop me," she said. "I know my rights, and I'll take this matter all the way to the king if you make me. We'll see what that scandal does to the impending Dumarque-Smythe alliance."

That was as close to extortion as Rosalie had come, and it made her father angrier than she'd ever seen. It was terrifying to behold, but Rosalie was in this with both feet. If she backed down now, she'd be stuck inside Sina for the rest of her life. She was preparing to launch her next attack when her father suddenly said, "Fine."

Rosalie blinked. "What?"

"Fine," her father repeated, visibly taking control of his anger as he lowered himself carefully back into his chair. "The wise learn from history, but fools learn from experience. Since you seem determined to be a fool, I'm going to make sure you get the most out of your lesson."

"Meaning?" Rosalie asked warily.

"It means you get your wish," Lord Dumarque said, grabbing a sheet of official military stationery from the stack on his desk and writing a short note in sharp, angry strokes before stamping it with his seal. "Effective immediately, you're assigned to the Trost Gate Garrison."

"Trost?" Rosalie said, snatching the order out of his hands. "You mean the city that juts off the southern tip of Wall Rose? That Trost?"

Her father nodded. "You want to fight titans? You'll see plenty there. Though I'm sure they'll be nothing for someone of your elite training and determination."

His tone was mocking, but Rosalie was too busy staring at the letter to be insulted. The gate at Trost opened into the lost Maria territory. And it faced south, the direction that titans, for reasons no one knew, tended to come from. The monsters would be everywhere down there, which was undoubtedly the point. Her father had clearly given her the worst assignment possible in the hopes it would send her running back home.

Not going to happen.

"Thank you for this opportunity, General," Rosalie said formally, tucking the letter into her pocket before pressing her fist against her chest in salute. "I promise I'll make you proud."

"You might want to get moving," he said, glancing at the ornate silver water clock on his mantel. "Muster is at eleven, and it's a hundred and thirty kilometers to Trost."

He trailed off, lips curling into a smirk as he watched Rosalie realize she'd been set up. Even with the fastest carriage, it would be nearly impossible for her to make such a long journey in such a short time. But she wasn't so easily beaten, and after a brief collapse, the smile popped right back onto her face.

"Then I'd better be off," she said cheerfully. "Don't want to be late for my first deployment."

Lord Dumarque's smug smile slipped, leaving him scowling as Rosalie turned and marched out of his office. The moment she was alone in the hall, she took off running, yelling for the maids to help her pack.

None of her five siblings had travel plans that day, so Rosalie was able to procure the fastest horses in the stable and the most capable driver. The moment her trunks were packed, she had half the household loading them into the carriage before bounding in herself. Only when the doors were shut and the horses were racing down the estate's manicured lanes did the tension finally start to leave her body.

"I did it," she whispered, slumping back against the carriage's velvet padded seat. "I won."

"What was that, ma'am?" the driver yelled back through the curtained window.

"Nothing," Rosalie said, lifting her voice so he could hear her over the clatter of the horses. Then her face split into a grin. "Go faster."

The man tipped his cap and whipped the horses, increasing their speed as they careened off the Dumarque's private lane onto the cobbled road that led toward Wall Sina. As they got closer, the street grew crowded with traffic. The gate especially had a massive queue of carriages and wagons waiting for inspection, but the Dumarque seal on the carriage door got them past all that. The moment the guards saw that a noble was coming, they ordered everyone to the side so that Rosalie's carriage could pass straight through.

Smiling at the hour delay she'd just avoided, Rosalie opened the carriage shutter and stuck out her head as they passed under the mountainlike shadow of Wall Sina for her first look at the world beyond.

The gate by the Dumarque estate opened into the walled city of Ehrmich, which looked disappointingly like the cities inside Sina. It had the same elegant brick houses, wide streets, manicured gardens, and well-dressed townsfolk. Everything was slightly shabbier than the interior cities she was used to, but Rosalie saw nothing truly remarkable until they passed through the second gate on the other side of town, riding out of the walled border city into the rolling countryside of the true Rose Zone.

The moment they left the wall, everything changed. The tall buildings and neatly trimmed hedges gave way to more modest homes of fieldstone and wood. Working farms and golden fields full of wheat surrounded the road, which was now dirt instead of cobblestone. The sudden change caused the speeding carriage to bounce wildly, almost sending Rosalie spilling out the window. Laughing, she gripped the frame and leaned out even further, eyes wide as she watched the countryside she'd only seen from her roof fly by.

The countryside out here was lovely and rugged, dotted with charming villages and farms. Rosalie especially liked the forests, which grew wild and huge, their trees' gnarled branches exploding with fall color—nothing like the carefully managed arbors back in Sina. Another day, she would have been telling the driver to stop every few feet so she could explore. But the sun was already worryingly high, and Rosalie's eyes were locked on the horizon ahead, where the smooth white stone of Wall Rose had already grown larger than she'd ever seen it. Rosalie could make out the massive gate, its dark shape like a pockmark in the endless wall.

Even at top speed, changing horses twice along the way, it still took three hours for the carriage to reach Wall Rose. By the time they entered its shadow, the towns had stopped being charming, or even true towns. These were the refugee camps, squalid clusters of connected hovels built by the people who'd fled the breach of Wall Maria when the titans came through. According to the proclamations of King Fritz, they were supposed to be temporary, but the shanties didn't look like they were going anytime soon. They were also still surprisingly full. Rosalie couldn't imagine why anyone would choose to remain in such terrible conditions.

As they started maneuvering through the traffic in front of the gate that would take them into Trost, Rosalie sat back down on the velvet seat and pulled out her map. It was a simplified diagram showing the three walls as perfect circles rather than the meandering ovals they actually were, but Rosalie liked the clarity. It was the driver's job to worry about specific roads; she just wanted to estimate how far they'd come. Rosalie traced her finger across the heavy line that marked Wall Rose, and found the city that jutted off it.

Each of the three great walls had four gates, one for each cardinal direction. And each gate city, Trost included, was protected by its own rampart, a semicircle of wall that jutted off of Maria, Rose, or Sina. On the map, the gate cities appeared as half-moon-shaped bumps, like flower petals. But small as they appeared on paper, each petal was enormous, packed with buildings and surrounded on all sides by a half-circle of fortifications just as tall as the main walls they were attached to.

Ostensibly, the fortified towns were there to protect the gates. But the truth, as Rosalie had learned from her instructors, was far more sinister. The border towns existed because titans were drawn to people. By concentrating large populations in heavily fortified cities, the designers of the walls had ensured the titans would attack there instead of spreading out along the entire length of the wall, which would be impossible to defend.

The effectiveness of this strategy had been proven five years ago at the southern Maria gate town of Shiganshina. The titans had indeed been drawn to the city, exactly as planned.

Only the walls hadn't held.

Scowling, Rosalie put her map away and looked up at the white expanse of stone that now dominated her forward view. This was the closest she'd ever been to Wall Rose. Unsurprisingly, it looked exactly like Wall Sina. All the walls were made of the same material: enormous, fifty-meter-tall monoliths of gray-white stone joined together by even taller vertical ribs. Details of their construction were a royal secret, but they were said to be stronger than any other material humans could produce. They didn't look breakable to her, but then, the titans hadn't come through the walls. According to the survivors of Shiganshina, the monsters had broken through the gate, let inside the city by an attack from a new titan so huge, it was known only by its size.

The Colossal Titan's appearance had been a game changer. For a hundred years, titans had been little more than boogeymen who lurked beyond the walls, out of sight. Rosalie's nurse had even claimed they didn't exist anymore, except when they snuck in to gobble up naughty children who wouldn't go to bed. All through her childhood, Rosalie had believed that, and then word came that Shiganshina was overrun.

Caught unprepared, the walled city had fallen in a matter of hours. The unstoppable horde of monsters had poured through the broken gate in Wall Maria, turning the entire ring of land between Maria and Rose into their killing ground.

With all the farmland in Maria lost and so many homeless people to feed, the kingdom's resources had been stretched past their limits. Safe inside Sina, Rosalie hadn't seen the famines, but her father had hardly come home at all that first year. He'd been too busy putting down riots with the Military Police. He never talked about those fights, but from her rooftop perch Rosalie had seen the plumes of smoke rising in the distance. She'd joined the academy the very next spring, and now, four years later, she was here, at the edge of everything.

Just as at the Sina gate, the Dumarque seal on Rosalie's carriage was all it took to bypass most of the traffic and ride through into Trost. Throwing open her window again, Rosalie stuck her head out for her first look at a real frontline city. Given where they were located, she'd always assumed the outer cities were like the refugee camps that surrounded them—savage pits full of desperate people stabbing each other over bread—but aside from being more crowded, Trost didn't look that different from Ehrmich.

Like other cities inside Rose, the wide streets here were well paved and lined with multistory brick and half-timber buildings. There was a market square bustling with vendors selling everything from live chickens to dresses and a massive military building that took up an entire block at the town center. According to the map, there was a river as well, but though Rosalie could smell the water, she couldn't see anything through the tightly packed buildings. She was wondering how much longer it would take when the racing carriage suddenly lurched to a stop right in front of the sealed outer Trost Gate.

Despite her hurry, Rosalie could only stare. She'd never seen a closed gate before. Like all the others, it was a huge slab of brick decorated with a giant white stone carving of a woman's face, the Rose of Wall Rose. But where the other gates were always raised to let traffic through, this one was lowered all the way to the ground, and the street leading up to it was blocked off by a ring of permanent cannon emplacements, their giant iron barrels pointed at the lowered gate. It was the clearest sign yet that she was actually at the front. There were titans just on the other side of that gate, and next to it was the base she'd been assigned to.

The closed gate was bracketed by two brick towers, the left of which was connected to a fortified square of long, rectangular stone buildings squeezed right up against the massive Trost wall. A flag bearing the Rose Garrison insignia hung limply above the fortress's squat wooden guard house where two soldiers in tan Garrison uniforms were leaning against the raised portcullis, trying not to get caught playing cards.

Target finally in sight, Rosalie leaped from the carriage and raced across the empty street, calling for her driver to bring in her things as she shoved her father's letter into the hands of the first soldier she reached. The startled guard seemed confused by her hurry, and by her white Academy uniform. The moment he saw Lord Dumarque's signature, however, all questions were forgotten. He let her in at once, pointing her to the stone-paved training yard where several other nervous young soldiers were already waiting. Rosalie had barely joined them when a sergeant came out and yelled for everyone new to fall in line and get up the tower stairs.

They were going to the Wall.

🏵 🏵 🏵

Rosalie had been on top of Wall Sina several times during her training. But Sina just looked down on the tame fields and genteel towns
of the inner Rose Zone. This wall looked out over a world she'd
never seen.

She was standing at parade rest with a dozen or so other recruits
atop Wall Rose. The wall was wide enough for two of her family's
carriages to drive side by side with room to spare. But even standing
on the Trost side, behind the cannon emplacements, Rosalie could
see acres and acres of open fields stretching out in front of her. The
terrain was wildly overgrown from five years of neglect, but she
could make out the remains of a road running from the sealed gate
below them to what had once been a town. Crushed and abandoned
now, there had clearly been houses and shops down there. The brisk
wind carried scents she'd never experienced before: musky, earthy
odors with a hint of decay.

She just wished her fellow recruits had been half as impressive.
Given the famous brutality of the Training Corps, she'd expected
crack soldiers, but the men and women standing around her looked
scrawny and underfed, their eyes lowered meekly. The sight was
enormously disappointing, but Rosalie had hopes she could change
things by setting a good example. She'd killed thousands of practice
targets with her cannon during training, knew all the best strate-
gies and tactics. She only had six months before her marriage, but
if she worked at it, Rosalie was sure she could spread her Academy
knowledge to the soldiers here. Once they had the benefit of the same
training she'd gotten, they'd win Maria back in no time.

She was already making plans when a line of Garrison officers
marched out onto the wall in front of them. Unlike the recruits, they
all wore full vertical maneuvering gear. The complicated system of
leather straps crisscrossed their uniforms from their necks to the tops
of their high boots. The trigger grips were holstered tight under their
shoulders, and the long, boxy, rectangular sheaths that held their

spare sword blades hung from their thighs where the extra weight wouldn't throw them off-balance.

Seeing the full gear gave Rosalie a pang of excitement. It had been weeks since she'd suited up and used her own gear. She was wondering when she'd be assigned a set of her own gear when a shout cut through the air like a cannon blast.

"Soldiers!"

Everyone jumped, the recruits pulling themselves into tight formation as a sour-faced man with wiry brown hair, small deep-set eyes, and a captain's insignia on his jacket stepped forward.

"I am Captain Woermann," he bellowed. "Commanding officer of the Trost Garrison. I don't care why you came to my division, but from this moment forward, you are my burden to bear."

He walked along the line of recruits as he spoke, staring down his nose like they'd already disappointed him.

"For various reasons, all of you have been allowed to join our ranks outside the normal training schedule," the captain went on, his nasal voice rising high and hard over the cold wind. "But don't expect any special treatment! As winter recruits, you'll have to work twice as hard to catch up with those who've been here since the spring. Our charge is the defense of Trost, a city vital to the security of the Rose Zone. This wall—" he stomped his foot on the stone "—is all that stands between the titans and humanity. As soldiers of the Garrison, you will defend it at any cost, including your life and your equipment, in that order."

Someone at the end of the formation snickered, and Woermann whirled around. "You think I'm joking?" he roared, stomping down the line until he was nose to nose with the soldier who'd laughed, a rail-thin, freckle-faced recruit who looked more like a boy than a man. "Answer the question!"

"No, Captain," the solider said, his whole body shaking.

Woermann leaned in until he was breathing down the boy's

throat. "Let me make this perfectly clear. You are the least valuable thing on this wall. If I want more hungry mouths to feed, there are plenty down in Trost. You could all die today and be replaced tomorrow, but this—" he slapped his hand against the gleaming metal flywheels at his waist that held the coiled wires for his vertical maneuvering gear "—is another matter."

The captain straightened up and resumed walking down the line, glaring at each solider in turn. "When you go on duty, you will all be issued equipment, including your own set of vertical maneuvering gear. The metal and engineering that goes into that gear is more valuable than your lives. If a single screw goes over that wall, I expect you to dive after it. Is that understood?"

"Yes, Captain!" the soldiers answered.

Rosalie had to force the words out. No one at the Academy had ever spoken to her like this. They'd yelled at her, of course—it was the military—but even at their angriest, her instructors never implied that the soldiers were worthless. But Woermann wasn't finished.

"You are the Garrison!" he cried, marching back to the front of the formation. "The human shield that protects humanity! Each and every one of you is expected to give up your life without hesitation. If I learn that one of you has been a coward or has endangered equipment to save your own hide, I will shoot you myself. Is that clear?"

The wall was silent.

"*Is that clear?*"

"Yes, Captain," the soldiers answered quietly.

Satisfied, Woermann walked away, his aides falling in behind him. As they marched down the tower stairs, another officer—a short woman with steel-gray hair, a weathered face, and a wiry body as taut as her maneuver gear cables—stepped briskly forward to take the captain's place at the front.

"Greetings, recruits," she said in a confident voice loud enough to be heard from the ground. "I'm Gate Lieutenant Brigitte Morris, and I'm in charge of the Trost Gate, its base, and the daily patrol of all surrounding walls. In few moments, I'll be dividing you into your units, but first, we have some business to take care of."

The recruits began to shuffle nervously. Confused, Rosalie watched as Lieutenant Morris walked to the edge of the wall. The Maria edge, the one that dropped into the lands where the titans roamed. For a moment, it looked like she was going to walk right off, but she stopped just short, planting her boots on a red mark someone had painted between cannon emplacements. She stood barely an arm's length away from the edge of the wall.

"This is the Red Line," Brigitte announced. "It marks the place on the wall from which you can first see the enemy."

She paused to let that sink in, but she didn't need to. The recruits were already frozen in place, their eyes locked on the scuffed red paint beneath the lieutenant's feet. Rosalie's eyes were there as well. She'd wondered why she hadn't seen any titans while she was scanning the countryside. Now, though, she realized why. There were no monsters in the fields because they were already here. Now that no one was yelling, Rosalie could actually hear a scraping noise coming from somewhere below. She realized this was the sound of giant fingers rasping across the brick of the gate. The noise seemed to go straight through her.

Brigitte wasn't finished yet. "No other gate commander does this," the lieutenant went on. "But I'm different. Five years ago, I was an officer at Shiganshina. I was there when the Colossal and Armored Titans broke through the gate. There were many tragedies that day, but the worst for me were the hundreds of soldiers who died unnecessarily because, due to the Garrison's old practice of keeping soldiers off the walls, none of us had ever seen a titan before. We didn't know what we were fighting, and when we confronted them for the first time, too many soldiers panicked, forgot their training, and became titan food."

She said this matter-of-factly, but the recruits around Rosalie were already backing away. One girl actually looked a little green.

"To keep that mistake from ever happening again," Brigitte continued, "I require that all new recruits see a titan face-to-face before they begin active duty. There's no shame in being afraid, but panic is another matter. I need to know you can handle yourselves when the time comes, so when I give the order, you will step up to the line and look the enemy in the eye. If you panic or otherwise fail to keep control, you will be sent back to Supply HQ and given a job off the wall with a commensurate drop in pay. Ready?"

The recruits murmured a faint reply, and the lieutenant lifted her arm. "First five on the end, advance!"

The five recruits shuffled forward until their boots touched the edge of the scuffed red line. Rosalie held her breath. She didn't know what she was waiting for, but it was obvious when it happened. Even just looking at their backs, Rosalie knew the moment the recruits saw the titans.

It went over them like a wave. Some froze in place. Others fell, their legs giving out as they tried to scramble backward. The girl who'd turned green actually threw up before running away, her eyes so wide Rosalie could see the whites all the way around. It seemed like a sorry showing, but Lieutenant Brigitte just shrugged and yelled, "Next!"

Five by five, the recruits stepped up to the Red Line. Some did better than others, but no one came away unaffected. Even soldiers who didn't fall left with pale faces and haunted eyes. It was horrifying to watch, but Rosalie didn't let herself look away. This was what she'd wanted, to fight at the front. Maybe the other recruits hadn't had the opportunity to see detailed illustrations of titans like she had. Or maybe their obvious lack of feeding had left them with delicate constitutions. Either way, Rosalie was determined to do better.

Rosalie moved automatically when the lieutenant ordered her

forward, but her feet seemed to grow heavier as she neared the gash of red paint. With every breath, she reminded herself that she'd trained for this. She'd seen drawings and diagrams of titans every day since her very first at the academy. She knew how to kill them, and she was on top of a fifty-meter wall, well out of their reach. There was nothing to be afraid of. She reached the Red Line, then leaned just enough to look straight down over the edge of the wall . . .

And into the eyes of a titan.

Even in her shock, Rosalie's military training kicked in, classifying the titan at about eleven meters. Taller than the mature oak trees in her uncle's hunting park. She forced herself to keep looking, and saw that smaller monsters were clustered at its feet. Four- and five-meter-tall titans, who barely came up to the larger monster's waist.

Other than their size, they looked human, at first. The biggest one had a human man's wrinkled, bearded face. It had human eyes, and human hands, reaching up the wall toward Rosalie like a toddler trying to grab candies off a shelf. And that was where things went wrong, because while Rosalie's brain told her she was looking at a giant man, something else, some much deeper instinct, knew there was nothing human about that *thing*.

It started with the shape. Titan body types varied, but their human-contoured bodies were always distorted, as if they wanted to mock humanity by their very appearance. This particular giant had a torso that stretched far too long compared to its limbs and a head that was two sizes too big for its body. Its wagon-wheel-sized eyes were the same brown as Rosalie's, but empty. There was no intelligence, no spark of recognition as they fixed on Rosalie. Just the bright gleam of manic joy. A perfect match for the toothy, open-mouthed grin spreading across its hideous face.

As the monster's jaws opened, the hot reek from its cavernous mouth rose up the wall, making Rosalie's stomach churn. The stench of decay was worse than dead cattle in high summer. As its mouth stretched wider, Rosalie could see where the smell was coming from. The titan's thick lips and huge, flat teeth—each one as large as her bedroom window—were crusted with the brownish-red of dried blood. The stain ran down its beard as well, forming a clotted mat in the tangled hair. In it, Rosalie saw chunks of half-chewed, rotting flesh, one of which looked suspiciously like a human foot.

Rosalie stumbled backward, her lungs gasping for air that no longer seemed to exist. The titan's eyes followed her movement, and it licked its bloody lips with a tongue as wide as the carriage she'd ridden in, sending a fresh blast of hot, putrid air wafting up the wall. It hit Rosalie in the face, and she slapped her hand over her mouth, fighting not to vomit.

As she tried desperately not to be sick, she told herself over and over that the titan couldn't reach her up here on the wall. But that logic couldn't beat past the instinct that was screaming at her to run. To flee all the way back to her room inside Wall Sina.

That was what cleared Rosalie's head. Running home with her tail between her legs was intolerable. She clenched the hand covering her mouth into a fist. She couldn't fail now. Not after fighting so hard to get here. Not when she hadn't even begun.

With that, Rosalie yanked her arm down and forced herself to look at the bearded titan again.

She would shoot it through the mouth, she decided. One good cannon shot to the back of its throat would blow right through the spine and destroy the weak spot at the rear of its neck, the only sure way to kill a titan. She was imagining how its headless body would tumble like a felled tree when a firm hand gripped her shoulder.

Rosalie jumped, turning with a start to see Lieutenant Brigitte standing beside her. "You all right, solider?"

When Rosalie nodded, the lieutenant smiled. "Welcome to the Garrison," she said, clapping Rosalie on the shoulder. "Just make sure you replace that uniform with a standard issue one before tomorrow."

"Yes, ma'am," Rosalie said, but the lieutenant had already moved on to the next soldier, who was crying on the ground.

Farther down the wall from the recruits, a pair of seasoned veterans sat on top of a large stationary cannon, enjoying the show.

"Lot of pukers this time," the older one quipped, taking a bite of the green apple in his hand. "I swear, they get worse every year."

"They're just soft," said the other one, a young, black-haired soldier with hard blue eyes. "But they'll toughen up, or they'll die." He nodded at one recruit in particular. A well-groomed girl with an athletic build who was staring at the titans like she wanted to bite their heads off. "That one's trouble, though."

"Who? The blonde girl?" The old veteran squinted down the wall. "She looks nice enough."

"Too nice," the young soldier said, hopping off the cannon. "Nice hair, nice skin, nice clothes." He shook his head. "Trust me, she's bad news."

"Which means you'll take care of her, I suppose," the old veteran chuckled. "The Black Cat of Trost strikes again."

"Someone has to keep the wall clean," the young soldier said, grabbing the handles of his vertical maneuvering gear. "I'm off to collect my victims. See you after dinner, Cooper."

Cooper waved, but the black-haired soldier was already gone, using the gas-powered cables of his maneuvering gear to swing down the Trost side of the wall like a diving falcon.

CHAPTER TWO

The shaking started the moment Rosalie left the top of the wall.

It reminded her of when she'd fallen off her horse as a child. She'd been fine while it was actually happening, but when all the servants rushed over, she'd started sobbing, blubbering over bruises she hadn't even noticed until that moment.

Rosalie didn't cry now, of course, but the fear stayed under her skin like an ache, making her heart pound as she climbed down the gate tower's rickety spiral stairs back to the training yard. She was still trying to shake it when someone dropped a heavy stack of metal and leather equipment into her arms.

Rosalie grunted in surprise to see she was now holding a full set of vertical maneuvering gear. Everything was there: the gas canisters, the wire-coiled flywheels, the dual-trigger handles and cables, the belt and the leather harness that attached it all to a soldier's body. It was standard military issue, but it looked so . . . used.

"I think there's been a mistake," she said, holding out her arms again to show the dented metal and worn leather to the scarred, sour-faced veteran who'd shoved them at her. "This set isn't up to—"

"All equipment assignments are final," the man grunted. "Gotta problem, take it up with yer sergeant."

"And who is my sergeant?"

"Squad number's on yer gear," the veteran said as he added two rectangular cases to the top of Rosalie's pile, each one longer than her arm. The leather-covered boxes were so battered, it took Rosalie a moment to realize these were the sheaths for the hardened steel sword blades that attached to her maneuvering gear handles. She was looking to see if they even had blades in them when the veteran shoved her to the side. "Keep moving! Don't hold up the line!"

Irritated and making a mental note to report the soldier's unprofessional demeanor, Rosalie walked away from the crowded door where the tower opened into the yard. She found a quiet spot to take a look at the rest of her equipment.

She didn't much like what she saw.

Vertical maneuvering gear gave human soldiers a fighting chance against a titan in combat. It was a marvel of technology: a compact, gas-powered turbine that could fire barb-ended steel cables—colloquially called "hooks"—with enough force to embed them in stone or wood . . . or a titan's flesh. When the powerful motor retracted the cables, the soldier was pulled forward, upward, or in whatever direction the cables were anchored.

By properly targeting the cables, and with skilled use of timing and momentum, a soldier could essentially fly freely through the air, countering a titan's size and strength with speed, maneuverability, and precision. Cannons could demolish a titan's head or limbs, and swords could slice the weak spot at the backs of their necks. But the agility provided by maneuvering gear was what kept you alive. It was the single most important piece of equipment a soldier possessed. And the set the Garrison had just issued Rosalie seemed little more than garbage.

She wrapped her hands around the handle-like triggers that controlled the cables' firing and release. These were bigger than what she was used to, the grips painfully sharp where the leather padding had worn away. By design, the triggers resembled sword hilts. In combat, soldiers attached replaceable blades to them, allowing them to wield swords against the titans while keeping both hands on the maneuvering gear controls. But Rosalie wasn't even sure she could fit a sword into these hilts. Not only were the mechanisms loose, the metal clamp that held the blades in place was dented, like something had been chewing on it.

Rosalie dropped the triggers in disgust. This was absolutely unacceptable. Whoever had inspected this gear deserved to lose their job. Another soldier would have been doomed, but thankfully, Rosalie had packed her own set of gear from home. She just had to find the barracks and locate where her driver had put her luggage. She was about to go searching when a sharp finger tapped her on the shoulder.

Rosalie turned around to find herself face-to-face with a poof of curling, red-brown hair. She was staring at it in confusion when the soft fluff bobbed to reveal a sharp-eyed, extremely short girl with bushy eyebrows, endless freckles, and a sour not-quite-frown that dominated her skinny face.

"Squad Thirteen?" she asked in a heavily accented voice, pointing at Rosalie's gear.

Rosalie glanced down at the sad pile of broken equipment in her arms, which did indeed have the number 13 scratched into the vent fan's steel casing.

The freckled girl whirled around. "EMMETT! I found one!"

On the other side of the yard, an equally short boy with tanned skin and close-cut chestnut brown hair waved and started toward them. He was already wearing a full set of maneuvering gear that was almost as battered as Rosalie's, only Emmett seemed to be trying to take his apart as he walked, fiddling with his triggers as he shuffled across the yard.

While he took his time, the girl turned back to Rosalie. "I'm Willow Whittaker," she said, looking Rosalie over. "Seems we're squadmates."

Rosalie nodded.

The stranger arched an eyebrow. "And your name is?"

"Oh, yes, of course," Rosalie said, flustered. "Rosalie Dumarque."

She paused, waiting for the inevitable gasp that always came after the Dumarque name, but Willow just kept going like she'd said nothing remarkable.

"What's your assignment? This is Emmett—" She grabbed the distracted young man by the shoulders and yanked him over before he could walk into a wall. "We're from the same town. Where're you from?"

Rosalie blinked. That was a lot of information and questions to throw at a stranger. Obviously, this girl hadn't been taught any kind of etiquette, but Rosalie was careful to keep judgment out of her voice. If they were squadmates, six months would be plenty of time to smooth Miss Whittaker's rough edges.

"I'm from Sina," Rosalie said quickly. "And I'm the cannoneer." No one had actually told her that yet, but Rosalie knew that Garrison wall squads were typically five-person teams: a medic, an engineer, a gunner, a nonspecialist soldier, and an officer. Since she'd chosen cannon tactics as her specialty at the academy and earned the highest scores in her class, her role was obvious.

Willow let out a low whistle. "Sina, eh?" She flashed a crooked-toothed grin. "Fancy! Is that why you're in that weird uniform?"

"This is the Royal Academy dress uniform," Rosalie explained, straightening her elegant coat, which looked rather sad after the carriage ride. Willow and Emmett were both wearing the standard sand-colored trousers and jacket of the Garrison, with the shield-and-two-roses insignia on the sleeves and back. "I suppose it does stand out," she admitted. "But it *is* a regulation uniform."

"Whatever you say, beanpole," Willow said with a shrug. "White doesn't seem very practical for battle dress to me, but it definitely won't be good if our new sergeant catches you out of your gear as well."

"Oh, no," Rosalie said quickly, holding up the battered maneuvering gear she'd been given. "No, no, no. I can't wear this."

Willow elbowed Emmett, who finally stopped fussing with his own equipment. He reached out to shake Rosalie's hand, grabbing her palm and pumping it several times before finally letting go. "Hi! I'm Emmett," he said cheerfully. "What's that about your gear?"

Rosalie was so shocked at his forwardness that she could only stare. Even her brothers would never take her hand like that without permission. Like Willow, Emmett had a rough, undisciplined air about him, but unlike his sharp-eyed companion, his open smile was genuine and disarming.

"It's terrible," she said, showing him the battered metal. "Are you our medic?"

Given his pleasant demeanor, that made the most sense, but Willow snorted. "Why would a medic care about your maneuver gear?" she asked, rolling her eyes. "He's the engineer. I'm your medic."

Rosalie paled. "You're the medic?"

"I set bones proper," Willow said with a smile that made her shiver. "More important, I don't faint when I see a titan. I saw you up on the Red Line. You looked like you were going to pop."

Rosalie's face began to burn. "I did *not* almost faint."

"Then why was the lieutenant over there holding you up?"

"Go easy on her, Willow," Emmett chided, moving in to take a look at Rosalie's gear. "Maybe that was her first titan."

"Of course it's her first titan," Willow said, smirking. "She's from Sina. I bet she didn't even think titans were real before today."

"I thought nothing of the sort," Rosalie snapped. "I know titans are real. I came here to kill them."

"Well, you're off to a good start," Willow said mockingly. "What's your strategy? Faint so the titan will come closer and drop its guard before you puke on its feet?"

Rosalie was usually willing to let things slide, but there was only so much one could take. "Say that again," she growled, stepping into the stance she'd learned in hand-to-hand combat training.

"Whoa," Emmett said, jumping back. "Easy. Let's not get tossed in the cooler on the first day, okay?"

Rosalie was about to remind him that Willow had started it when the girl began to laugh. "Relax, beanpole," she said, slapping Rosalie on the shoulder. "I was just making fun of you. Are you always so serious?"

"Not usually," Rosalie said, glancing down at the dirty finger prints Willow had left on her epaulets. "But I'm not usually insulted to my face."

Willow shrugged. "Better than behind your back, right?"

There was a certain sense to that.

"Stop looking at me like that," Willow said, waving her hand. "I respect that you didn't back down, Rosalind—"

"Rosa-*lee*," Rosalie corrected.

Willow shrugged. "Whatever. Anyway, if you can't learn to take a ribbing, you're going to have a hard time. I don't have the spare materials to patch you up if you're going to swing every time someone here insults your princess suit."

She scooped her bag off the ground and flipped open the top to show Rosalie the cache of rolled-up bandages, sutures, compresses, and other first-aid paraphernalia inside. "See?" she said, holding up a bandage. "This has to last us until summer, so if you want your scraped knees bandaged, you'd better stay on my good side, Dumarque."

The idea that one bag of medical supplies was supposed to last an entire squad six months was ludicrous, but at this point, Rosalie was too tired to care. "I'll do my best," she grumbled, turning back to Emmett, whom she'd now decided was hands down her favorite squad mate. "Can you do anything about my gear?"

"It's not so bad, actually," he said, reaching into his bag for a pair of pliers. "Not as bad as mine, anyway. A few adjustments and it'll be ready to go."

Emmett was able to pry most of the dents out of her trigger handles. He couldn't do much about the mangled grips, but he fixed the clamps so that her sword blades wouldn't fall out. That was something, she supposed, but although he could pry the mechanical parts of her gear into place, he couldn't do anything about the straps.

Vertical maneuvering gear was designed to distribute the incredible force required to lift a solider into the air at high speed equally across the person's body. Proper fit was critical. If the turbine that sat on the small of her back slid to one side during flight, the resulting imbalance could rip her arm off. But even when Rosalie pulled them past their last notch, the straps that cinched the gear to her shoulders were far too loose. When she reached her arms behind her back to see if she could tighten them further, the whole apparatus slid toward the ground, throwing her off balance.

Emmett was there in a flash, catching the gear's turbine before it struck the stone courtyard. Rosalie was left to fall, landing painfully on her rear end. Face burning, she looked up to see Willow snickering.

"Where did you say you trained?" she asked as Rosalie got back to her feet. "You act like you've never put on maneuver gear before."

"I've put it on hundreds of times," Rosalie snapped. "This is just the wrong size."

A few tries and some creative application of twine later, and her gear was in place: two reeled wire coils on either side of her waist, control triggers holstered under her arms where she could grab them easily, sword sheaths hanging from her hips, and the gas-powered turbine that powered the whole thing secured at the small of her back.

"There," Emmett said, stepping aside as Rosalie put her white military academy uniform jacket back on. "Try not to put too much weight on your left side, and let's just hope our sergeant doesn't send you off the wall today."

"I'm going to have a talk with our sergeant," Rosalie muttered, tugging at the knotted string that kept her straps in place. "It's an absolute disgrace that any soldier should have to wear this." She craned her neck, looking around the crowded yard. "Which one is he, anyway?"

"Don't know," Emmett said. "Haven't seen him yet."

With a frustrated huff, Rosalie reached out to pluck the sleeve of a lanky soldier walking toward the mess hall. "Excuse me, do you know where we go to find our officer?"

"He should have found you," the soldier said, doing a double take at Rosalie's polite tone and another when he saw her academy uniform. "You're one of the new recruits?"

"Yes," Rosalie said proudly. "We're squad thirteen."

"*Thirteen?*"

He said that the way someone else would say 'firing squad,' and Rosalie shifted nervously. "Is something wrong?"

"No," the soldier said, shaking his head. "But you might want to notify your next of kin. Squad thirteen is Jax's unit, and his soldiers never finish a tour."

"What does that mean?" Willow demanded, pushing her way forward.

"He means they're dead," said a new voice.

The soldier who'd been talking to them froze. From his expression, you'd have thought a titan had climbed over the wall. When Rosalie turned around, though, she only saw a man.

The sergeant was just a hand taller than she was, but the way he stood made Rosalie feel like he was looming over them. He was dressed in the same tan uniform and maneuvering gear as the rest of the Garrison, but he wore his like he never took it off. His thick black hair was ragged, as if he cut it himself using a dagger and no mirror. The sergeant didn't look that much older than she was, but his face was hard in the way Rosalie associated with grizzled veterans. Pity, too, because he would have been handsome if he'd been a bit softer. He had a good, strong jaw, and his nose, though once broken, was still mostly straight. A smile would have helped enormously, but the man didn't look like he did that very often. The only lines on his face were from scowling, as he was now, glaring at the gossiping soldier with blue eyes that looked more like chips of broken glass than anything that belonged in a human face.

"Finished?" he asked the lanky soldier.

The soldier didn't reply. He just turned and bolted.

"Sergeant?"

The hard blue eyes flicked to her, and Rosalie flinched before she could stop herself. "My name is Rosalie Dumarque, and—"

"Don't care," he said, turning to address Willow and Emmett instead. "I'm Sergeant Jackson Cunningham. It's my responsibility to keep you idiots in line so long as you're on my wall. I've only got two rules: do your job, and don't talk back. Stick to those, and we won't have any problems."

"Yes, sir," Rosalie said, pressing her fist against her chest in salute. "As I was saying, I'm Rosalie—"

"Did I ask?" he snapped, whipping back to her. "I'll get your name when I want it, Private Rich Girl. Right now, the only thing I want is for you to get your fancied-up carcass to the top of that wall. We've got a cannon that needs to be moved, and it ain't going to push itself."

"But we're still one short, sir," Willow said. "A wall squad should have five—"

"I know how many soldiers are in a bleeding squad," Jax snarled. "But the new recruits broke up unevenly, so I volunteered to take the short straw." He glowered at Rosalie. "The very short straw."

Willow gaped at him. "You mean you're going to make us do a full squad's work with only four people?"

"Yes," he said, turning his glare on her. "That's the job. Do it or get out."

Willow snapped her mouth shut. Emmett said nothing. When Rosalie remained quiet as well, Jax nodded like he'd won and pointed at the stairs. "We're moving cannons today. If you work half as well as you complain, we'll be done in time for dinner. Now *move!*"

The cannon was already on the track when they got there.

It was a big one, too. Not quite as large as the twelve-pounders pointed at the closed gate on the street below, but the iron barrel was still as long as Rosalie was tall. Add the wooden brace that kept it locked to the iron rails running along the top of the wall, and the whole thing had to weigh a ton, which made the fact that Jax expected the four of them to move it all the more insane.

"Right," Jax said, resting his hand on the cannon's iron muzzle. "Our orders are to move this big bastard two kilometers to the wall's western bend. Blonde Girl and Freckles, you push first. When one of you drops, Short Boy there will take over."

Rosalie couldn't believe it. "You expect the two of us to push that?"

"I expect you to follow orders," Jax said, looking down on her. "It only gets harder from here, Private, so if you have a problem, I suggest you find somewhere else to play."

Narrowing her eyes, Rosalie stomped around him and positioned herself behind the cannon. Willow joined her a few seconds later, her previously sour face looked decidedly nervous as she placed her hands beside Rosalie's on the cart. But no matter how they tried, the cannon didn't move.

"Push . . . Dumarque . . . " Willow gasped. "Pretend . . . you're shoving a . . . butler down the stairs . . . "

"I *am* pushing," Rosalie gasped. "It's supposed to take . . . five people to . . . "

Emmett moved to help, but Jax stopped him, reaching out to give the cannon a push with his own boot instead. The extra shove was enough to finally to get the thing rolling, creaking down the rails at a snail's pace.

"Come on," Jax chided, strolling beside Rosalie and Willow as they struggled to keep the momentum going. "We'll be up here all night if you don't put your backs into it."

Rosalie kept her mouth shut and her head down, forcing the cannon down the rails through sheer stubbornness.

Willow was having a harder time of it.

"This is . . . ridiculous," she panted, her freckled face bright red with exertion. "We're going to . . . pull something . . . if we keep this up."

"We can do it," Rosalie whispered back, blinking the sweat out of her eyes. "He's just hazing us."

"He's . . . killing us . . . " Willow flopped forward against the cannon. "I can't anymore," she gasped. "Just bury me here."

"Don't stop," Rosalie hissed, grabbing her. "That's exactly what he wants us to—"

A shadow fell over them.

"What's this?" Jax asked in an infuriatingly superior voice. "Slacking already?"

"She's not slacking, sir," Rosalie said, glaring up at him. "The cannon's just too heavy. We need help."

"Sorry, Princess," he said, leaning closer. "We ain't got no servants up here. Pushing cannons is part of the job. If you can't do the work, get off the wall."

At that, Willow's flushed face went white and Rosalie gritted her teeth. "It's not failure if two people can't do a job meant for five," she said angrily. "If you actually care about moving the cannon, perhaps you should assign the correct number of soldiers to the job. *Sir.*"

"Big words from someone who can't even be bothered to put on the correct uniform," Jax snapped back, reaching out to smack the gold fringe sewn onto Rosalie's sleeves. "You joined the Garrison, not a costume party. Where's that get-up from, anyway? The Fancy Lady's Pony Club?"

"It's the uniform of the Royal Military Academy," Rosalie said proudly, "where I graduated first in my—"

"The *Royal* Military Academy," Jax repeated mockingly. "Oh, well, a *thousand* pardons, Your Grace. You, short stack." He pointed at Emmett, who'd been hovering behind Willow to catch her if she fell. "Take over for her ladyship. It seems her hands are too delicate for cannon pushing."

"I can do my job!" Rosalie said angrily, holding her ground as Emmett tried to take her place behind the cannon. "I just can't do one meant for three other people!"

"Yet you complain enough for five," Jax said, pushing her out of the way as he stepped behind the cannon. When he was in position, he ordered Willow to move as well, "before she had a heart attack."

Unlike Rosalie, the medic didn't argue. She gladly stepped aside, clutching her chest as she struggled for breath. Emmett took his place beside Jax, looking nervously at the giant cannon in front of them. Rosalie still didn't see how they were going to move it. Emmett wasn't any bigger than Willow, and though Jax was definitely bigger than Rosalie, he wasn't superhuman. Or, at least, that's what she'd assumed before he braced his feet and shoved the cannon down the rails.

"And that's . . . how it's done," he said through gritted teeth, walking the cannon down the rails at a slow—but still much faster— pace. "That's how . . . a soldier works. Learn something from it, and maybe today won't be a waste."

Rosalie couldn't say a word. She was too busy gaping at Jax, who, despite Emmett's best efforts, was basically pushing the cannon by himself.

"Wow," Willow said. "He's *strong*." She wiped her brow with her sleeve. "No wonder they let him go out a man short. He's like two soldiers."

Rosalie nodded silently, hurrying down the wall before Jax accused her of slacking again.

Jax pushed the cannon all the way to the two-kilometer mark. The moment he locked it into position, Rosalie hopped up behind it. Determined to make up for her failure as a cannon pusher, she threw herself into preparing the gun for battle. Turning the crank on the side, she lowered the cannon to the optimal firing position. She even leveled it off, using the smaller fine adjustment crank to maneuver the barrel to a perfect forty-five degrees.

When the gun was where she wanted it, she leaned over the wall's edge to note the elevation of this particular section compared to those around it. Height and drop off were important variables if you wanted the cannon's explosive shells to hit a titan's neck, the only target that would kill it. With that in mind, Rosalie went ahead and triangulated what she felt was the most likely shot—directly ahead, twenty meters from the wall's base—and scratched the firing angle into the cannon's wooden brace with the point of her pocket knife. She was trying to think of anything else she could do to be useful when Emmett came over to join her.

"Nice math," he said, looking down her sighted barrel. "But how did you figure out the shot without a reference?"

"The wall is the reference," Rosalie replied, tapping her foot on the stone. "No matter where you are, the walls are always fifty meters tall. Twenty meters out from the base is the sweet spot for accuracy on this make of gun, so by putting those two together, I was able—"

"To calculate the firing angle," Emmett finished, flashing her a huge smile. "Nice."

Rosalie beamed proudly. "My advanced cannoneering instructor made us triangulate firing angles on demand every day for three years. If you got it wrong, you had to run twenty laps. I hated laps, so I learned not to be wrong."

"If you spent so much time studying cannons, why're you so bad at pushing them?"

Rosalie jumped. She hadn't heard him approach, but when she turned around, Jax was right behind her.

"Isn't this our lucky day?" he said, his blue eyes colder than ever. "We got our very own expert come down from Wall Sina to teach us how to point a cannon."

The sneer in his voice made Rosalie bristle. "With respect, sir, I wasn't trying to brag. I was only answering Emmett's question."

"Why shouldn't you brag?" he asked mockingly. "You've got *advanced training*. How kind of you, Miss Sina, coming all the way down here to share your knowledge with us lowly wall guards. Should I prostrate myself at your feet now or later?"

"That's not what I meant," she said furiously. "And my name is Rosalie."

"Your name's whatever I say it is, Private," Jax said, his voice low and dangerous. "Right now, it's Disappointment. I'd have thought an elite solider from the Royal Military Academy would have herself together, but you can't even put your vertical maneuvering gear on straight. Just look at this."

His hand darted down, snatching something off Rosalie's belt. By the time she moved to stop him, Jax was already dangling one of the metal gas canisters that powered her maneuvering gear carelessly from his fingers.

"Here's your problem," he said, holding the silver cylinder just out of her reach. "I'm sure you had servants to take care of this sort of thing back at the Royal Academy, but here on my wall, you're responsible for your own gear. Leave it flapping about, and—" He snapped his hand back, tossing her gas canister over his shoulder. "—it could fall off anywhere."

Rosalie's stomach lurched. The silver metal canister spun through the air, flashing in the sunlight. She jumped to grab it, but it was far too late. The canister had already sailed over the Maria side of the wall. She sprinted to the edge just in time to see it land with a distant clatter in a copse of overgrown bushes at the edge of the field below.

"Oh no," Jax said. "Now look what your carelessness has done."

"*My* carelessness?" She whirled on him. "You did that on purpose!"

Jax didn't bother to deny it. He just looped his fingers through his belt and sneered down at her with a look of hatred so deep, Rosalie had no idea where it had come from. "Go get it," he ordered.

Rosalie swallowed.

"Um, sir," Emmett said nervously. "Going off the wall on the titan side is strictly—"

"Did I ask your opinion?" Jax said, keeping his eyes on Rosalie.

"This is between me and Princess Dumarque."

Emmett cringed at the threat in his voice, and Rosalie crossed her arms over her chest. "So you do know my name."

"I could hardly miss it with the way you were telling everyone," Jax said. "But your fancy breeding won't do you any good out here. I don't bother listening to Woermann's speeches anymore, but I'm sure the old skinflint's policy of putting equipment over soldiers hasn't changed. A lost canister's enough to get you docked half pay for the rest of the year, not that soldier's pay matters to someone like you. I'm sure your daddy can buy you out of any trouble, but I don't need spoiled little rich girls who are only here for tourism in my squad."

"That's *not* why I'm here," Rosalie said, stepping forward. "I—"

"I don't care!" Jax yelled in her face. "You want to shoot the big cannon and kill a titan for your trophy collection, do it on your own time! But so long as you're on this wall, you'll do your bloody job just like the rest of us. Now get down there and get your equipment, 'cause I ain't getting it for you!"

"Fine!" she yelled, grabbing her spare gas canister and screwing it into her maneuvering gear. When the rubber seal locked into place, she grabbed her worn-out control handles from their holsters and stepped to the edge of the wall. "Be right back."

"Wait!" Emmett cried. "There's a—"

But Rosalie had already jumped, falling straight down the wall toward the dead grass below.

If she hadn't been so angry, she would have felt terrified. For all the hundreds of hours she'd spent training in vertical maneuvering gear, jumping off a tower was a far cry from plummeting off Wall Rose wearing mangled gear that was probably older than she was. The first time she squeezed the triggers, nothing happened. It wasn't until she squeezed with all her might that the cables finally fired, shooting from the coils at her hips to stab their barbed hooks into the stone of the wall.

The sudden stop a second later when the line caught was enough to knock her breath out. Her body was used to being jerked around, but she'd fallen a lot farther than she meant to. She was dangling only five meters above the ground. If she'd cut it any closer, she would have landed splat in the grass.

Heart pounding at how close she'd come to a very messy and stupid death, Rosalie eased back on the loose triggers to lower herself the rest of the way to the ground. She fell with a thump into the tall grass at the wall's base, looking around for any sign of danger, but saw nothing. Now that she was down in it, the Maria side of the wall was even more hauntingly empty than it looked from above. Even the sounds of the city were gone, leaving only the soft rustle of dead leaves.

And the distant boom of giant footsteps.

Rosalie's heart slowed to a crawl as she scanned the empty fields for the source of the sound. When she found it, she let out a small breath. There *was* a titan out there, a behemoth shape almost a kilometer away. If it came closer, though . . .

Rosalie set her jaw. If it came closer, she'd kill it. Killing a titan on her very first day would show her father how wrong he'd been, and it would certainly shut Jax up. For now, the titan wasn't even facing her direction, so Rosalie triggered her metal cables to dislodge the anchor hooks from the wall.

The dented control handles worked if she applied enough pressure, so she kept squeezing until both cables retracted and were safely in place, coiled in the cases that hung at her waist. With everything ready to fire again should she need to make a quick escape, Rosalie dropped into a crouch, keeping her eyes on the distant titan as she crawled through the knee-high grass to the bushes where she'd last seen her canister.

Even with their leaves shed for winter, the brambles were a tangled knot. Rosalie could barely wedge her arm through the thorny

branches, and she certainly couldn't do it while holding her maneuvering gear handles. She slid them back in their shoulder holsters
and tried again, pressing her shoulder into the undergrowth as she
wiggled her hand through birds' nests and spiderwebs until, at last,
her fingers closed around the cold metal cylinder of her gas canister.

She almost cried in relief. It was too quiet on this side of the wall.
There was no sound, no movement. Just the fall of titan feet rum-
bling like distant thunder, making her hands shake as she struggled
to fit the canister back into the harness on top of her blade sheath.

When the cylinder finally slid into place, Rosalie grabbed her
control handles and whirled, squeezing both triggers to fire her
hooks and haul herself back over the wall, but the cables didn't fire.
Cursing the idiot who'd let the Garrison assign such deteriorated
gear, Rosalie squeezed harder, gripping the triggers until her knuckles were white. This time, though, the extra pressure did nothing.
She was banging the control handles together in an attempt to jos-
tle whatever had broken back into place when a gust of hot wind
brushed the top of her head.

Wind that smelled of rotting meat.

Rosalie froze. She didn't turn around, didn't lower her handles,
didn't dare breathe as her eyes slid up to see the titan standing directly
above her. Not the one in the distance. This titan was much bigger,
and it was *here*, looking down at her from at least fifteen meters up
with brown, childlike eyes and a drooling smile that showed off
every single one of its flat, bloodstained teeth. It had a beard as well,
the matted hair dangling so close over Rosalie's head that the flakes
of dried blood falling from it landed on her face.

The feather-light brush set her body shaking uncontrollably. It
was the titan from this morning. The one she'd seen at the Red Line,
only now she wasn't out of its reach. She was on the ground, practically standing between its feet, standing and staring while the titan's
smile grew wider, its empty eyes shining in delight as it reached

down to grab her.

It wasn't until those giant hands were close enough and she could see the dried blood under the paving-stone-sized fingernails that Rosalie's training finally beat through her terror. Her body moved before she could think, diving between the titan's legs. When she reached the other side, she slammed the handles of her maneuvering gear into the sheaths hanging from her waist.

Fortunately, this equipment did work. Thanks to Emmett's tinkering, the locks clicked exactly as they were supposed to, and when she raised her arms, the handles were equipped with two hardened steel blades, the straight edges gleaming as she whirled around to face the titan.

To do what, Rosalie wasn't sure. She'd managed to pull her swords, but now that they were out, the blades in her hands looked dull as butter knives, and her triggers still weren't working. She couldn't fire hooks into the titan and haul herself up its body to slash the weak spot on the back of its neck, as she'd been trained to do. With blades this useless, Rosalie wasn't sure she could cut the thing at all.

Fear came roaring back. She was trapped on the ground outside the walls with maneuver gear that wouldn't fire and swords that couldn't cut. She could try running, but a titan this big could travel farther in one step than she could in twenty, and she had nowhere to run. There was no cover in the open field, no trees to climb or buildings to hide in. Just the wall she couldn't climb, and the titan she couldn't kill.

With heart pounding, Rosalie rolled away, rising in a defensive position. It seemed impossible that things had gone so bad so quickly. Already, the titan was reaching for her again, its face distorted with a glutton's smile.

Rosalie's legs shook so badly, she couldn't even run.

The next time Lieutenant Brigitte made a recruit step up to the

Red Line, it would be Rosalie's severed foot stuck in the monster's beard.

Struggling not to cry, Rosalie braced her swords so she could at least scratch the creature before it ate her.

A shadow flashed over her head so fast that Rosalie couldn't look up to see what it was. A heartbeat later, the bearded titan's head jerked back as if yanked by a string. That was the only warning Rosalie got before a splash of scalding liquid hit her, leaving her vision bright red. She'd been splattered with the titan's burning blood, she realized as she staggered backward. That was all she managed to process before the titan fell on its face in the grass beside her, the back of its neck sliced open in two perfect, precise cuts.

Rosalie hit the ground next. Her legs gave out, dropping her to the bloody grass beside the titan's motionless body, which was starting to steam. She was staring at it in horrified wonder when the shadow fell over her again.

"Get up."

Rosalie lifted her head to see Jax looming above her, his swords dripping with the titan's smoking scarlet blood.

"Are you deaf?" he snarled when she didn't move. "I don't see any limbs missing, so get *up*."

With a shuddering breath, Rosalie pushed herself to her feet. When she was standing, Jax turned back to the wall. "I assume you know how to climb up as well as down?"

"I . . . I do," Rosalie said, her voice shaking horribly. "But my . . . my gear. It won't, it's not . . . " She stopped, frustrated and mortified. Her mouth wouldn't make the words. She couldn't force herself to be better. Couldn't do anything.

Jax shook his head with an angry huff. "Come on," he said, moving to her side. His arm snaked around Rosalie's waist, yanking her toward him as he turned them both to the wall. "Hold on tight," he ordered. "We don't have time to do this twice."

Before Rosalie could ask what they were doing, Jax fired the left hook of his maneuvering gear into the wall. The moment the metal barb stuck in the stone, he hit his trigger and reeled them up at blinding speed. When they got close to his first hook, Jax fired from his right hip, hitting a spot near the top with his other line. After that, it was all a blur until he dumped her unceremoniously on the stone at the top of the wall.

She fell in a heap, smacking her head painfully on the rails behind the cannon. Willow was at her side at once, squeezing her limbs and asking questions in a serious medic voice that Rosalie's ears were ringing too loudly to make sense of. All she could do was lie there and shake, staring dumbly at Jax as he took a cloth from his pocket and began casually cleaning his blades. When the twin lengths of razor-sharp steel were spotless, he shoved them back into their sheaths and turned away, walking down the wall toward the base without so much as a look over his shoulder to see if his squad would follow.

CHAPTER THREE

Thanks to Jax's angry, silent walking, they made it back to the gate a full half hour before the dinner bell. Rosalie was braced for a dressing down, but to everyone's surprise, Jax said he was letting them off early.

It was a welcome relief. Rosalie's body ached from scalp to toes, and her stomach was so empty it felt like it was caving in. She should have gone straight to the lieutenant to report Jax, but that would have been a sorry thing to do to the man who'd saved her life, even if he was the one who'd endangered it in the first place. Rosalie was just happy she'd finally stopped shaking. She was following the others toward the stairs when Jax called after her.

"Oy, rich girl."

Suppressing a long sigh, Rosalie turned around to find him glaring at her. "You need to get that fixed," he said, nodding at the maneuvering gear under her arms. "Hit the quartermaster before dinner and tell him I said to give you new gear. Blades, too, 'cause yours are less than useless. And while you're down there, get yourself a uniform that doesn't look like a costume."

Rosalie blinked at him. "Does this mean you're not kicking me out of your squad?"

"Don't put words in my mouth," Jax snapped. "Squad equipment is the sergeant's responsibility, and I ain't about to get docked pay because you were stupid enough to accept broken gear. Now get to the armory and get it fixed. Same goes for the rest of you." He glared at Willow and Emmett. "If anything's broken, take this time to get it *un*broken. Report back here at dawn tomorrow fixed up and ready to work, or find yourself another job. Dismissed."

He fired his maneuvering gear as he finished, shooting the hooks into the edge of the wall and swinging down to the stone yard fifty meters below.

Willow rolled her eyes. "What's his hurry?"

"Probably has to give his report," Emmett said with a shrug. "He killed a titan. I'm pretty sure there's paperwork for that."

"Then he should take the stairs like a normal person," Willow huffed. "I think he's just showing off."

"He's doing a good job," Rosalie muttered as she jealously watched Jax's perfect landing. She couldn't manage a landing like that from a straight fifty-meter jump even with working gear.

"I'm going to turn this garbage in," she said, smacking her useless control handles.

"You should eat first," Emmett said authoritatively. "You can go to the quartermaster any time, but first in line for dinner is a rare event."

Rosalie's stomach growled loudly at the mention of dinner. "What are we having?"

"The board said bread, ham, and cream soup," Willow replied.

"The bread's likely gritty, and the ham's probably turned, but no one can mess up cream soup."

Gritty bread and questionable ham fit Rosalie's low expectations for Garrison cooking, but cream soup didn't sound too bad. "What's in it? Besides cream?"

Willow laughed. "There's no cream in cream soup, idiot! It's called that because the potatoes make it white. Honestly, can you imagine how much it would cost to feed cream to this many soldiers? I can't even remember the last time I had milk."

"I can," Emmett said happily. "Your tenth birthday. Your Gran served it with your cake."

"That's right," Willow said, her face wistful. "It was such a good cake."

"We should go get in line," Emmett said excitedly. "If we get first choice, maybe we can get a slice of ham that isn't too green yet!"

He hurried down the stairs with Willow close on his heels. Rosalie followed more slowly, shaking her head in bewilderment. She couldn't remember the last time anything had made her as excited as her squadmates were about a chance to eat unspoiled pork and deceptively named potato soup. She didn't want to be a killjoy, though, so when the three of them reached the bottom of the gate tower, Rosalie told Emmett and Willow to go ahead without her.

"Are you sure?" Emmett asked. "This might be the only time ever we're first in line."

"I really want to take care of my gear problem," Rosalie said. "I'll catch up."

Willow shrugged. "Suit yourself, but don't blame us if there's nothing left. Come on, Emmett."

Given the choices, Rosalie didn't care if she never ate again. This time, though, she kept her opinion to herself, waving farewell to her squadmates as she walked toward the armory.

Like most Garrison bases, including the one near her home, the Trost Gate base was arranged in a defensive square. A protected stone corridor connected the base to the gate and its towers, but the heart of the fortress was a paved yard surrounded by four long, stone-and-wood buildings. At Trost, these were the mess hall, two barracks, and the armory, a three-story warehouse built right up against the wall itself.

Unlike her father's Military Police stockpiles, which were shrines to rifles and artillery, the Garrison's armory was almost entirely dedicated to maneuver gear. There were cannon supplies and a truly impressive cache of ammunition up in the loft, but the main floor was devoted to vertical maneuvering gear and the machines needed to keep it running.

One wall was occupied entirely by the giant air compressors used to fill the gas tanks. Another corner held the sharpening wheels for the blades. The rest of the warehouse was stacked with crates full of spare parts, all of which looked just as battered as Rosalie's. She didn't see a single piece of equipment that wasn't dented, scratched, or damaged in some way. She didn't see the quartermaster, either, but Rosalie never had any intention of asking for a new set. She simply dumped her broken gear into the bin marked "Scrap." Her blades were salvageable, so she set them down at the sharpening wheel before making her way to the uniform wall.

Her white Royal Military Academy jacket went straight into the trash, as did the stiff, high-necked dress shirt beneath it. Even if titan blood stains could be removed, Rosalie wanted no reminders of today's failure. Shivering in her undershirt, Rosalie grabbed a folded set of Garrison standard dress: a sand-colored military jacket, the waist cut high to accommodate the maneuver gear, and durable light-gray trousers that were tailored for moving in battle, not posing in a parade line.

The jacket's coarse fabric was horribly itchy without a proper field shirt underneath, but at least now she looked like a real Garrison soldier. She was hurrying out of the armory to find her luggage—which included what might well be the only properly maintained set of vertical maneuvering gear in all of Trost—when she turned a corner and walked face first into Captain Woermann.

"I'm so sorry, sir," she said, dropping into an automatic curtsy despite the fact that she wasn't wearing a dress. The captain didn't seem to notice her awkwardness. In fact he looked even more flustered than she was as he dropped into a low bow.

"Lady Rosalie," he said, his nasal voice desperate. "Please accept my sincerest apologies for not welcoming you properly. I didn't know you were in Trost until I received your father's letter this afternoon. I am dreadfully sorry you were shoved in with the common soldiers. Had I known you were here, I never would have allowed—"

"It's fine, sir," she said, cutting him off before he made things any more uncomfortable. "I came on extremely short notice, and I enlisted to be a common soldier, so there's no need to apologize."

"But you're a Dumarque!" Woermann cried, his deep-set eyes scandalized. "The king's own cousin! I could not possibly permit a lady of your rank to serve on the wall. It would be an insult to your illustrious—"

"It's *fine*," Rosalie said again, more sharply this time. "I'm grateful for your concern, Captain, but serving on the wall is what I came to Trost to do."

The captain's scowl deepened. "With respect, my lady, this is no place for someone like you. Our frontline soldiers come from the lowest walks of life. They're refugees, riff-raff, people for whom the guarantee of a good meal and steady pay is reason enough to risk their lives. Such desperate, dangerous people always resent those of us who are more successful, and I simply couldn't face your father if something happened to you."

He sounded deeply concerned, but it was all Rosalie could do not to roll her eyes. Really? Fear of the jealous commoners? That was what he was going with? She'd heard better arguments from her maids when they were trying to get each other in trouble. But ridiculous as this was, it wouldn't do to be rude to the captain of Trost, so Rosalie plastered on her best fake-sincere smile.

"Thank you so much for your concern," she said sweetly. "But all of my fellow soldiers have been wonderful so far. A trait which I'm sure is due to your leadership. With you in command, I'm certain I'll be perfectly fine here in Trost. Now if you'll excuse me, it's been a long day, and I'd like to get to dinner."

That was probably laying it on too thick, but Rosalie was tired and had no patience for this conversation right now. She was about to finish him with a dazzling smile and make a break for the mess hall when Woermann said, "I hear you're having trouble with your sergeant."

Rosalie paused midstep.

"Jackson Cunningham, right?" the captain went on. "He has quite the record. I've tried to discharge him several times, but for some reason, Lieutenant Brigitte insists on keeping him around. Of course, if *you* asked me, that would be a different matter." He smiled. "I'd be happy to discipline him for you, if you'd like."

"You'd do that?"

"Of course," he said. "Anything for Lord Dumarque's daughter."

Rosalie made a show of thinking it over, but she'd played this game before. Men like Woermann were always trying to worm their way into her father's good graces, and offering favors to Rosalie was a popular tactic. So popular that Rosalie considered it lazy. Woermann wasn't even trying to bribe her in a new or interesting way. He was just offering preferential treatment, which would have been insulting if it hadn't been so easy to defuse.

"Thank you for your concern, Captain Woermann," she said,

giving him a flawless rendition of her mother's "you're a useful moron" smile. "But I'm afraid you've been misinformed. I've had no problems at all with my sergeant."

Woermann's eyes widened. "I'm . . . I'm surprised to hear that," he said, regaining his composure. "How fortunate. Though if you do find yourself in need of assistance, Lady Rosalie, I trust you'll come to me."

Unwilling to promise any such thing, Rosalie gave him a final smile, saluted, and escaped, walking toward the mess hall as fast as she could without breaking into a run.

Across the yard, unnoticed, Jax Cunningham slipped out of his hiding place behind a stack of supply crates and stalked silently in the other direction.

"I don't like this," Jax muttered.

"Really?" Cooper chuckled. "Because I'm *loving* it."

Jax glowered at the lanky old wall guard. "Would you kindly shut up?"

They were on top of the gate, which, since titans didn't move at night, was utterly empty now that the sun was down. Normally, the solitude made this Jax's favorite place. At this specific moment, though, he would have paid money for someone to walk up and distract Cooper, who had a dangerously delighted gleam in his eyes.

"It's about time you messed up," the old soldier said, poking Jax in the shoulder. "You've only been up here for two and a half years, and already you've gotten yourself promoted to sergeant, beaten my record for titan kills, and collected enough dirt on every soldier in the Garrison to run this place better than Brigitte. Honestly, you were getting insufferable, but now your habit of spying on everyone has finally come back to bite you. You heard the rich girl refuse to rat you out to Woermann with your own ears! She could have strung you out to dry, but she didn't. She covered for you. That means you're in her debt, and that, my friend, is priceless."

"It ain't funny!" Jax snarled as Cooper began to cackle. "She's not just some rich girl. She's actual nobility, the king's bloody cousin! They could hang me just for talking to her, let alone everything else I did."

Cooper nodded enthusiastically. "I don't think the law has a specific punishment for kicking members of the royal family off the wall, but I'm certain they'll come up with something." His scarred face brightened. "Maybe you'll be drawn and quartered! I read about that once. They tie each of your limbs to a different horse, and then they send the animals running in different directions, ripping you—"

"I get the idea," Jax groaned, rubbing his face. "I have to get her off the wall. Woermann's been looking for a chance to boot me since I made sergeant, but with Lady Dumarque here, it's only a matter of time before he finds an excuse to hang me. And you know he'll do it."

"Without batting an eye," Cooper agreed. "But Woermann's the least of your worries. Rumor is Daddy Dumarque's a big name in the Military Police. If you get his daughter eaten, your end will be worse."

"That's not my fault!" Jax cried. "How was I supposed to know she'd be stupid enough to jump off the wall without testing her gear first?"

Cooper thought for a moment, turning to stare at the fields below where the silhouettes of a dozen titans stood motionless in the moonlight. "I don't think it's a matter of stupid. She's just from a different world. One where, when someone hands you something, you expect it to work. It probably didn't even occur to Lady Rosalie that the Garrison would assign her broken gear." He smiled wistfully. "That's the beauty of being noble. You have the luxury of expecting decency from others."

"Well, that's lovely for her," Jax said. "But what am I supposed to do?"

"Get her reassigned," Cooper suggested. "Privates beg to get out of your squad all the time. Let her go be someone else's problem."

Jax looked at him in horror. "Are you mental? A girl like that serving with the sort of trash that builds up here?" He shuddered. "She'd be safer with the titans."

"Plenty say the same about you," Cooper reminded him. "But you're hardly the first man willing to shoot himself in the foot to keep a pretty girl close by."

"That's not what this is about!"

The old soldier shrugged. "Whatever you need to tell yourself. Just get her off the wall before she gets you hung and I have to find a new grump to spend my evenings with."

Jax rolled his eyes. "Thanks, Cooper. That's a big help."

"What are friends for?" Cooper asked, standing up. "Join me for dinner? It's cream soup night."

"No thanks," Jax said. "Cream soup lost its charm last year, and it ain't exactly a friendly room for me down there."

"It's a lonely life for the Black Cat of Trost," Cooper said, pressing a hand dramatically to his chest before turning toward the stairs. "I'll save you some ham if there's any left. And Jackson?"

Jax looked up.

"Get rid of her fast. Nobles are as delicate as the flowers they're always naming themselves after. Sooner or later, something will take a bite out of her, and then Woermann will take it out on all of us."

"Don't worry," Jax assured him. "I'll have her running back to Sina by the end of the week."

"That's my Jax," Cooper said with a smile. "See you tomorrow."

Jax waved and turned away, listening to his friend's footsteps as he descended the stairs. When the sound of boots vanished, Jax pulled a hand-sized, cloth-bound, extremely battered book out of his jacket pocket. After a furtive glance down the wall to make sure he was alone, he opened the book and began to read, moving his finger slowly along the page to track the words in the bright moonlight.

CHAPTER FOUR

Her belly full of tasteless potato soup, Rosalie limped her way into the women's barracks to find her trunks waiting. All five of them.

The largest two leather-bound cases sat on her bunk, almost too tall to fit beneath the mattress above. The other three were stacked in the aisle, blocking the way. A half dozen recruits were gathered around, and they did not look happy.

"I say we pop the locks and dump 'em," growled one girl, who was nearly as tall as Jax, with even larger shoulders.

"Do they even got locks?" asked another, chewing on a piece of her own stringy black hair as she pondered. "I never seen boxes like these before."

"I say we shove 'em out the window," a third voice joined. "And when the idiot they belong to shows up, we'll shove her out, too!"

The laughter that followed was not pleasant. Rosalie was wondering how best to approach when the tall girl noticed her.

"Oy," she said, jerking her head at the trunks. "You know whose
these are?"

"Somebody thinks she deserves three times as much space as
everyone else," the black-haired girl added. "Can you believe?"

Rosalie's face began to warm. She looked around the barracks,
but there were no cabinets or chests. This was nothing like the academy dorms. There was barely enough room for people to sleep, much
less store belongings. The girls in front of her didn't seem to have any
possessions but the clothes on their backs.

"I'm sorry," she said, folding her hands in front of her. "There's
been a mistake."

"Oh, it's a mistake, all right," the tall girl said. "And we're waiting to see whose stuff this is so we can correct it." She took a men-
acing step. "Do you know whose junk this is?"

Rosalie wanted to back away, but more soldiers stood behind
her now.

"You're new, ain't you?" the black-haired girl said. "What's your
name? Where's your bunk?"

Rosalie swallowed. "I'm—"

"Oh, *there* they are!" cried a voice from across the room.

Everyone turned at the shout. Rosalie saw Willow jogging toward them through the packed grid of beds.

"Sorry 'bout that, girls," she said as she elbowed her way into the
circle, "those are the medical supplies I've been looking for all day.
That idiot supply sergeant—you know, the one who would be kinda
cute if it wasn't for that missing ear?—he botched the paperwork."

"These are medical supplies?" the tall girl asked, looking skeptically at the closest trunk, whose leather straps were tooled with a
whimsical floral pattern. "You sure?"

"'Course I'm sure," Willow said, making a show of inspecting the trunks before turning back to Rosalie. "Can you believe they dumped them on your bunk, Rosalie? Idiots." She rolled her eyes and placed her hands on the smallest trunk. "Come on, let's get them moved. I need to see you in the infirmary anyway. Sometimes getting sprayed with titan blood has lingering effects."

The crowd surrounding Rosalie jumped back. "*Titan blood?!*"

"Yup," Willow said, tilting her head proudly toward Rosalie. "My squadmate here found one in sector nine today. Had her swords out and everything. Course the sergeant had to swing in and claim the kill. You know how officers are."

"That was you?" the black-haired girl cried, practically pushing her face into Rosalie's. "I heard about that. My name's Henrietta, and—"

"Yeah yeah, you can suck up while you help us move these," Willow said, tapping a trunk with her boot.

"Hold on," the tall girl said, grabbing Henrietta, who'd already stepped forward to help. "Moving stuff ain't our job. Why should we help you?"

"Because if you don't, it'll be here taking up space forever," Willow said. "I'd move 'em myself, but as you can see, I'm obviously not capable." She held her bony arm up to the bigger girl's, which was easily twice the size. "But you're built like an ox, so stop being a prig and give us a hand, 'cause if I don't get these moved, Sergeant Cunningham is going to be hopping mad at all of us." At the mention of Jax's name, the air seemed to go out of the room. Then everyone was scrambling for the trunks, leveraging them on their shoulders and hauling them away as fast as they could go.

When everything was safely stowed in the supply room, Rosalie slumped onto her bunk. "Thank you," she whispered to Willow, who sat beside her.

The smaller girl shrugged. "'S nothing. Squadmates gotta stick together, and I need you alive to help keep Jax off me."

"Seems everyone wants to keep Jax away," Rosalie said. "Why are they so scared of him?"

Willow leaned closer, dropping her voice to a whisper. "I did some digging at dinner. The whole base is convinced our sergeant's a murderer."

"*What?*"

"They're saying he's killed ten squads and four officers," Willow went on. "One of the cooks even claimed Jax fed his brother to the Gobbler."

"That can't be true," Rosalie said authoritatively. "They'd hang him. And I don't even know what a Gobbler is."

"It's the name of a local aberrant titan," Willow said. "Really awful one, apparently. A lot of the squads from the Jax stories end up in his mouth."

"Thank you again for coming to my rescue," Rosalie said sincerely. "Those girls were ready to tear me apart because of those stupid trunks."

"They'd be right to," Willow said with a snort. "Who the hell brings that much stuff to a military barracks?"

"Just me," Rosalie said, burying her face in her hands. "The same soldier who gets cornered by a titan in an open field and can barely draw her swords."

"Now hold on," Willow said, smacking Rosalie's hands away from her face. "I'm happy to call you out for being a pampered rich idiot who packs for a job at the Garrison like she's going on holiday, but what happened over the wall is nothing to be ashamed of. There's soldiers who've been here for years who've never been that close to a titan. You stood your ground better with broken gear than Henrietta and her big-shouldered friend could have managed with brand-new sets."

Rosalie couldn't keep her voice calm anymore. "But I didn't *do* anything!" she cried. "I let a fifteen-meter-tall giant sneak up on me, and then I froze like a cornered deer." She looked down at her empty hands in disgust. "I'm supposed to be better than this. I'm a Dumarque! If my father found out I'd gotten all that training only to turn into a coward the one time it actually mattered, he'd disown me!"

"At least you've got a father left to care."

The bitterness in Willow's voice knocked Rosalie out of her self-loathing. "I'm sorry," she said, feeling worse than ever. "I didn't think—"

"You never do," Willow said, standing up. "Get some sleep, bean-pole. Bell rings at sunup, and you've got a lot of unpacking to do."

"Any idea why Sergeant Jerk got us up early?" Rosalie asked, digging through piles of sheathed blades for ones that weren't dull as spoons.

"Real early," Willow grumbled, glaring balefully at the dark sky through the armory door. "It's not even false dawn yet."

"No idea," Emmett said, grabbing metal canisters for himself and Willow before walking to the compressors to fill them up with gas. "I saw Jax briefly in the barracks after practice last night, but he didn't say anything."

Rosalie looked up in surprise. "There was practice last night?"

"Just me and Willow," Emmett said. "We practice on our own as much as we can since we're not the best with maneuvering gear."

"He means we suck," Willow said sourly, walking over to grab some blades for herself.

"You can't be that bad," Rosalie said helpfully. "You got into the Garrison."

"I don't need your condensation," the medic snapped, jamming blades angrily into her sheath.

She clearly meant "condescension," but Rosalie didn't feel the correction would be appreciated. "What's she so prickly about?" she whispered to Emmett.

The scrawny engineer shrugged. "That's just Willow. She'll die before she says something nice, but she's a good person." He smiled. "She appreciated what you did for her yesterday, by the way."

Rosalie blinked. "What I did?" Because from her recollection, Willow had been the one saving her skin.

"With the cannon," Emmett explained. "When she was practically dying, you started an argument with the sergeant to let her catch her breath. Clever move."

"I wish I'd been that clever," Rosalie said. "Honestly, I was just angry."

Emmett shrugged. "It still worked. Good thing, too. Willow can't stand it when she can't do something, but her arms have never been the same after the titans attacked our village."

He said that so casually, Rosalie almost didn't catch it. "Wait," she said, freezing. "You and Willow, you're from Maria?"

"Born and bred," Emmett said proudly. "Our families' farms were right next to each other, right up against the outer wall. You'd think that would have made us experts, but we didn't even hear them coming."

He laughed it off, but Rosalie's eyes were the size of coins. "Did they . . . did they attack you?"

Emmett nodded slowly. "They took out Willow's house first. One of them grabbed her out of her bed. He was going to rip her arms off, but she slipped out of his grip and ran to my place. We were just getting out of the house when more of them came." He lowered his eyes. "Willow and I were the only ones who made it."

Rosalie took a deep breath.

"Is that why she has trouble with maneuvering gear now?" she said quietly, watching Willow dig through piles of dull blades with ever louder curses. "Because the titan hurt her arms?"

"No," Emmett said with a laugh. "We're bad because we've always been small. The two of us were the village runts. Her arms still work, they're just not as strong as they should be. Something to do with damage inside, but I'm not the medic, so I don't rightly know what. You'd have to ask her for the details."

Rosalie couldn't see herself doing that. Ever. "Thank you, Emmett."

"You're welcome," he said brightly. "I just want you two to get along. We all need to stick together if we're going to survive the wall."

"Or our officer," Willow said, laughing as Rosalie jumped. "Let's go."

Willow's words proved prophetic. After Jax mocked Rosalie mercilessly for the baroque ornamentation on her maneuver gear—she'd retrieved her old academy-issued set from her luggage, then bribed a guard to send back everything else except her hairbrush, books, and a spare set of warm underclothes—the sergeant was all too happy to inform them of a "special assignment." They were going to be assisting the Supply Corps in their annual cleanup by scraping the summer's layer of dried bird droppings off the wall.

The Maria side of the wall.

"I just don't see why we have to scrape it into buckets," Rosalie said angrily, clutching the bright silver cables of her new vertical maneuvering gear with one hand as she stabbed the sharp edge of her trowel into a particularly stubborn bit of dried muck with the other. "Cleaning is one thing, but why are we saving bird poop?"

"It does make good fertilizer," Emmett said, his face deathly pale as he struggled to balance on his own cables.

"More like a good waste of time," Willow grumbled, her own face even paler as she tried to stay still.

They were hanging off the edge on the Maria side. When they'd started before dawn, the titans weren't an issue, but now that the sun was coming up, the monsters were moving again. A small group had already gathered below, their stupid eyes watching hungrily as Rosalie and the others scraped away at a year's worth of filth.

"This isn't even our job!" Willow said, bracing herself against the wall with both feet. "Cleaning is Supply Corps work!"

It was pretty disgusting, but Rosalie decided she preferred scraping dried poop to enduring Jax's mockery. He'd ridiculed her gear's decorated straps for five solid minutes, calling her "carriage horse" and asking if she'd brought ribbons to tie in the titans' hair.

As if he could hear her thinking, Jax chose that moment to poke his head over the edge of the wall. "Pick up the pace!" he yelled. "We're not going back until this whole side is done, so if you want to eat tonight, you'd better scrape faster!"

"You didn't let us eat breakfast," Willow muttered, stabbing her trowel into a large white streak of droppings. When she tried to yank it out again, though, the motion upset her already precarious balance, forcing Rosalie to stick out a foot to steady her squadmate before she flipped over.

"Thanks," Willow grumbled, her sour voice shaking slightly as she eyed the titans thirty meters below, their hands already raised to catch anyone who fell.

"You're welcome," Rosalie said, trying not to look too confident as she hit her shiny new triggers with one hand, reeling herself up to the top of the wall to empty her bucket into the cart.

By midafternoon, Rosalie's arms burned from all the scraping, and her core was watery from holding herself upright in her vertical maneuvering gear for eleven hours straight. She couldn't tell if her aching muscles were shouting down her empty stomach or if all her discomforts had merged into a single throbbing agony. Either way, there'd be no relief. Jax had already told them they'd have no lunch. When she voiced her disbelief, he'd said:

"You don't look like you've ever missed a meal in your life. But this is the wall, not a picnic. There's no food and there won't *be* any food until the work gets done, so I suggest you stop grousing and get to it."

Rosalie could still hear those hateful words in her head as she hauled herself over the lip of the wall to dump her bucket full of droppings into the collection wagon. When she landed on her feet, though, she spotted something unexpected.

A new squad was walking toward them along the top of the wall. They all wore uniforms bearing the Supply Corps insignia, and their wagon was piled with buckets and trowels just like the ones Squad 13 was using. For a soaring moment, she thought they'd come to help. Then, as always, Jax opened his mouth and ruined everything.

"Took your sweet time, Markus!" he called, lips curling into a sneer. "What happened? Got lost on the way out of the tavern?"

The new squad's leader, a short, potbellied man with a flushed red face, flashed Jax a sneer of his own. "I wasn't exactly in a hurry, you crazy bastard. What kind of demented sergeant volunteers his squad to do two weeks' worth of cleaning in one day?"

"Because it doesn't take us two weeks on account of we're not lazy wastes of space," Jax replied. "Case in point, you were supposed to be here at noon. What were you doing? Stopping for a drink every block between headquarters and the wall?"

"That's most unkind," Markus said, winking at his men, who did indeed look suspiciously wobbly on their feet. "We got here fast as we could, and it's not like you needed us." He waved at the cart of bird dung that Rosalie, Emmett, and Willow had been filling all morning. "You're almost done already."

"No thanks to you," Jax snapped, crossing his arms. "We'll be done in half an hour. Since you arrived just in time to do nothing, you can push our cart back for us, assuming you idiots can manage two carts at once without falling off the wall."

The way he said that made Rosalie frown. From the notation on his sleeve, Markus was also a sergeant, which meant Jax had no right to give him orders. She fully expected Markus to call him out, but to her surprise, the older man didn't say a word. He just ordered his men to start shoveling bird droppings from Squad 13's overloaded cart into their empty one.

The one-sided exchange was so odd, Rosalie actually went up to Jax when it was over, swallowing her anger, and asked, "What was that about?"

To Rosalie's surprise, he answered without mocking her. "Markus used to be a wall sergeant like me, and then I caught him drunk on the job. I could have gotten him kicked out of the Garrison, but I fudged my story and he ended up in Supply Corps instead."

That explained a lot. "So he owes you."

"Everyone owes me," Jax said bitterly. "Because everyone up here is trash. Bribes, drunkenness, extortion, corruption, good old incompetence—I know it all, and I use it."

"Why?" she asked, genuinely curious. "I mean, if they're all so bad, why not just have them tossed out?"

"Because then I'd have to do it all over again on a whole new crop of idiots."

Rosalie scowled at that, and Jax sighed. "Look, Princess, this isn't a nice job for nice people. It's dirty and hard and there's a good chance you'll end your career in a titan's belly. The only reason anyone does it is because the Garrison pays twice what anyone else does, and even mouth-breathers like Markus have families to feed. Not that you'd know anything about that."

Rosalie ignored the barb and stayed on target. "Is that why you covered for him? Because he had a family?"

"I didn't *cover* for him," Jax said angrily. "I'm blackmailing him because a drunken idiot under my boot is safer than a drunken idiot running around loose."

That made a strange sort of sense. "Do you have a family to feed?"

"That's none of your damn business!" Jax roared. "*Get back to work!*"

Rosalie backed away, but inside she was smirking. That was the first time Jax had answered her questions rather than just insulting her. She hadn't missed the softness in his voice when he'd talked about feeding families, either. Or how he'd boasted to Markus about his squad doing in a day what normally took the Supply Corps two weeks.

If he was a cynical man, rather than just a horrible one, maybe he could be reasoned with. The possibility made Rosalie grin as she hopped down off the wall to help Emmett and Willow finish the final stretch.

❀ ❀ ❀

As Jax had predicted, it took their squad half an hour on the nose to finish. It was still an hour before sunset, too. Plenty of time to get back for dinner. When they hauled themselves triumphantly to the top of the wall, though, Jax was the only one waiting.

"Where's the Supply Corps squad?" Rosalie asked, looking at the abandoned carts.

"Where they always are when they have five free seconds," Jax said bitterly. "Down in Trost having a drink."

She gaped at him. "And you're not writing them up?"

"Oh no, they're dead," Jax growled. "But Supply Corps operates out of HQ. That means Markus works under Woermann, and the captain doesn't listen to my reports. I'm still telling Brigitte, though. It's not her jurisdiction, but she's a sneaky old fox. She'll find a way make those slackers pay."

Rosalie certainly hoped so. If her father had discovered one of his Military Police squads abandoning their post to go drinking, he'd have had them all shot. Rosalie was feeling a bit like shooting someone herself when Markus and his team finally made their way back up the wall five minutes later.

"For the love of—" Jax marched over to grab Markus, who was so drunk he was having trouble staying upright. "What kind of idiot gets falling-down drunk on the wall?"

"Don't be such a stick, Jaxy," Markus slurred in his face. "It's just a bit o' fun. Here." He fumbled a flask from his pocket. "Have a drink. Might make you more likable."

Jax smacked the flask out of his hand. The other drunken soldiers cried out in dismay, but it was too late. The flask had already tumbled over the edge of the wall, which meant the drink was gone, and now they were mad.

"What'd you go and do that for?" one of them yelled, turning to Markus. "Sergeant!"

"You done messed up now, Cunningham," Markus growled, pulling a well-honed knife from inside his jacket. "I don't care what you got on me. You give orders like you're a damn captain, but you're no better than the rest of us, you sorry piece of—"

He cut himself off with a strangled cry as Jax calmly grabbed his hand, bending his fingers backward until the knife clattered to the ground.

"That's enough out of you," Jax said calmly, giving Markus's fingers one last shove before letting go. "Men as stupid as you are when you're sober shouldn't drink, Markus," he said as the other sergeant dropped to the ground, cursing and clutching his swelling hand. "My squad's done with their work and yours, so we're leaving.

Why don't you lie there a moment and collect what little wits you've got, then you can—"

Rosalie didn't see which of Markus's men started it. They all seemed to come to the decision to jump Jax at the exact same time, charging him with a chorus of drunken roars. Jax dodged the attacks without batting an eye, ducking under one man's fist while sidestepping another's kick. The third had gone for a tackle, but he must have been even drunker than the others because he missed Jax entirely, running straight past him. When he turned around for another try, his foot slipped, sending him stumbling sideways . . .

Right off the titan side of the wall.

CHAPTER FIVE

The moment the soldier disappeared, everyone went silent. Even the falling man didn't scream. It was so quiet, Rosalie could hear the whistle of his body as he plummeted, followed by a wet *plop*.

"*Hans!*" Markus shouted, lunging for the edge.

Jax raced after him like a shot, grabbing Markus seconds before the drunken idiot threw himself off the wall as well. Once he'd locked his arms around the bigger man's barrel chest, Jax became still. When she ran over to help, Rosalie saw why.

The falling man hadn't hit the ground. He'd landed in a titan's open mouth.

It was a big one. Fifteen meters tall at least, with a distended potbelly, distorted thin arms, and a boy's innocent face.

Its huge gray eyes were crossed in an effort to look at the man moving groggily on its tongue. The fallen soldier had managed to lift his head and look around, his drunken face confused as he spotted the wall of giant teeth above him. He was still staring when the titan's mouth snapped shut.

The damp crunch, and then the echoing *clack* of its teeth snapping together, were sounds Rosalie knew she'd never be able to forget. The next was even worse. The titan's throat flexed, moving with a gulp as it swallowed the man whole.

"NO!" Markus cried, lurching against Jax's grip. "Damn you monsters! I'll—"

"Shut up!" Jax snarled, wrestling Markus away from the edge, but not fast enough. His screaming had already caught the titans' attention. The crowd of monsters Squad 13 had been attracting all day as they cleaned was now swarming the wall, throwing themselves against the stone in a frenzy to reach the humans on top.

"That's just brilliant!" Jax yelled, throwing Markus down on the stone. "You just had to go and kick the hornets' nest, didn't you?"

Markus rolled away, clutching his wounded hand and screaming obscenities at the top of his lungs. Jax kicked him in the ribs for good measure and turned to Willow.

"You're the medic," he snapped. "Fix his damn hand and shut him up before his noise brings more."

Willow nodded frantically, throwing open her medical bag and grabbing a roll of bandages, which she proceeded to shove into Markus's mouth.

"What about us?" Rosalie asked as Willow struggled with the raging drunk. "What do we do?"

"*You* do nothing," Jax said, drawing his blades. "Just stay here and try not to die while I clean this mess up."

"Are you crazy?" she cried, pointing at the giants slamming their bodies into the wall. "There's a dozen titans down there, one of which is fifteen meters. Fighting that alone is suicide! *Stupid* suicide, seeing how we've got a cannon right over there."

She started toward the cannon emplacement only a few meters away, but Jax stepped in front of her. "You are *not* using that cannon!"

"Then why have it?" Rosalie yelled back. "Why do we have any of this if you're determined to kill titans by yourself?"

Jax eyed his razor-sharp blades with a sneer. "Who's going to help me?"

"Us!" Rosalie shouted at him. "Your squad!"

"You're not my squad," he said in disgust. "You're just recruits. You're not even good recruits." He jerked his head toward Emmett and Willow, who were both trying to hold Markus down. "They can barely stay upright in maneuvering gear, and you're just a little girl playing solider."

Rosalie clenched her fists. "I'm not playing," she said through clenched teeth. "I trained four years for this."

"At the *Royal* Military Academy, which is inside Wall Sina, as far from the front as it's possible to get. You don't know anything about fighting titans. You couldn't even stand up in front of one yesterday. All you'll do is get in my way."

Rosalie winced as the memory of her failure came back sharp and hot, but she was too mad to stop. "So you'd rather die?" she cried. "You'd rather throw your life away than let us attempt to help?"

"*Death's the job!*" Jax shouted, his blue eyes flashing with real anger. "You don't get it, do you? We're not heroes. We're disposable! We're up here to die so they"—he pointed at the city behind them—"don't have to. You think I should give you a chance because you're going to try really hard? That doesn't matter. Nothing matters except protecting this wall and the people behind it!"

He turned his back to her and set his feet for the jump. "If you're not willing to give up everything for this job, go home and stop wasting the time of those of us who are."

Rosalie clenched her jaw. "That's not—"

But Jax was already gone. She heard his maneuvering gear fire a second later, the clink of the hooks as they dug into the stone wall. The sound was still echoing when Rosalie turned and ran for the cannon.

He was wrong. They weren't up here to die. They were here to live. To fight and protect so everyone could survive. *That* was the Garrison's job, and she was going to prove it.

First, though, she had to get the cannon in position.

This gun was in far worse shape than the one they'd moved yesterday. The loading cap was so rusty, Rosalie had to kick it to open it. The firing chamber was a bit better, but when she ran to the ammunition crate, only two high-explosive shells sat at the bottom.

Rosalie was certain there was a special place in hell for the person who left only two shells in the stockpile for a frontline cannon, but she had no time to curse him for it. She was already shoving the first one into the cannon. Sealing the rusty loading cap was harder than opening it. The cannon didn't look like it had been cleaned all year. There was even an old mud-wasp's nest in the hole where the locking pin should go. Swearing under her breath, Rosalie knocked it clean and jammed the lock into place. When she grabbed the crank to turn the cannon to the correct position, though, the handle fell off in her hand.

"We've shut up the angry man," Willow reported, running over. "What's going on? Where's Jax?"

"He jumped down to fight the titans alone," Rosalie said. She stuck the handle back on, but the crank still didn't budge. "I'm trying to give him fire support, but the gear is stuck."

"It's rusted together," Emmett said. "Let me try."

He and Rosalie pulled together. Willow joined in as well, but even the three of them weren't enough to get the cannon turning.

"Does *nothing* on this wall work?" Rosalie yelled, slamming her hand on the cannon's barrel, which was still pointed in the entirely wrong direction. She was about to kick the crank with her boot when Emmett stopped her.

"I have an idea."

He ran over to the carts and returned holding two of the flat-bladed iron trowels they'd used to scrape bird dung off the walls. Before Rosalie could ask what he meant to do with them, Emmett shoved the first trowel into the rusted teeth of the wagon-wheel-sized gear that turned the cannon. He wedged the second trowel beside it, then grabbed the boxy sheath containing his sword blades off his hip and turned it sideways, placing the length of it across the short handles of both trowels. When everything was in position, he leaned all his weight on the sheath, using it like a lever to put pressure on the trowels until, at last, the rust gave way and the gear turned with a deafening *clunk*.

"Emmett," Rosalie said, her face breaking into a smile. "That was brilliant!"

Emmett retrieved his trowels with a flourish. "Give me a lever long enough, and I shall move the world."

That sounded like a quote, but Rosalie had no time to ask from where. Now that the cannon was moving, she had to aim it before their idiot sergeant became titan food. Thankfully, turning the big gear had loosened the others as well. The crank still stuck and slipped, but she was able to maneuver the cannon more or less into the position she wanted: twenty degrees to the west and straight down the wall.

Right at Jax.

Rosalie's hand froze on the crank. Just as she had been yesterday, Jax was standing on the ground at the base of the wall, staring up at the fifteen-meter titan who towered over him. *Only* the fifteen-meter titan, because all the smaller ones were dead. The crowd of titans that had followed them all day as they cleaned the wall was now lying on the ground, their necks cut clean through.

Given his broken swords and the blood on his arms, Jax was clearly the reason why. But though he'd mowed his way through the dozen smaller titans in the time it had taken Rosalie to get the cannon working, he hadn't touched the big one yet. Before she could wonder why, Jax exploded into motion, sprinting for extra momentum as he fired the left cable of his maneuver gear into the flesh of the monster's shoulder. The child-faced titan didn't even flinch. It just turned to follow Jax, its big hands reaching out in a clumsy attempt to catch him as he reeled himself up to land in the crook of the titan's shoulder, his swords already in position to stab the weak spot at the nape of its neck.

Like the bearded titan yesterday, the monster's head snapped back the moment Jax's blades came down. It fell a moment later, toppling like a tree onto the bodies of the smaller titans. Jax hopped clear as it fell, firing his maneuvering gear at the wall to pull himself to safety as the titan crashed into the dead grass.

The whole thing couldn't have taken more than thirty seconds.

"Wow," Willow whispered, her voice trembling. "He killed them all."

Rosalie nodded silently, eyes as wide as could be as she watched Jax calmly drop back down to the ground to collect the snapped ends of his broken swords so they could be reforged. He must have broken all of the blades he carried, Rosalie realized. She was trying to calculate how many cuts he must have made to go through every blade in his sheath when the thick copse of fir trees at the edge of the field began to rustle.

"*Jax!*"

Her warning came far too late. A massive arm had already shot out of the fir trees, grabbing Jax in a hand big enough to tip a horse cart.

The new titan had a young woman's face and long, stringy black hair. It crawled out of the thick copse of conifers on its knees, its cracked red lips curling in a hungry smile as it saw Jax struggling in its fingers, twisting and stabbing ineffectively at the titan's hand with his broken swords. It wasn't as big as the one he'd just killed, but its palm was as wide as Jax was tall, leaving him no leverage to kick his way free as the titan lifted him toward its open mouth.

"I have to take the shot!"

Everyone jumped. Rosalie hadn't even realized she was shouting until the words left her throat raw, but she was moving too fast to care. She'd already cranked the cannon into position, smacking the barrel with her fist until it was pointed where she wanted.

The shot had to be exact. Drop off wasn't an issue for a shot this close, but even the shiny new cannons on Sina were famously inaccurate. With a rusted old tube like this, she'd be lucky to hit a titan standing right in front of her, which was why every other variable—the wind, the alignment, the tilt of the barrel—had to be perfect.

For once, though, the age of the Garrison's equipment provided an advantage. This was a classic iron ten-pounder, the mass-produced workhorse that had been the default example in all of her gunnery manuals. She licked her finger to estimate the stiff breeze from the northwest. When she had it, she smacked her hand against the barrel to slide it a hair to the left so that the muzzle was pointed at the front hollow of the female titan's throat, directly opposite the weak spot.

Exactly where she wanted.

"Fire!"

She yanked the firing line, and the rusty cannon rocked backward with a deafening boom. The sound was still echoing when the titan's head exploded like a ripe melon, splattering blood to the tops the trees behind it. But though the titan's head was gone, its hand was still wrapped around Jax like a vise.

"Why isn't it dead?!"

"Because you only blew off its head!" Willow said frantically. "Unless you take out the weak spot, titans can regenerate any damage!"

Rosalie thought she had gotten the weak spot. When she looked down at the titan's headless body, though, she saw Willow was right. For all the blood, the very bottom of the titan's neck was still there, and it was growing before Rosalie's eyes, the flesh creeping up from the bloody stump to form a new cranium.

It was exactly what they'd taught her in titan anatomy class. But now that Rosalie was seeing it with her own eyes, her brain was actively rejecting it. *How does anything live without a head?!* There was no sanity, no aspect of science or nature that could allow this, and yet it was happening. The titan had already regenerated up to the jaw line, its new bottom teeth poking up through the red flesh of its gums like white mushrooms. As its head regrew, the titan's hand squeezed Jax even tighter. As his face began to turn purple, Rosalie realized he'd been right. For all her training, she really didn't know anything about fighting titans. She couldn't, because fighting titans made no sense. There was simply no way to properly prepare for a creature that didn't care if you blew its head off.

"We have to get down there," she said, stepping away from the cannon. "We have to cut its neck before it regrows enough to finish killing Jax."

"Um, Rosalie?" Emmett said, pointing at the ground.

Rosalie jerked back. The monster in the fir trees hadn't been the only lurker. Two other titans had crept out of the brush as well. Neither was particularly big, but Rosalie hadn't even killed one titan yet. There was no way she was taking three by herself, and Willow and Emmett's lack of maneuvering-gear skills meant they wouldn't be much help. If they didn't do something fast, though, Jax wasn't going to make it.

"Just shoot it again!" Willow said desperately. "That's what you're here for, right?"

Rosalie shook her head. "The neck stump's too small a target.

I'm a good shot, but no one's that good. Even if I did land it, Jax would just get laid out for the other two to pounce on."

The two new titans had crept perilously close to the headless one now, their empty eyes locked on Jax like greedy children eyeing a sweet. If she'd had more shells, she could have taken them all out, but the ammo box had only one shot left. Rosalie loaded it anyway, focusing on sliding the silver canister into the barrel as she forced herself to be calm and *think*. There had to be a way to do this. Had to be a . . . Her head shot up, and then she whirled on Emmett so fast he jumped. "What's the lift capacity on vertical maneuvering gear?"

"Two hundred kilos," he replied without missing a beat. "Why do you ask?"

"Because I think I've figured out how we're going to do this." Rosalie pointed at the titan holding Jax. "I need both of you to shoot your hooks into its hand. Fingers, wrist, doesn't matter. Just get the hooks in somewhere they won't come out."

"Are the cables long enough for that?" Willow asked, looking at her spools. "I've never extended mine all the way."

"They should be fifty meters," Rosalie said. "Or one wall's worth. If each of you dangles down the wall on one cable, you should be able to get your other into that hand."

Neither Willow nor Emmett looked happy about the idea, but they did as Rosalie asked, securing the barbed hooks of their cables firmly in the stone at the top of the wall before lowering themselves down. When they were dangling at the halfway mark, they fired their cables at the titan. It took them a few attempts to land the shot, but eventually both had their hooks firmly buried in the flesh of the titan's fingers.

Not a moment too soon. Jax was no longer moving, and the titan's head had almost completely regenerated. No skin had grown yet, but its skull was fully formed and there were eyeballs in its sockets. At this rate, Rosalie estimated they had less than a minute before it fully healed. If they were going to do something, it had to be *now*, so the moment Willow and Emmett called that they were ready, she pulled the string, firing the cannon.

But not at the titan's neck.

Just as before, the cannon rocked on its supports, echoing with a boom across the overgrown fields. Unlike before, though, it wasn't the titan's head that exploded. It was its arm.

The high-explosive shell landed perfectly below the titan's elbow, blowing a hole straight through the forearm and separating the hand that was crushing Jax from the rest of the monster's body. The blast sent the clutched fist flying into the air, but Willow and Emmett were already on it, reeling in their cables as fast as the flywheels could go.

Even with the two of them, the extra weight of Jax and the titan's hand was almost more than the motors could take. Now that she had taken her second shot, Rosalie jumped in as well, swinging down the wall and shooting her free cable into the titan's severed flesh between the thumb and the wrist.

"Pull!" she shouted, hitting the triggers on her maneuvering gear to reel herself back up the wall. *"Pull!"*

The air was filled with the whine of metal on metal as their cables reeled in. The titan's severed hand was enormous. Rosalie had no idea how much it weighed, but their gear was chugging the whole way. Even after the three of them made it to the top, it took all the gas left in their cylinders to raise the severed hand holding Jax to the wall's edge. Then they had to pull themselves, grabbing the titan's fingers and tugging with all their strength until, at last, the smoking fist flopped onto the top of the wall.

The moment it landed, everyone fell over. Rosalie was the first back to her feet. She slammed the handles of her maneuvering gear into the blades at her thighs, drawing her hardened steel swords with a clang of metal and slamming them into the sinews of the titan's still-clenched fingers.

"Jax!" she yelled, hacking at the already withering flesh. "Hang on! We're getting you out!"

He gave no answer, but Rosalie wouldn't have heard one. She was too busy cutting the fingers off, slicing each one at the joint to break the titan's rigor mortis grip until, at last, the hand fell open and Jax collapsed gasping onto the stone.

Rosalie slumped to the ground as well, her body heaving in exhaustion while Willow ran in to check on Jax, who was coughing up a storm. Beside them, the titan's chopped-up hand was starting to steam, releasing a horrific stench. On the grass below, the titan who'd grabbed Jax had fully regrown its head and was staring in confusion at the blown-off stump of its severed arm. It was not, however, looking at them. None of the titans were. There was no more pileup, no more threat to the safety of the wall, which meant . . .

"We did it," Rosalie said, panting and grinning at her squad. "They're not beating on the wall anymore! We're safe!"

"We're alive," Emmett said, looking down at Willow, who was rubbing Jax's back to help him breathe. "We're alive!"

They were better than alive. They'd won. They'd protected the wall. They'd saved Jax. Markus's soldier had fallen due to his own foolishness, but no one else had died. Their squad was safe. They could all go home. Everything was fine!

"We won!" she cried, hugging Emmett, who'd come over to help her up. "We did it! We—"

She stopped with a gasp. Jax was suddenly right in front of her, his face terrifying in its anger.

"*Who told you to fire the cannon?!*"

CHAPTER SIX

Rosalie sat nervously on the cold bench, shuffling her feet on the brick floor as she waited for the desk sergeant to call her name. It was her first time in the western tower, which housed the controls for the gate as well as the offices of the woman who controlled it: Gate Lieutenant Brigitte Morris.

She wasn't sure how long she'd been waiting. The guardroom's only window had been bricked over years ago, but it had to be late evening. Everyone else in her squad had already given their report and been dismissed. She was the last one, sitting with her hands balled anxiously in her lap until, finally, the scruffy soldier who served as the gate lieutenant's secretary called her name.

Rosalie jumped to her feet, but the veteran just pointed down the hall at the lieutenant's office. Stomach sinking, Rosalie marched out of the guardroom with her head held as high as she could manage, opening the battered door with a quiet click.

The gate lieutenant's office was smaller than she'd imagined. As the officer in charge of the Trost Gate and the forward walls, Lieutenant Brigitte was outranked only by Captain Woermann himself. In Rosalie's experience, that kind of power meant perks like a spacious office and nice furniture, but Brigitte's cramped workspace looked more like a root cellar. It had windowless brick walls, a low board ceiling, and a brick floor worn down by decades of boots. The only furniture was an ancient wooden desk and a little iron heater in the corner. There wasn't even a chair for visitors, not that Rosalie could have used it. As a subordinate here for a chewing out, her duty was to stand and take it.

When the door closed, Brigitte tucked the papers she'd been reading into a drawer and leaned forward, planting her elbows on her now-empty desk as she scowled at Rosalie. "Do you know why you're here, Private?"

"Yes, ma'am," Rosalie said, keeping her back straight and her eyes locked on the detailed map of the gate and the surrounding landscape pinned to the wall above the lieutenant's gray-haired head. "I fired the cannon despite my officer's direct order not to."

"You fired it *twice*," Brigitte corrected, leaning back in her chair. "Do you understand why firing the cannons is such a big deal?"

Jax's explosion earlier had given her a hint, but before he could explain why he was so mad, Markus's squad—who'd fled when Jax went over the wall—had come back with a bunch of soldiers and everything had gone crazy. Too crazy, in Rosalie's estimation. What was the point of even having cannons if shooting one got you treated like a criminal? The confusion must have been clear on her face, because Brigitte sighed.

"Cannon shots on the wall mean danger," the lieutenant explained. "Trost sits in the same southern position on Wall Rose that Shiganshina occupied on Wall Maria when it fell. There's not a soul in this city who doesn't know that, or who doesn't understand what the sound of a cannon could mean. The only reason the people of Trost are able to live their lives in peace is because we keep that fear from them. That's the Garrison's job. We don't just walk the wall. We *are* the wall. So the next time you decide to play hero, Private, I suggest you find a quieter way to do it."

Rosalie lowered her eyes, feeling like she was going to cry. As the soldiers were marching them back along the wall, she'd noticed the streets of Trost seemed oddly active, but she'd never considered that it could be panic, or because of her.

"I'm sorry," she whispered. "I didn't think—I didn't know that I—" She took a deep breath. "Did my actions cause damage to Trost?"

"No," Brigitte said solemnly. "The local military police kept things from getting out of hand this time, but panic of the sort you could have caused is one of the most dangerous situations we face out here. The titans will eat us if they ever break through, but fear can make us eat ourselves. You attacked Trost as much as you did the titan when you fired that cannon. That's a violation of your oath of service to the Garrison, and you must face consequences for it."

"Yes, ma'am," Rosalie said shakily. "I understand what you're saying, and I don't disagree, but . . . "

The lieutenant cocked a gray eyebrow. "But?"

"I don't see what else I could have done," Rosalie finished. Because if she was going to stick her foot in her mouth arguing with an officer, she might as well go for the knee. "If I hadn't shot the cannon, Jax would have—"

"I'm well aware of what Sergeant Cunningham did," Brigitte said angrily. "Your squadmates told me what happened. There's no question in my mind that your actions saved the life of Sergeant Jackson Cunningham, but that doesn't excuse the fact that you disobeyed a direct order and fired the cannon without permission.

These are offenses that must be punished. I won't have anyone saying I went easy on you because you're Charles Dumarque's daughter."

The mention of her father made Rosalie's blood run cold. "You're not going to tell him about this, are you?"

The lieutenant looked disgusted. "This is the Garrison, not boarding school. Unless they die in combat, I don't make a habit of talking to my soldiers' parents. You're going to have to face this on your own."

Rosalie nodded and pulled herself straight, meeting the old lieutenant's eyes as she braced for the worst.

"Rosalie Dumarque," Brigitte said formally, "as a trained cannoneer, you automatically entered the Garrison as a private first class. As of tonight, you are demoted to private second class."

She'd been expecting that, but Rosalie still couldn't stop from wincing. Private second class was the lowest rank in the Garrison, but Brigitte wasn't finished.

"I'm also continuing your assignment to Jackson Cunningham's squad."

Rosalie blinked. "I—I'm sorry, ma'am. Is that . . . it that part of my punishment?

"No," Brigitte said. "It's Cunningham's." Her expression softened to the point that Rosalie thought she looked almost amused. "Jax has been a frustration of mine for a long time, but ordering his squad to stand down while he faced a dozen titans alone is one of the cockiest, *stupidest* stunts he's ever pulled."

Rosalie clenched her jaw.

"Your use of the cannon was unauthorized and very poorly thought out, but the rest of your solution was brave, creative, and effective. We need more soldiers who aren't afraid to use their brains. Cunningham tells me you don't belong here. The fact that you passed the Red Line is proof enough for me that you're serious, so until you break another rule, you stay right where you are." Her lips quirked into an actual smile. "You and Jax will have to learn to get along."

"Yes, ma'am," Rosalie said, relieved.

"And your entire squad has kitchen duty tomorrow for keeping me up late dealing with this rot," the lieutenant added grumpily, pulling out her papers again. "Dismissed."

The paved training yard was dark and empty when Rosalie finally left Brigitte's tower. All the soldiers were still at dinner, lingering over their meager rations to stretch their one hour of free time before bed as long as possible. Given the hollowness in her stomach, Rosalie should have joined them. But hungry as she was, sitting down next to her fellow soldiers like nothing had happened felt impossible. So she sank on the steps leading up to the wall and tried to sort out how everything had gone so wrong.

She'd come here to use her superior training in the fight against the titans. Instead, she'd nearly gotten eaten, disobeyed orders, almost started a riot, and been demoted to the lowest rank the Garrison had—and that was just in her first two days.

Rosalie sank lower on the step, dropping her head into her hands. All those big words to her father about showing these poor, under-educated soldiers how it was done, and she was the one who'd been shown up. No wonder everyone here thought she was playing soldier. She didn't know the first thing about life in the Garrison, as the last two days had clearly shown.

Sniffing, Rosalie forced herself to sit up and dry her face. This sort of thinking was unbecoming of a Dumarque, and it didn't help anything. If she quit now, all she'd do was cement her defeat, and it was far too early for that. Obviously there was a lot more to fighting on the front lines than she'd assumed. But she could learn. All she needed was someone to teach her, and though the thought made her stomach sink, Rosalie knew just the person for the job.

With that, she hauled herself off the step and set out to look for Jax.

Finding him proved much harder than anticipated.

The soldiers on watch were eager to talk to Rosalie now that word had gotten out that she was one of *those* Dumarques, but none of them knew where Jax was. When Rosalie asked if he'd gone into town, the men had laughed for a solid minute. Apparently, Jax never left the base, not even on his nights off. Not even during paid leave, which was absurd. As training for her inevitable marriage, Rosalie had helped her mother manage their household staff for three years, and she'd never had an employee choose to spend their vacation at their job.

Things only got odder from there. The other sergeants said Jax never came down to play darts or cards. The cooks said he never ate in the mess hall. According to everyone she asked, Jax never went anywhere or did anything, at least not with other people. Rosalie was starting to think he was a ghost who appeared only to torment recruits when she bumped into a veteran happy to help.

A handsome old tower guard with steel-gray hair and a battle scar across his left cheek, Cooper not only claimed to know where Jax was but seemed delighted to give Rosalie directions. He was so helpful, she was a little nervous she was walking into a prank. But when she followed his directions to the top of the Trost Gate, there was Jax, sitting alone with his back against one of the big cannons, reading a battered, pocket-sized book by the light of the full moon.

"I don't know what you think you're doing, Private," Jax said without looking up. "But I'm not obligated to see you until tomorrow, so kindly piss off."

Rosalie set her jaw and walked out onto the gate until she was standing beside him. "Sir," she said, keeping her voice as clear and genuine as she could, "I'd like to apologize for my actions today."

"Are you deaf? I said *piss*—" He stopped suddenly. "Wait, what?"

"I'm sorry for firing the cannon and for disobeying your orders," Rosalie clarified, bowing formally, from her waist, as she would before a nobleman. "I thought I was doing the right thing, but I did not fully understand the situation. It was arrogant and wrong of me to assume I knew best, and I am very sorry for the trouble I caused you and the people of Trost. I promise to listen next time and obey your orders exactly."

She ducked her head even lower to show her sincerity, but when she straightened up, Jax was staring at her in bewilderment. The expression lasted a full five seconds before collapsing back into his usual sneer.

"If it were up to me, there wouldn't be a next time," he grumbled, closing his book. "I don't even understand why you're here. You've got money and a family who cares enough to spend it on you, and I've been hearing all about how famous your dad is. A girl like you could get posted anywhere she wanted. Woermann would probably give you his captaincy if you asked nicely enough, so why do you insist on bothering us? What do you want?"

Rosalie looked him straight in the face. "I want to fight the titans."

"Oh, well, mission accomplished," he said sarcastically. "You shot one into bloody chunks. Now go home."

"One isn't enough," she said, desperate to make him understand. "I want to push them all back. You keep harping on about how rich my family is, but the titans don't care that Dumarque is an ancient and noble house. If we don't fight them, we'll be just as dead as everyone else."

"Good."

"*Not* good," she said, clenching her fists. "Why can't you see that we're all in the same boat?"

"'Cause I never been in a boat," he snapped, rolling to his feet. "You want to help the war against the titans? Go home and tell your rich dad to up the Garrison's budget. Some decent gear would do a lot more good than you prancing around on the wall shooting cannons."

"I *am* going to talk to my father about the situation here," Rosalie said angrily. "The lack of proper equipment for the front lines is deplorable. But that's not the only thing I can do. You told me earlier that I had no idea what I was doing, and I see now that you were right. I don't know anything about life on the wall, but that doesn't mean I can't learn. I want to get better, to fight the titans as well as you do."

Jax rolled his eyes. "Save your flattery for someone who cares."

"I'm not trying to flatter you," Rosalie said earnestly. "I saw what you did today with my own eyes. You killed ten titans in the time it took me to unstick a rusted cannon. That's the sort of soldier I want to be. One who can fight the titans and win."

"There's more to it than that," Jax snapped.

"Then teach me," Rosalie said, stepping closer. "You accuse me of being ignorant, but the cure for ignorance is to learn. If I don't know anything, instruct me. Show me how to be a proper Garrison soldier by your standards, and I promise I'll never be a burden to you again."

Jax stared down at her, his blue eyes gleaming black in the moonlight before he turned away. "No."

"Why not?" Rosalie demanded.

"Because I don't like you."

"How can you say that?" she asked. "You don't even know me. How can you dislike someone you don't even know?"

"I'll dislike anyone I want!" he cried. "You nobles might own all the land left in the world, but you don't own me!"

"I'm not trying to own you," Rosalie explained patiently. "I'm just asking you to—"

"And I'm saying no," Jax snarled, crossing his arms tight over his chest. "First, I don't want to, and second, it ain't my job. Recruits are supposed to come to the wall fully trained. If you want someone to hold your hand, there's a thousand idiots downstairs who're dying to teach *Lady* Rosalie Dumarque whatever she wants to know. Go bother one of them. I'd transfer you myself, but Brigitte thinks it's funny to tie you to my back. But don't ever assume that just because I'm forced to be your sergeant means I care, because I don't. The only thing I want from you is for you to be gone. That clear enough for you?"

"I'm not asking you to like me," Rosalie said firmly, meeting Jax glare for glare. "All I want is a chance to prove I belong on this wall. Just give me one month. If you teach me, I swear I'll do anything you say. I will listen and work hard, and if you still think I'm not serious by the end, I'll leave. I'll resign from the Garrison with no questions asked, and you'll never have to see me again."

Jax tilted his head like he wasn't sure if that was a joke or not. "*Anything* I say?"

"Well, obviously I won't commit treason or do anything criminal," Rosalie said quickly. "But if it's important to the wall and my training, then yes. Pretty much anything."

"You sure you 'bout that?" Jax said, leaning in until he was looming over her. "The rumors about me ain't all true, but they're not all wrong, either. If you're stupid enough to sign on knowing that, I'll teach you just for the joy of watching you fail, but understand this'll be a hell of your own making. I'm not playing around."

"Neither am I," Rosalie said, glaring back at him.

Jax arched a dark eyebrow, and then he stepped back with a shrug. "Your funeral, then," he said, putting out his hand.

Not having spent much time around commoners, it took Rosalie several seconds to realize he wanted to shake on their deal. Once she did, she grabbed his calloused hand hard, trying to squeeze his fingers just as painfully as he squeezed hers.

"Training starts first thing tomorrow," Jax said when he let go. "Be up here one hour before the bell, and if you're not waiting when I walk up the stairs, you're done."

"I'll be here," she promised. "You won't regret this."

From the look on his face as he walked off, Rosalie suspected Jax already did.

C H A P T E R   S E V E N

In the predawn dark of the next morning, Rosalie got to the top of the wall fifteen minutes before Jax had told her to be there, and she still beat him by only a hair.

When he saw her waiting, her torch already set in the holder by the cannons, his face turned sourer than an old grape. He didn't even say hello before ordering her to start on jumps, and not the sort done with maneuvering gear. These were regular old jump squats, crouching down until her thighs were parallel to the ground before leaping as high as she could. The moment Rosalie landed, he ordered her to do it again, over and over and over until her legs were on fire.

Jax didn't even bother to watch. He just sat on top of one of the big stationary cannons, eating an apple and reading his book, which she could now see was an ancient copy of the Garrison's Rules and Regulations manual. He yelled whenever the sound of her feet hitting the ground slowed to anything less than a frantic pace, but otherwise he didn't say a word. If he hadn't been so obviously trying to discourage her, Rosalie would have been furious at him for wasting their time. She knew his game now, though, and she doggedly played along, jumping to the absolute edge of her ability until the morning bell rang.

She collapsed on the ground, panting as spots danced in front of her eyes. She was debating whether to throw up when a hand suddenly appeared in front of her.

When she looked up, Jax was standing over her with a grudging look on his face. "That wasn't as bad as I expected," he admitted gruffly. "Another few months and you might be passable."

"A compliment?" Rosalie asked as she grabbed his hand. "What's wrong? Are you sick?"

Jax scowled and yanked her to her feet. He let go as soon as she was standing, returning to his cannon to grab a small packet wrapped in brown paper.

"Here," he said, tossing it at her.

Rosalie grabbed it out of the air right before it hit her in the face. "What's this?"

"Breakfast," he answered, hopping back up onto the cannon to finish his apple. When her eyes widened, he looked away with a sneer. "Don't act like it's your birthday. I'm not feeding you because I want to. It's just there's no way you'll make it to breakfast with your legs in that condition, and Lieutenant Brigitte threatened to dock my pay if I starved any of you again."

That was a lot of excuses, but Rosalie let it be. She was too busy ripping open the packet, her mouth watering when she saw two slices of honey-smeared bread and a small apple. "Thank you," she said as she shoved the bread into her mouth.

Jax waved the words away and hunched lower, staring down at his book like he was trying to burn a hole through the page.

"Do you enjoy reading the Garrison Rules and Regulations?"

His jaw clamped tight. "Why do you want to know?"

"Just making conversation," Rosalie said, pulling out her pocket knife to slice the apple into wedges. "But since you asked, I noticed you reading it last night as well, and I was wondering why. It doesn't exactly seem like a riveting choice."

"It's not exciting, if that's what you mean," Jax said sourly. "But knowing the rules and regs inside and out is key to surviving up here, and it ain't as though I've got anything else to read."

Rosalie stopped cutting mid-slice, her jaw falling open in horror. "You don't have any books?"

The moment the words were out of her mouth, Rosalie knew she'd stepped in it. "No, I don't," Jax snarled, his face turning red. "Books cost a lot of money, and some of us got more pressing concerns, like food and not freezing to death. Not that you'd know about that."

"I'm sorry," Rosalie said immediately. "You're right, that was thoughtless of me."

Her quick apology seemed to throw him. "Yeah, well, don't do it again," he grumbled, turning away.

Rosalie couldn't help herself. "What if I gave you a book?"

"I don't want your damn charity."

"It's not charity," she said. "You're giving up your free time to train me. It's only fitting that I offer something in return. Since you're my officer, it's against regulation for me to pay you money—"

"Section one, article fifteen, paragraph two," Jax recited. "Regulations Regarding Bribery."

"—but it doesn't say anywhere that I can't loan you a book," Rosalie finished. "I kept several when I sent back my—" She stopped. Jax had never mentioned the incident with her luggage, which could only mean he didn't know about it. Not wanting to lower his already rock-bottom opinion of her, Rosalie skipped ahead. "Anyway, I'd be happy to let you borrow one."

Jax glared at the ground, his face a dark cloud. But the promise of reading material that wasn't a rules book must have been a strong temptation, because a moment later, he gave her a sideways look. "What you got?"

Rosalie popped her last apple wedge into her mouth to hide her grin. "A bit of everything," she said, limping toward the stairs. "Let me go down and get them, then you can pick the one you want before we report for kitchen duty."

"You mean before *you* report for kitchen duty," Jax said. "I told Brigitte you volunteered to fill in for me."

"What?!"

"Consider it part of your training," he replied smugly, getting more comfortable on his cannon. "Bring your library up tomorrow and I'll have a look. Until then, I believe Cook's expecting you in the kitchens."

Rosalie shot him a killing look. But she was the one who'd promised to obey his every command, so she swallowed her pride and started down the stairs, hobbling as fast as her aching legs would go.

Despite being considered a punishment by both Jax and Brigitte, kitchen duty wasn't actually that bad. It mostly involved sitting in the warm mess hall peeling potatoes, practically a holiday compared to scraping bird poop while dangling over titans.

Rosalie took a while to figure out how to cut the slippery potato peel quickly without also cutting her fingers. Once Emmett showed her how to slice away from herself, though, things got much better. So much better, they actually finished early. Rosalie was headed for the barracks to catch up on all the sleep she'd missed when Emmett caught her sleeve.

"Rosalie," he said, his voice oddly serious, "can we borrow your maneuver gear?"

"Why?" she asked, surprised. "We're off duty."

"That's why we're asking," Willow said, wiping the last of the slimy potato starch off her hands. "Off duty is the only time we can practice, and we need it bad. If you hadn't helped us, we'd both've fallen off the wall during cleaning yesterday."

"It's hard to isolate problems when you're working with broken gear," Emmett piped up. "Your suit is quality, though. If we use it, I'm hoping it'll help us figure out why we're so bad."

"Emmett and me didn't even want to be in the Garrison," Willow continued, "but it was the only branch of the military we could get into with our low maneuver gear scores."

"We did pretty well on everything else, though," Emmett said hopefully. "If we can just improve our maneuver gear skills, I bet we can still transfer next year."

"Transfer to where?" Rosalie asked. "The Military Police?"

That was where most recruits wanted to go, but Emmett and Willow were both shaking their heads.

"Who'd want to work there?" Willow said scornfully, wrapping her arm around Emmett's shoulders. "We're gunning for the Survey Corps."

Rosalie couldn't have heard that right. "You want to join the Survey Corps?"

Emmett nodded excitedly. "They're why we signed up for the military in the first place. Unfortunately, Survey Corps has the highest requirements of any branch when it comes to maneuver gear. I thought we were done for when our scores came back, but then Willow had the idea to join the Garrison instead."

"It's brilliant," Willow said proudly. "Working here gets us gear, lodging, food, and an excuse to practice our maneuvering. And we get paid. It ain't much, but it's better than the nothing you get in the

Training Corps." She smiled at Emmett. "We're hoping to get our skills up enough to put in for a transfer next summer."

Rosalie was gaping in horror now. "It's a clever plan," she admitted, voice shaking. "But . . . why? Maybe you haven't heard, but the Survey Corps is a death sentence! They're the smallest branch of the military, but they have a higher casualty rate than all the others put together. I don't think they've ever had a mission where someone didn't die. Why would you ever want to join—"

"Because they're the ones who go beyond the walls," Emmett said without missing a beat. "And that's where we want to go, too."

"That's where the answers are," Willow said, scowling at her. "Haven't you ever wondered where the titans come from? Why they're here? How they're able to regrow a head after it gets shot off by a cannon?"

"It *is* mysterious," Emmett said. "But everyone's too caught up in killing them to wonder about it. The Survey Corps are the only ones who try to find out."

"They're the ones who explore," Willow said excitedly, her face breaking into the most earnest smile Rosalie had ever seen from her. "Don't you want to know what's beyond the walls? There's a whole world out there! Haven't you ever wondered what it looks like?"

"All my life," Rosalie said, remembering the view from her roof.

"Exactly!" Willow said with a grin. "So can we borrow your gear or not?"

Rosalie grinned back. "Let me get it from my bunk."

As promised, Rosalie brought her books to her early-morning training session the next day. Jax looked them over while she killed herself doing pushups; he settled on a historical novel for his first read. It was one of Rosalie's favorites, a sordid, bloody drama about a wronged nobleman who destroys his family, his fortune, and his future in the reckless pursuit of revenge.

Rosalie expected Jax to rip right through it, but by the end of their first week, he'd barely made it past the first few pages. When she offered to loan him a new book since he clearly didn't like this one, he'd snapped at her that he liked it fine. He was just taking his time. When he still hadn't finished chapter one by the next week, though, Rosalie grew suspicious.

"Are you *sure* you like it?" she asked for the tenth time when he'd called a halt to her exercises (lunges, this time—hundreds of them) "I promise I won't be insulted if you don't."

"You think I care about insulting you?" he snapped. "I like it fine."

"Then why are you taking so long?" she pressed. "Really, it's okay. I can loan you another—"

"I'm not a good reader, all right?"

Rosalie's lips pressed into an O, and Jax dropped his head with an angry sigh. "I don't care if you judge me," he said sullenly. "I know I'm not up to your standards, but I'm damn good by mine. Most Garrison soldiers can barely read at all. Your book has a lot of words I don't know, so it's going slow. But I like it fine and I'm going to finish it. Just stop rushing me."

"I'll stop," Rosalie promised, looking down at the paper-wrapped breakfast he brought her every morning. "But . . . isn't it frustrating?"

"Of course it's frustrating," he said. "But I'll get there. Always do."

Rosalie nodded, rolling her apple thoughtfully between her fingers. "What if I helped you?"

He looked away with a snort. "I don't want your help."

"Why not?" she asked. "You're helping me get stronger. Why shouldn't I help you in return? That way we'll both get something we want and be better for it."

"You and your bloody trades," he muttered, glancing at the

barely started book in his hands. Then, quietly, he asked, "You won't tell anyone?"

"I swear I will not," Rosalie replied, crossing her heart. "We can meet up here in the evenings. No one goes on the wall at night, and it probably won't be for long. Once I get you through the rough bits, I'm sure you'll have no problem reading the rest yourself."

Jax was silent for a long time after that, and then he nodded. "All right," he said. "Meet me here tonight after dinner, and if you tell anyone about this, I'll push you off the wall."

Rosalie swore up and down that she would not, which was how, starting that night after supper, Jax took over her evenings as well, waiting for her between the cannons with her book clutched in his hands.

After that, they fell into a pattern. Every morning before sunrise, they'd meet on top of the gate for training, and every evening they met there again to read. Rosalie wasn't sure if it was the power of a good novel or if she'd just worn him down through sheer exposure, but over the next few weeks, Jax became considerably more pleasant to her.

Not nice. He was never that. In fact, their morning training sessions became more brutal since Jax had started paying attention, adding maneuvering gear challenges and sword practice on top of exercising her to death. He corrected her form ruthlessly, smacking her limbs every time she moved out of position, and he still refused to call her by her proper name. It was always "princess" or "rich girl" or "hey, you."

Jax's training was harder than anything she'd endured at the academy. For weeks, Rosalie could do nothing right. Then, slowly, his corrections became smaller. Her limbs got stronger, which made the exercises feel less brutal. Her sword work improved as well, and her balance in maneuvering gear improved enormously, to the point where the rest of the squad started to notice.

When Jax let them off work late one evening after a long patrol, Willow and Emmett cornered Rosalie in the doorway to the tower stairs, demanding to know whom she was practicing with. Rosalie dodged their questions as best she could, but they were dogged, and soon enough, the truth came out.

"Jax?" Willow cried. "You've been training with *Jax*?"

"Not so loud!" Rosalie hissed, looking over her shoulder at Jax, who was talking with another sergeant just a few meters down the wall.

"Isn't he trying to get you kicked out?" Emmett said, only slightly quieter. "I thought he hated you."

"Why didn't you invite us?" Willow asked at the same time. "You know how bad we need help!"

"Because I barely got him to train me," Rosalie said. "He wouldn't even think about it until I'd promised to do everything he said and that I'd quit the Garrison if I didn't live up to his expectations."

Willow looked horrified. "You gave him that much power over you?" She shook her head. "You like to live dangerously."

"He was trying to get rid of me anyway," Rosalie argued. "This way gives him a guaranteed out, which means he can stop sabotaging me during patrol. Plus, I get training. You've seen how good he is."

"He's good at killing titans," Willow agreed. "But you're an idiot for handing him your career. Even if the rumors about him being a murderer are mostly bollocks, we've seen his crazy with our own eyes, and he *hates* nobles."

"He'll work you to death for the fun of it," Emmett agreed. "Then flog your corpse for good measure before he kicks you out."

"He's not *that* bad," Rosalie said, chuckling.

"Not that bad?!" Emmett cried. "He just made us push a cannon all the way to the junction with the main wall!"

It had been a long walk. Thanks to Rosalie's new muscles, though, she hadn't noticed the distance like she used to. A fact that didn't escape Willow.

"Do you think he'd train us, too?" the medic asked.

"Willow!" Emmett cried, horrified. "You just said he was crazy!"

"He is," Willow said. "But you can't argue with his results." She pointed at Rosalie. "If he can turn this spoiled creampuff—"

"Hey!" Rosalie said.

"—into a hardened wall veteran, imagine what he could do for us!" She considered what she'd just said. "This could be our chance."

"Our chance to die," Emmett muttered.

Willow crossed her arms over her chest. "Do you want to get into Survey Corps or not?"

Emmett slumped in defeat, and Willow's smile softened. "There's my Emmett," she said, giving him a soft punch on the shoulder before turning to Rosalie. "We're in."

At that, Rosalie felt panic. Inviting other people into the delicate truce she'd formed with Jax was starting to feel . . . wrong.

"It's no fun," she warned them. "You have to be on the wall an hour before the bell, and the exercises are brutal. Terrible, really. And who knows if he'll agree to teach you."

"Oh, he'll say yes," Willow assured her. "Lieutenant Brigitte herself praised Emmett and me for training on our own just last week, and Jax never goes against the gate lieutenant. She's the only person on this wall he actually listens to."

"And he *is* always yelling at us to stop being terrible," Emmett added, his face grim, like he couldn't believe he was arguing for this.

"Good point," Willow said excitedly. "We've got him cornered. He has to train us."

"Right," Rosalie said, stomach sinking. She wanted to remind them that, just a few minutes ago, they'd been horrified at the very thought of Jax training anybody, but Willow was already jogging toward the sergeant, waving her arms over her head to get his attention. Rosalie was too far away to hear what she said, but Jax's face turned murderous a few moments later, and Rosalie ducked into the stairwell before he could look for her.

"I'm going to dinner," she said as she ran down the stairs. "Let me know what he says, Emmett!"

"If we survive," Emmett called nervously after her.

When Rosalie climbed back up the wall that evening for their regular reading time, she could feel the waves of anger coming off of Jax.

"I'm sorry," she said as soon as she saw him. "I know I shouldn't have told Willow and Emmett about our training sessions without talking to you first, but they put me on the spot. I didn't want to hurt their feelings."

"I'm not mad about that," Jax said, dragging his hands through his thick black hair, which was getting longer as the winter dragged on. "I would've included them from the start if I'd been thinking. They need the work more than you do. It's just . . . "

He trailed off with a frustrated huff that Rosalie wasn't sure how to interpret. "Just what?"

"Nothing," he said, sitting down between the cannons. "Let's just read."

Relieved, Rosalie dropped down on the stone beside him, thumbing her book open to where they'd left off the night before. Since it would be taken the wrong way if her books were found in Jax's possession, they'd agreed Rosalie should keep track of them. This meant Jax could only read when they were together, but that was for the best since his reading needed a lot more work than Rosalie had realized. He was fine with small words, but the larger ones tripped him up, which made for very rough going on a book as complicated as the one he'd chosen.

But frustrating as it was watching someone stumble their way through a story she'd read a hundred times, Rosalie was keenly aware that this was her best chance to worm her way into Jax's good graces. She was patient as a saint: following silently as he read aloud, correcting him gently when he got stuck, never making fun. And it worked.

In the few weeks since they'd started, Jax had gone from half a page per night to whole chapters. Now they were almost at the end, and even though Rosalie knew the story by heart, seeing Jax experience it for the first time was almost better than reading it herself. He tried to downplay his excitement, but no one could read about the fiendish cleverness and self-destructive drive of the Count of Monte Cristo's quest for revenge without getting caught up in it.

By the time they reached the final chapter, Jax was plowing through the text without even a sideways glare at Rosalie when she corrected him, which she was having to do less and less. It didn't hurt that when he wasn't snapping at her Jax had a lovely voice, deep and rich and full of emotion. It was the sort of voice you could fall into, which she must have, because when the bell rang for lights out an hour later, Rosalie was surprised to find she'd scooted from her spot a respectful distance away to sitting practically in his lap, pressed up against his arm in her eagerness to see the page.

She darted away the moment she realized her mistake, face burning. "Sorry."

"It's all right," he replied, his own face oddly dark in the torchlight. "Damn that bell, though. We were just getting to the good part."

"It's *really* good," she promised with a smile. "Something to look forward to tomorrow."

She could hardly see in the dark, but Rosalie would have sworn he smiled back at her. Actually smiled, not a smirk or an evil grin. She was about to call him on it when Jax suddenly reached into his pocket.

"Wait," he said, pulling out a folded envelope. "I almost forgot. You got a letter today."

His words instantly killed Rosalie's good mood. "Really?" she said at last. "I was wondering"—*dreading*—"when one would come."

She took the elegant envelope and tore it open with shaking fingers, holding the parchment up to the light. To her enormous surprise, it wasn't a scathing note from her father demanding she come home. "It's from my mother," she said, squinting at Lady Dumarque's cursive, which, as always, was so elegant it was nearly impossible to read. "She wants me to come home for our Longest Night party."

"Sounds like fun," Jax said, leaning over in a subtle—but not nearly subtle enough now that Rosalie knew his habits—attempt to read over her shoulder. "I'd forgotten Longest Night was coming up."

So had Rosalie. It didn't seem possible that she'd been in Trost that long, but when she added up the weeks in her head, they were only three days away from the winter solstice.

"Getting leave won't be a problem," Jax went on. "The whole Garrison gets off for Longest Night. Command throws a big party every year with a bonfire and free drinks and everything. Supposed to be good for morale, but the whole thing usually ends in a brawl." He wrinkled his nose. "Probably a good thing you're missing it."

"Trust me, I'd much rather be in a brawl here than at one of my mother's parties," Rosalie groaned. "They're so boring. I'm not allowed to talk about anything except the weather, my dress, shops my mother approves of, and how eligible my youngest brother is."

"At least the food will be good," Jax said. "I've heard stories about noble parties. Don't you have whole roast pigs with apples in their mouths?"

"Not at our house," Rosalie said, slightly scandalized. A dead pig on a table? Her mother would faint. "But the food *is* very good, I'm just not allowed to eat any of it. Have you ever tried to eat while wearing a corset?"

"Can't say that I have," Jax replied, arching an eyebrow. "How do you manage to make being rich sound so terrible?"

"Everyone has problems, I suppose," she said with a shrug. "But at least I won't have to make the journey home alone. Mother's enlisted Ferdinand to escort me."

"Who's that?" he asked. "Your butler?"

Rosalie shook her head, folding the letter back into the envelope. "He's my fiancé."

Jax jerked away so fast she jumped. "You have a fiancé?"

"Well, yes," Rosalie said, utterly caught off guard. "Of course I do. Why do you think I was allowed to come down here?"

"You said you wanted to fight titans!"

"That's what *I* wanted," she said. "And I had to fight hard to get that much. But my father would never have allowed me to enroll in mixed company if I was single. That's just ridiculous."

"The Garrison's full of single girls!" Jax cried, staring at her like she'd betrayed him. "You're the one being ridiculous, having a fiancé you never even mentioned!"

"I wasn't trying to keep it secret," Rosalie said defensively. "It just never seemed important."

"How is getting married not important?" Jax demanded, crossing his arms. "Do you like him?"

Rosalie had to stop and think about that one. "He's fine, I suppose," she said at last. "Honestly, I don't know him very well. We've been engaged since I was eleven, but I've only met him a handful of times."

This seemed to mollify Jax somewhat. "So he's a stranger," he said, and then his scowl darkened. "What kind of father engages his eleven-year-old daughter to someone she doesn't know?"

"I was a bit young," Rosalie admitted. "But that's not unheard of. All noble marriages are arranged, and this one's a good connection for both of our families. The Smythes have been extremely obliging. They could have made me get married the moment I turned sixteen, but they gave me a whole year to do what I liked. Once I graduated from the academy, I chose to spend it here." She smiled wistfully. "Really, I've had far more freedom than any of my sisters. I'm grateful to the Smythe family for being so understanding."

"You're grateful to them for not forcing you into marriage the moment they could?" Jax said angrily. "Can you not hear how messed up that is?"

"It's not messed up!" she cried. "I'm doing this for my family! I'm a Dumarque. I have a duty to my house and my—"

"Hang your house," Jax said. "What about their duty to you? Say what you want about us Maria folk, at least we look out for our own."

Rosalie sucked in a breath. That was going too far. "My father's looked out for me since I was born! All noble families do this. It's perfectly normal."

"There's nothing normal about forcing your daughter to marry a man she hardly knows," Jax said stubbornly.

"Well, we are clearly going to have to agree to disagree," she said in a cold voice.

"Nothing doing," Jax snapped, his low-class Maria accent becoming even thicker in his anger. "I'm never going to agree with something that treats you like you're cattle, and I don't understand why you're willing to, either. I mean, what the hell, Rosalie? You're smarter than this."

Rosalie was too angry to meet his eyes. She just pulled her outrage around her like a cloak and marched down the stairs, stomping away with such fury, she completely missed the fact that Jax had finally called her by her name.

CHAPTER EIGHT

Rosalie didn't go to practice the next morning.

She stayed in bed, lying with her eyes open in the dark until the bell sounded. Willow and Emmett must have gone without her because she didn't see them at breakfast, which she ate alone, sitting on the end of a bench in the mess hall while soldiers with hopes of impressing a genuine noble desperately tried to make conversation.

When she put on her gear and reported to the wall for duty, Jax was already there, coaching Emmett and Willow on the best ways to land from a single-anchor suspension. It was a surprisingly friendly scene, at least until she arrived.

The moment Rosalie stepped onto the top of the wall, Jax snapped at the others to wrap up and get ready for assignments. To Rosalie, though, he said nothing. He just grabbed his paper-wrapped breakfast and stomped off toward the cannon they were scheduled to move.

The rest of the day was more of the same. Emmett desperately tried to fill the void with lively stories about his and Willow's history as the least popular children in their Maria village. But though the tales were funny, no one laughed. Eventually, he petered out, and the whole squad lapsed into sullen silence, speaking only when necessary. When evening came, Jax dismissed them early and clomped off to his sulking spot by the cannons—the place Rosalie had started thinking of as *their* reading spot.

She didn't go to reading that night. And she skipped practice again the next morning.

It was harder the second time. Rightfully angry as she was, Jax's coaching had been her idea. She didn't think he'd use this as an excuse to claim she'd broken their deal, but skipping practice was only hurting her.

Except . . . it was getting difficult to ignore the nagging question that had been weighing on her since her mother's letter arrived: *What was all this training for?*

Without question Jax's work had made her a better soldier. But Rosalie knew now that her dreams of turning the war around had been foolish, childish fantasies. So what was she doing here? She'd put everything she had into this, but no matter how good she got at killing titans, her tour of duty would be over at the start of summer. After that, she'd be a wife, and she'd have no reason to use these skills ever again. Why was she acting like she had a future here? Was she playing solider, as her father claimed?

The uncomfortable questions kept Rosalie awake all night. When she couldn't stand being in bed any longer, she got up and went to practice by herself in the yard, using the armory roof as a launching platform for the exercises Jax had been teaching her before he'd decided to be an idiot. It might be for nothing, but at least the work kept her from stewing and let her avoid awkward questions as Willow and Emmett walked by on their way to morning training.

Thankfully, today wasn't the usual schedule. Today was the day of Longest Night, the festival celebrating the winter solstice. It was the most important of the winter holidays with parties held all over the city, but the Garrison's celebration was the biggest of all. With the exception of a few skeleton crews to keep the wall functional, every soldier had been pulled off work to help with the preparations. Tables were moved out of the mess hall to hold the epic amount of food the kitchen was cooking. On the street in front of the blocked gate, a tower of logs had been built for the bonfire that traditionally burned all night. Rosalie was in the courtyard helping the cooks set up the table that would hold the traditional winter cakes when someone tapped her on the shoulder.

She glanced up to see one of the guards from the front gate, and standing behind him was a prim older woman dressed in somber black velvet whose familiar, disapproving face made Rosalie want to drop what she was doing and run.

"Mrs. Brixton," she said instead, forcing a smile. "What are you doing here?"

The old woman's scowl deepened at Rosalie's false cheerfulness. Before she could scold her for it, though, Jax appeared between them, glaring over the old lady's graying head at the guard cowering behind her. "Who's this, Private? What're you thinking, letting civilians in here?"

"Sorry, sir," the guard said nervously. "But she had a letter from the captain, and she wouldn't leave."

"Of course she wouldn't," Rosalie said, stepping around Jax with an angry look. "This is Lady Dumarque's personal maid, Mrs. Brixton."

"I don't care if it's Lady Dumarque herself," Jax snapped. "This is a military base. Civilians are—"

"Lady Rosalie," Mrs. Brixton interrupted, speaking over Jax.

"Your mother has sent me to prepare you for tonight. I've brought your dress."

She nodded back at the large trunk the driver was pulling out of the hired carriage in the alley, and Rosalie's eyes widened. "Mother wants me to dress here?"

"There's nowhere else to do it," Mrs. Brixton said, looking down her nose at Rosalie so sternly, she might as well have added *you stupid girl*. "Mr. Ferdinand Smythe will be here to pick you up in less than an hour, and you can't meet your fiancé in *that*." She reached out to pluck the coarse sleeve of Rosalie's uniform with the expression of someone who'd just touched a corpse.

"I would have arrived sooner so we could wash your hair, but this young man"—she turned her scowl on the guard, who cringed—"has wasted so much of my time, that's no longer an option. We'll just have to make do with a good stiff brushing."

The memory of Mrs. Brixton's "good stiff brushings" gave Rosalie an involuntary shiver, but nothing could be done. This was her duty, so she turned with a sigh, looking at Jax directly for the first time in two days.

"Sergeant," she said, "it seems I have a pressing family engagement. May I have the rest of the day off?"

She half expected Jax to deny her out of spite, but he just waved his hand. "Do what you want. Just be back for roll call tomorrow, or I'm reporting you AWOL."

"Yes, sir," Rosalie said, startled. "Thank you, sir."

But Jax had already turned away, stalking through the crowded yard while the other soldiers scrambled to get out of his way. Rosalie was still watching him go when Mrs. Brixton grabbed her by the arm and dragged her into the barracks to change.

❦ ❦ ❦

"She has a fiancé."

Cooper said nothing, just kept maneuvering his end of the slatted wooden table they'd been asked to carry.

"She's getting dressed up for him right now," Jax continued angrily. "In the barracks with her fancy mother's fancy maid who showed up for work wearing a dress nicer than anything my own mum ever laid eyes on."

"That's her world," Cooper said with a shrug as they dropped the table and went back for the benches, hoisting one under each arm. "You knew she was noble. You damn well wouldn't shut up about it. The real question is why seeing the proof now makes you look like you want to kill something."

Because he was a damn fool.

Jax dropped the benches with a crash that made a nearby group of laughing soldiers jump. He had to get away from all these damn happy people and the festival cheer that was already invading the yard, but he didn't know where to go. His favorite hiding place at the top of the gate was ruined. He'd gone up there last night, and all he'd been able to think about was how Rosalie wasn't there with him.

"It's my own fault," he said bitterly. "I let myself get distracted and forgot what nobles are like. Always stepping on people, always trading yours to get theirs. Rosalie's no different. Just look at her hair. No one has hair that shiny without eating like a king while others starve."

"I confess, I have not made a study of her hair," Cooper said, his face splitting into an evil grin. "And it's 'Rosalie' now, is it?"

"Shut up."

Cooper raised his hands. "I'm just saying. You claim she's a typical noble, but I've seen the way you train her. You've pushed her hard enough to kill a man twice her size."

"Because I'm trying to make her leave."

"And yet she doesn't," Cooper said, his infuriating smile growing wider. "She keeps coming back for more, and she's been spending her evenings with you as well. That's a lot of time with someone you claim to hate."

"I don't hate her," Jax said defensively. "I hate what she is. You should've seen the way she talked about her family. I wouldn't be surprised if this fiancé of hers didn't demand to check her teeth before he—"

"Sergeant Jax?"

Jax whirled around to see Emmett standing on the other side of the table they'd just set down. He was looking even more nervous than usual. "Sorry to interrupt, sir. But there's a man at the front gate asking for Rosalie."

"What man?" Jax demanded.

"I'm not sure, but he's offering money to the guards to get her for him." He bit his lip. "It didn't seem right, so I figured I should tell you."

"You figured right," Jax said coldly, giving the still smirking Cooper a deadly look as he tugged his uniform straight. "Thank you, Emmett. I'll take it from here."

The short boy nodded, his tanned face relieved, but Jax was already jogging across the busy yard to the base's front gate, where a well-dressed man with perfectly coiffed brown hair was waiting impatiently beside an enormous red-lacquered carriage.

"Can I help you?"

The moment the stranger turned around, Jax hated him. He was in his late twenties, dressed in a sweeping fur-lined coat that was too long and heavy even for this cold, wet weather. His kid-leather boots were clearly never meant to be worn outside a ballroom, and the embroidered cloth at his neck was so white and fluffed up, it looked like someone had pegged him in the throat with a snowball. He was undeniably handsome, Jax had to admit, but there was something unsavory in his face that his perfectly symmetrical features couldn't paint over.

It was his expression, Jax decided. Even when he smiled, he had a strain around his eyes, like the rest of the world stank and he was fighting to endure it. Between that and the fancy carriage, it wasn't even a surprise when the man introduced himself as Ferdinand Smythe. "I'm here to pick up my fiancée," the man said, giving Jax a sly smile, like they were sharing a secret, "Lady Rosalie Dumarque, youngest daughter of the famous Military Police general Lord Charles Dumarque. We're going to a *very* exclusive private party at the Dumarque estate inside Sina, and we'll be more than fashionably late if she doesn't hurry. If you can get her here in the next ten minutes, I'll make it worth your while."

He jingled the coin purse at his belt, but Jax just leaned back, making himself comfortable against the courtyard gate. "That's too bad. Private Second Class Dumarque was just dismissed from duties. I'm her sergeant, Jackson Cunningham, and I might have some more work for her to do before she goes, so I'm afraid you're in for a wait."

"Come now," Ferdinand said with a laugh. "We both know Dumarques don't do actual *work*. But this is a fortuitous meeting. I've been meaning to talk to her sergeant."

Jax's fingers slipped covertly to the knife in his pocket. "You have?"

The lordling nodded. "I've been living in fear ever since Lord Dumarque informed me that he'd allowed Rosalie to go to the wall. I know Captain Woermann won't let her get into any real danger, but I'm still very concerned about her well-being."

"You are?"

"Of course," Ferdinand said gravely. "The Garrison is a dangerous place. What if she gets damaged? Everyone knows Rosalie's not the prettiest Dumarque, but there's an enormous difference between a homely bride and a disfigured one. What if she breaks her nose? Or gets a scar? I'd be stuck with that for life."

"God forbid you have a damaged bride," Jax said in a flat, cold voice.

"*Exactly*," Ferdinand said, pulling a gold coin out of his purse. "That's where you come in. You're her sergeant. You control where she goes and what she does. We can help each other."

He grabbed Jax's free hand, the one that wasn't currently in his pocket gripping a knife, and pressed the coin into it. "A gift for your service," he said with a wink. "And there's a lot more where that came from if you can keep her face decent until our wedding. Just have her peel vegetables or something." He frowned. "Actually, forget the vegetables. Rosalie can be a klutz sometimes. The first time I met her back when she was eleven, she fell off her pony *five* times. Poor little thing would probably slice off a finger if you gave her a knife."

Jax curled his fingers around the coin until they made a white-knuckled fist. The urge to punch this man in the mouth grew stronger with every word he said. Before Jax could act on his violent impulses, though, he heard the familiar beat of Rosalie's footsteps behind him.

The surge of relief that followed surprised even him, but something was off. The rhythm of her steps was too short, like her feet were hobbled together. When Jax turned to see why, he immediately regretted it.

He'd known Rosalie was a lady from the first moment he'd laid eyes on her, but he'd never actually seen her look the part. Until now.

The first thing he noticed was her dress. It was huge and rose-red with bits of lighter pink ribbon on the neck and sleeves. Her swaying skirt was so padded with petticoats that the bottom hem stuck out wider than her shoulders, creating a stark contrast to her waist, which had been cinched so small Jax didn't know how she could breathe. Her hair was piled high on top of her head in smooth waves that had been dusted with something to make the normally bright-blond color look paler, like iced honey. Her face was dusted too, powdered until the freckles across her nose vanished, and her lashes were darkened and her lips painted until they were the same red as her dress. Her feet were shoved into ridiculously tiny shoes, which explained her trouble walking, and her cheeks were as pink as a porcelain doll's.

It all was incredibly beautiful. Maybe the most beautiful thing Jax had ever seen. But she looked absolutely nothing like herself.

And he hated it.

"Rosie!" Ferdinand cried, turning away from Jax as though they'd never spoken. "Darling, you look terrible." He grabbed her hands. "Your nails are a tragedy. What have you been doing, clawing your way up the wall?"

He laughed like this was hilarious, and though a healthy crowd of dumbfounded soldiers had gathered to witness the spectacle of Rosalie in a dress, no one joined in. Rosalie didn't even lift her eyes from the ground, though she did snatch her hands back.

"Sir Ferdinand," she said, dropping a curtsey so quick, Jax would have missed it if he hadn't been staring at her. "We should go. It's not wise to be late to my mother's parties."

"And whose fault is that?" Ferdinand asked, grabbing her arm. "If you'd stayed at home like a sensible girl, we wouldn't have to go through all this."

Rosalie let him steer her toward the carriage, avoiding Jax so pointedly, she might as well have been glaring at him. The driver hopped down to open the door as Ferdinand handed her in. Mrs. Brixton got in next, bounding into the carriage as though she couldn't stand to be in Trost for a second longer. Ferdinand climbed in last, pausing to tap his purse at Jax before he swung inside. As soon as he was seated, the driver shut the door and climbed back to his perch behind the horses. The carriage lurched forward a second later, rattling down the short alley that served as the base's entrance and into the busy street beyond.

Jax watched them drive away, clutching the coin in his fist tighter and tighter until, with an explosive motion, he hurled it after them, sending it flying as far as he could into the crowd.

Ferdinand talked the entire drive to Sina.

Rosalie tried to pay attention, but he just went on and on, recounting the latest gossip about people she didn't know. It was incredibly tedious, but more than that, it made her worried. The ride was the longest they'd spent together since their engagement announcement when she was eleven and he nineteen. Rosalie couldn't recall much from that meeting, other than he'd seemed fine enough then. She didn't know if Ferdinand had changed or if her eleven-year-old self's judgment had been grossly mistaken, but she was feeling less "fine" about the man sitting across from her as each moment passed.

Fortunately, Ferdinand's conversation didn't require participation, so Rosalie leaned her head against the cold glass window, watching the year's longest night fall over the villages and fields of Rose. By the time she spotted the familiar walls of Ehrmich, outside was pitch black. Even the decorated city felt dark, the candles sputtering in the windows as the carriage drove past the already rowdy street parties and through the gate in Wall Sina to the well-lit private road that led to the Dumarque estate.

The stone house on the hill was as lovely as ever, especially with the torches and bonfires lit for the festival, but Rosalie hadn't remembered Dumarque Manor being so . . . big. The entire Garrison base could have fit on the front lawn, and the stables were as large as the mess hall. She was still trying to wrap her head around her home's size when the carriage came to a halt on the pea-gravel drive.

The moment they stopped, the doorman leaped from his little shelter by the front stairs to open the carriage door. "Welcome home, Miss Rosalie," he said cheerfully, extending a gloved hand.

Rosalie plastered a smile over her face, letting the old man help her down from the carriage as she tried desperately to recall his name. He'd been their doorman since before she could remember, greeted her hundreds of times. How did she not know his name?

Because you never learned it, came the answer. Because he was just the servant who opened carriage doors, and she'd never thought to ask.

Hot shame filled her. Jax would have known the man's name. So would Rosalie, if the doorman had been a solider. She knew all of the Garrison guards' names, but not the man who'd worked in her family's house all her life.

"Rosie?"

She looked up to see Ferdinand standing beside her, his boot tapping impatiently. "Today, please. We're already late enough."

With a soft thank-you to the footman whose name she was now determined to discover, Rosalie linked her arm through her fiancé's so he could escort her up the steps and into the blindingly bright ballroom.

Her mother had outdone herself. Thousands of candles lit up the giant marble room until it glittered. The tables lining the rear wall were so laden with food, the white cloths beneath were no longer visible. One entire corner had been dedicated to cheeses, while the other was dedicated to wine. Servants moved between them constantly, passing out plates and delicate crystal goblets with the silent, effortless elegance that was expected at one of Sina's great houses.

They were the only ones who were silent. The manor was packed, and loud. Ferdinand led Rosalie to the reception line where they greeted her mother, who was radiant as ever in her trademark pale blue, a color chosen specifically to show off the complete lack of gray in her perfectly coiffed blonde hair. Lord Dumarque stood beside her, equally impressive in his officer's dress uniform. Then came Rosalie's three sisters lined up like daisies on a string with Marigold at the end, looking slightly drunk.

None of them spared more than a nod for Rosalie or Ferdinand, but that was to be expected. This was not a time for sentiment. The entire point of this affair was to gather, galvanize, and impress potential assets to the family. Her brothers were already working the crowd, collecting gossip and observing their rivals for signs of weakness.

As soon as they made it past the family gauntlet, Ferdinand abandoned Rosalie to join his friends at the wine table, and she took her chance to escape. Duty prevented Lord Dumarque from leaving his post at the front door until all his guests arrived, but that didn't stop him from watching his youngest daughter like a hawk as she slipped through the glittering crowd to the banquet tables. She was hoping to eat something delicious so tonight wouldn't be a total waste, but as she accepted a silver plate from the white-liveried servant, Rosalie realized with a start just how much food she was staring at.

Even with the packed ballroom behind her, there was more here than could possibly be eaten in one night. The food piled in front of her surpassed what the entire Trost Garrison consumed in three days, and that wasn't counting all the platters Rosalie knew were being held in reserve in the kitchen in case something ran out. An empty table was considered a disgrace, so Lady Dumarque always ordered her chef to make twice as much as they needed. Then, when morning came and everyone went home, all that beautifully prepared food would be scraped into buckets and fed to the pigs.

This was standard practice for most big houses, but Rosalie had never thought about the waste before. Now, staring at the tables groaning under the weight of all that food, waste was all she could see. What would Willow and Emmett think if they were here?

What would Jax think?

"There you are."

Rosalie jumped. She hadn't noticed her father until he was right behind her. Bad move on her part, because the tightness in Lord Dumarque's jaw told her this wasn't going to be just a hello.

"Why aren't you dancing with your fiancé?" he asked, nodding back toward the main ballroom where couples were spinning to the music of the quartet hidden in the gallery.

"I don't feel like dancing," Rosalie muttered, turning away. "Please excuse me."

Lord Dumarque grabbed her arm. Not hard, but tight enough that yanking out of his grip would have caused a scene. She wasn't ready to go that far, so Rosalie let him pull her out of the banquet area and through a side door into the rose garden.

All the lamps were lit for the party, turning the winding brick pathways between the winter-pruned beds of roses into glowing streams of light. Pretty as it was, the midwinter night was too cold for guests to venture outside, which meant there was no one to see Lord Dumarque corner his youngest daughter like a wanted criminal.

"I didn't want to do this," he said as he shut the door behind them. "But you've given me no choice. I let you have your fun, Rosalie, but it's time to come home."

"It is *not* time," she said, glaring up at him. "We had a deal."

"Things have changed," Lord Dumarque said darkly, stepping closer. "Don't be thick, girl. We both know I didn't expect you to last one day on the wall, but you've held out for six weeks. If you were anyone else, I'd give you a commission for bravery, but you're my daughter, you're engaged, and people are starting to talk. You've made your point, all right? You proved me wrong. Now it's time to stop this madness and come home before you subject our family to any further ridicule."

"Ridicule for what?" Rosalie asked. "I'm fighting titans. There's no shame in that."

"You're serving in the Garrison as a common solider," he snapped. "Do you have any idea what an embarrassment it is for a lady of House Dumarque to be living and working with washouts and criminals?"

"They're not criminals!" she cried. "They're soldiers just like you and me."

"They are nothing like us," he said, straightening himself. "I am a general, and you're set to marry the only son of the wealthiest man in Rose. Now I've been very lenient with you. Some would even say I've spoiled you, but it's time to grow up. Lord Smythe has fallen ill. He's asked that the wedding be moved up, just in case he doesn't survive the winter."

Rosalie's eyes went wide. "What?"

"You're getting married," Lord Dumarque said. "Next month. Lord Smythe has already sent over your bride price to pay for your wedding clothes. It'll be a bit of a rush, but with the money he's laying down, merchants don't mind working nights. You'll have the biggest wedding in Sina."

He smiled as he finished, holding out his arms as though he expected her to leap into them, but Rosalie could only stare. "I don't care about merchants," she said, her voice shaking. "I'm not getting married next month. I can't! I signed a contract with the Garrison for the rest of the year."

"Already taken care of," her father said. "I've written Captain Woermann, and he's more than happy to give you an honorable discharge."

Rosalie clenched her fists. "I'm not leaving the wall!"

"Why not?" her father demanded. "What do you hope to achieve, an early death? Because you have to know by now that your harebrained scheme to singlehandedly turn the war around is hopeless."

Rosalie flinched. His accusation was too close to her own sleepless worries last night to dismiss. Lord Dumarque must have realized he'd scored a hit because he moved in closer, reaching to rest his hand on her head as he'd done when she was little.

"There, there, my dear," he said, patting her hair. "You made a good show, but the game is over. It's time to stop playing soldier and come home to do your duty."

His voice was deep and lulling, and for a moment the old instinct to obey was almost too much, but then Rosalie jerked her head out from under his hand.

"No."

Lord Dumarque's fingers curled into a fist. "Rosalie—"

"No," she said again, looking him straight in the eye. "I know my duty to the family, and I will do it, but only when I'm done serving my duty to the Garrison."

"You have no duty to the Garrison!" he shouted at her. "The Garrison is for impoverished farmers and refugees from Maria. It's not for people like us."

"How can you say that?" Rosalie demanded. "We need the walls, too."

"Exactly," Lord Dumarque snapped. "The walls protect us. The Garrison are merely the glorified janitors who maintain them."

"The Garrison fights the titans!" Rosalie cried. "They protect all of us, and they do it on nothing! There are soldiers on the wall right now with maneuvering gear that doesn't even work. That should be criminal!"

"The Garrison has perfectly adequate equipment for their job," he said. "It's older, yes, but you've seen how big Wall Rose is. The crown simply can't afford to buy new gear for every single soldier who—"

"Can't afford?" Rosalie threw her hand back at the closed ballroom door. "With the money you spent on this party, you could have bought new equipment for every soldier in Trost! The food you're wasting tonight alone could have fed my entire regiment. How can you possibly stand there and say there's no money when you're surrounded by it?"

"Because this is *my* money," her father snarled. "Yours, too, and there's not as much as you think. The loss of our lands in Maria left us deep in debt. Your marriage to Ferdinand Smythe was arranged to fix that, which makes it far more important than anything you could do on the wall."

"You're wrong," Rosalie said fiercely. "And I was, too. I thought if I brought my training down to the front, I could change the entire war. I know now that was foolish, but it doesn't mean *I* was foolish for wanting to fight. The titans are coming for all of us, rich and poor, noble and common. The walls are the only thing that stops them. There is nothing more important than protecting them!"

The words were for her father, but Rosalie was the one left shaking. "You want to know what I'm doing on the wall?" she said. "I'm fighting. I'm practicing and learning and getting better every day so I can help my fellow soldiers keep our enemies from breaking through. My contribution might be small, but it's all those small contributions coming together that keeps everyone safe. That's a noble cause, Father. Far more noble than preserving the Dumarques' ability to pay for parties full of food no one eats. I won't turn my back on that just so the Smythes can earn their connection to a noble bloodline a few months early!"

"Mind your tone," her father snarled. "You think I can't make you marry? You're my daughter. My *property*."

She'd heard him say as much before, but hearing it again now, after what Jax had said, made Rosalie angrier than she could ever remember being.

"I am *not* yours," she snarled back. "I'm the king's cousin and a noble woman in my own right! I signed that contract same as you. If you and Smythe try to change the terms without my permission,

I can take you before the king!"

"You could try," Lord Dumarque said smugly. "But I would win. I'm a respected lord. You're a girl who's putting herself in danger for no reason. The king would find in my favor."

"But would you want him to?" Rosalie said coldly. "Even if my case was hopeless, imagine how embarrassing it would be for Lord Smythe if I pleaded before the king and his entire court to let me avoid marrying his idiot son for another few months. He'd probably break the contract himself just to save face."

Her father looked at her in horror. "You wouldn't dare."

Rosalie crossed her arms over her chest, and her father's face turned scarlet. "You selfish child!" he roared. "You would disgrace us! Throw down your family into ruin and poverty for—"

"I'm doing no such thing," Rosalie said. "I never said I wouldn't marry Ferdinand Smythe, just that I won't be forced into it early. This is my family, too. I know how badly we need the Smythes' money, and I'm going to do my part, but I will not let you take what little time I have left in the Garrison."

"It's only four and a half months," Lord Dumarque said through gritted teeth. "What good do you think you're going to do in so short a time?"

"I don't know," Rosalie said truthfully. "But I'd rather risk Lord Smythe's anger than spend the rest of my life looking at those walls knowing I walked away from them."

Lord Dumarque was white with fury by the time she finished, but to Rosalie's astonishment, he didn't yell. He just stared at her for a long, long time, and then he dropped his head.

"Fine," he said, running a hand through his no-longer-perfect hair.

Rosalie blinked. "You're giving in?"

"What choice do I have?" he snapped. "You threatened to drag this before the king. I'd rather beg old Smythe on my knees for an extension than subject our family to that sort of public ridicule."

He gave her a grudgingly respectful look. "It seems your stomach is stronger than mine on this issue, so very well. As long as you swear that you will do your duty and get married in the end." He waited until Rosalie nodded. "I will allow you to serve out your remaining time in the Garrison. However, if you do anything to bring shame to our family or jeopardize your marriage contract with Ferdinand Smythe, I will drag you off that wall with my own hands. Do I make myself clear?"

"Yes, sir," Rosalie said, biting back her triumphant smile. "Now, what was that about a bride price?"

Her father blew out a breath. "Lord Smythe gave us funds to cover expenses for rushing the wedding. I'm not sure what happens now that you've refused, but—"

"But he already gave you the money," she finished. "How much is it?"

Given what her father had said about the "biggest wedding in Sina," Rosalie's expectations were high, but the figure Lord Dumarque named made her eyebrows shoot up. "*Really?*"

"Of course," her father said haughtily. "You're a Dumarque. Anything less would have been insulting."

"Excellent," Rosalie said, holding out her hand. "Give it to me."

Her father jerked back. "Are you insane?"

"Not at all," she said. "It's called a 'bride price,' not a 'bride's father's price.' That makes it my money to spend as I see fit."

"On *clothes*," he snapped. "Not on—" He stopped. "What are you even going to buy?"

"That's none of your business," Rosalie said. "But you were right earlier. It *is* time I stopped playing."

Her father looked at her outstretched hand in disgust, and then he reached past her to yank open the door to the ballroom. "We'll do it in my office. I don't keep money like that in my pockets, and

I'd very much like to be at the other end of the house from Lord Smythe right now."

He glared over his shoulder, making it clear that was her fault. Rosalie just smiled back, lifting her skirts so they wouldn't get in her way as she hurried after him.

C H A P T E R

N I N E

It was **the best Longest Night party Jax could re-member. There was dancing, tables full of food, a band that could actually stay in tune, everything he'd complained was missing from last year's cele-bration, and he was already sick of it.**

He'd tried to skip, but Brigitte dragged him down from the gate personally and ordered him to enjoy himself. Since that was impossible, Jax stuck to the bare minimum: sitting on a bench at the edge of the yard and drinking until he didn't care anymore, which wasn't working nearly as well as he'd hoped.

"You're doing this to yourself, you know," said Cooper, plopping down beside him to catch his breath. "There's lots of town girls here who don't know your reputation. If you didn't stare at everyone like you were planning how to stab them, you'd be up to your neck in offers."

"Don't want to dance," Jax said, glaring into

his mug of ale, which had stopped tasting good two refills ago.

"I bet you would if certain squad members were here," Cooper replied in a singsong voice.

Jax's fingers tightened on the wooden mug. "Shut up."

"Certain blonde ones," his friend went on. "Who selflessly devote their off hours tutoring the less fortunate."

"I said *shut up*."

Cooper rolled his eyes. "I don't see why you're so uptight about this. So what if you like Rosalie? Everyone likes Rosalie. She's nice and, more importantly, she's rich. If you didn't avoid the mess hall like the plague, you'd know that the entire male population of the base, and no small part of the female, has been scheming to get her attention all month. The only reason none of them have succeeded is because she spends all of her time with you."

"She's not hanging around me because she likes to," Jax said defensively. "We made a deal. I teach her to be better at fighting titans, she helps me with my reading. That's all it is."

"Right," Cooper said. "So you're sitting here drinking alone in the dark because you're pining for reading lessons."

"Are you trying to get me killed?" Jax demanded. "She's a noble lady, *and* she's my subordinate. Taking liberties with either leads straight to a hanging. Anyway, weren't you the one telling me to get rid of her?"

"That was before I realized you two had a thing," Cooper replied, pressing his hands over his heart. "What can I say? I'm a romantic."

"You're obnoxious is what you are," Jax snapped. He was about to change the subject by suggesting a trip to the cake table, Cooper's ultimate weakness, when he heard the unmistakable sound of a horse-and-carriage coming in fast.

Jax's first thought was that something had gone wrong. A holiday that revolved around public bonfires and drinking tended to go south pretty fast, but it wasn't the fire cart approaching. It was a hired coach, and the moment it rolled to something like a stop in front of the base gate, Rosalie burst out of it.

Jax rubbed his eyes. Surely he hadn't had *that* much to drink. When he looked again, though, she was still there. She was even back in her uniform, no more fancy dress. She'd wiped most of the make-up off her face as well, leaving a hard scowl behind as she marched straight through the center of the party toward the officers' table.

"Uh-oh," Cooper whispered. "Trouble in paradise, you think?"

Jax shoved his mug at Cooper and took off through the crowd. He was too far away to hear, but he could see Rosalie talking to Brigitte. It must have been serious, because the lieutenant set down her mug and motioned for Rosalie to come with her to the gate tower.

Keeping to the deep shadows thrown by the fire, Jax followed.

"Care to explain what this is about?" The lieutenant's voice was sharp, but not angry. She sounded more curious than anything as Rosalie handed her a large rectangular piece of paper. "What is this?"

"Money," Rosalie said, her normally cheerful voice hard as the stone under her feet. "I'm financing all new equipment for the Trost Garrison. Vertical maneuvering gear, ammunition, cannon parts, whatever you need."

Brigitte stared at the paper in silence. "This is . . . quite unusual," she said at last, folding the note and setting it on her desk like a precious jewel. "Has Lord Dumarque given his permission?"

"He doesn't have to," Rosalie said. "It's not Lord Dumarque's money. It's mine. I want to spend it on something that matters, and we can't win this war without functioning weapons."

"It would do a lot," the gate lieutenant said, opening the paper to look at the sum again. "But much as we need it, I must urge you to reconsider. I'm not going to ask what this sum was supposed to be for, but are you sure this is how you want to use it? Because once I take it, it's gone. With a budget like this, I can put in a rush order with the factory towns tomorrow."

"I'm sure," Rosalie said, standing even taller. "This is the front line against the titans. If it falls, everything falls. Making this wall stronger is the best investment I can think of, and this way I know for certain that I'll be leaving behind something worthwhile when my service is over."

"It will definitely help," Brigitte said, standing up. Then, to Rosalie's astonishment, she bowed, lowering herself from the waist. "Thank you, Private Dumarque. I swear your generosity will not be wasted."

Rosalie nodded, her cheeks red in the lamplight. Brigitte was already pulling out account books and shouting for someone to get the quartermaster to her office, so Rosalie took her chance to slip away. She'd just shut the lieutenant's door when Jax stepped out of the shadows beside it.

Rosalie jumped almost a foot into the air, covering her mouth to keep from shrieking in alarm. Jax pressed a frantic finger to his lips and pointed down the hall, away from Brigitte's door and the frenzy of confused-looking staff officers who were now rushing through it.

He turned on Rosalie to ask what the hell she thought she was doing, but she beat him to the punch.

"I'm sorry."

Jax blinked. "What?"

"I'm sorry," she repeated, her eyes sad. "About getting so angry the other night. You were right. My family did sell me. I suppose I always knew it, I just didn't want to think about it that way. But wrong or not, they're my family and they need me. I can't turn my back on them, so I've decided to make the most of a bad situation and give my bride price to help fund the Garrison."

"You shouldn't have to do that," Jax argued. "That's your wedding money, right?"

Rosalie shrugged, brushing a lock of hair behind her ear. "It was supposed to pay for my wedding clothes. This is a much better use. Like you told me once, buying new equipment for the Garrison will do a lot more good than one rich girl soldier."

Jax closed his eyes with a curse. He had said that, hadn't he? "I'm sorry."

Rosalie waved it away. "Don't be."

"No," he said, rubbing the back of his neck. "I shouldn't have said those things. You're not . . . " He sighed. "I've been unfair to you, Rosalie."

She gave him a frankly skeptical look, which he deserved. Calling the horrific way he'd treated her unfair was like saying the titans were a mere nuisance.

"Can I tell you a story?" He was half hoping she'd say no. But she nodded.

"I grew up out on the southern edge of Maria," he said, talking quickly before he lost his nerve. "My parents were woodcutters, but we didn't own the land. The forest belonged to a noble, and he let us live there in exchange for cutting his trees. He paid us in food for the timber. Not much, but we got by. Then, one day, there was an accident. My dad's legs got crushed by a falling log. He couldn't walk after that, which meant he couldn't work. And if he couldn't work, we couldn't eat."

"But it wasn't his fault," Rosalie said.

Jax shrugged. "When you're poor, everything's your fault. The foreman didn't care why we weren't bringing in our wood for the week. We didn't have it, and that made us useless. He called us vermin, said he was going to give our house to a family that could do the work. Something had to be done, so I took my dad's ax and went to work in his stead."

Rosalie's face was pale when he finished. "How old were you?"

"Eleven," Jax said. "But like I said, there was nothing else to be done. Dad was laid up and my mum had just given birth to my little sister, so it was up to me. I cut what wood I could reach and made up the difference by doing pretty much anything people would pay me for. In the winter, I used to walk behind the horse carts picking up dung so we could burn it for fuel instead of wasting wood we could trade for food."

He stopped there, waiting for her to look disgusted, but Rosalie just nodded for him to continue.

"I did that for a year," he went on. "Then, just when I was getting big enough to meet the quotas, the titans appeared."

He still remembered that morning, clear as lightning. He'd just stepped out of his house with his ax over his shoulder to go to work when he saw the titan in the road, its mouth gleaming wet in the bright sunlight as it swallowed what was left of their neighbor.

"It came to our house," Jax said, his voice shaking. "My dad couldn't run, so he got the thing's attention. It ate him while the rest of us escaped. But there were more. We tried to climb the trees, but they were faster than us. One got my mother. Bit her right out of the tree, like she was a piece of fruit. She was in its teeth when she thrust my baby sister at me and told me to run. So I did. I took my sister and I ran away fast as I could."

"You were right to run," Rosalie said. "You saved your sister's life."

"No," Jax said angrily. "I got us here, to Trost, but the city was already full. Refugees from Maria were everywhere, and there wasn't enough food to go 'round. I was just a kid. I had no money, nowhere to go. I couldn't take care of a baby. I couldn't even take care of myself. I couldn't do anything, so I . . . I gave her away."

The words hung like swords in the silence, and Jax dropped his eyes in shame. "I gave her away," he said again. "There was another family. They'd just lost their daughter, and they offered to take my sister off my hands. I didn't want to give her up, but we were starving. They had food and relatives willing to take them in up north, which was more than I could offer. So I . . . I let her go."

Rosalie took a deep breath. "Where is she now?"

"I don't know," Jax said. "I haven't seen her since that day. But I'm not telling you this for sympathy. I just wanted you to know I was wrong when I said Maria folk look after their own, because I didn't. I gave up my sister, my own flesh and blood. I have no right to criticize you or your family, because I did the same thing."

"It is *not* the same thing," Rosalie said fiercely. "You gave your sister to a family because you were starving. You helped her survive."

"But the crime's the same," he said, eyes glued to his boots. "I tried to make it right. When they announced they were sending people out to reclaim Maria from the titans, I signed up right away. They said you could keep whatever land you could claim. I thought if I had a farm, somewhere I could grow food, I could convince the family to give my sister back. I wasn't even afraid of the titans because we were going out on the king's orders. Surely, I thought, he would send soldiers and cannons to protect us while we resettled the land."

"But he didn't," Rosalie said quietly. "The reclamation of Maria was a disaster."

"It was a *scam*," Jax snarled. "They sent us out with nothing, knowing we would die! They couldn't feed everyone, but instead of making do with less for themselves, the nobility and the king disposed of us. Of the two hundred and fifty thousand who took the bait, only a hundred of us made it back. I don't even remember how I got back to the walls. I'd given up on my sister by then. Given up on everything. They'd taken it all."

"'They' who?" Rosalie asked. "The nobility?"

Jax shrugged. "The nobility, the king, the titans. They were all responsible. But I couldn't kill the king and his cronies, so I decided to go after the targets I could reach. At least they pay you for killing titans."

Rosalie looked down at her knotted hands. "I can see why you didn't like me."

"It wasn't that I didn't like you," Jax said. "I *hated* you from the moment I saw you. But I was wrong. You're not like the nobles who sent me out to die. You're a fine soldier, and I'm . . . " He sighed. "I'm sorry, Rosalie."

They stared at each other in silence, the red firelight flickering across their faces until, at last, Rosalie's lit up with a grin.

"What?" Jax asked, suddenly wary. "Why are you smiling?"

"Because," she said, grinning wider, "you finally called me by my name."

Jax winced. "I've been an absolute beast to you, haven't I?"

"You have, but your apology is cheerfully accepted."

"Yeah, well, don't get too happy about it," he muttered, shoving his hands into his pockets. "Just because you threw a king's ransom at Brigitte and I blubbered my life's story at you doesn't mean you're off the hook. You're still my soldier, and that's how I'm going to treat you. Though I was hoping we could start reading again. You can't leave me hanging on that ending. It's cruel."

"Do you want to finish now?" she asked. "We should have just enough time for the last chapter before dawn breaks."

"I'd love to," Jax said. "But are you sure? It's still Longest Night."

"I've had enough Longest Night for one year," she said, reaching for his hand. "Come on, let's go read."

The sudden curl of her bare fingers around his made Jax's heart hammer. Sergeants did *not* hold hands with their subordinates, but Jax couldn't bring himself to let go. If anything, he held on tighter, jogging behing Rosalie as she dragged him out of the tower.

◈ ◈ ◈

At the Garrison headquarters building in the center of Trost, Captain Woermann was having a very different Longest Night.

He'd spent the evening jumping between parties, attending as many celebrations in Rose as possible as consolation for the fact that he hadn't been invited to a single event in Sina. He finished his rounds just before dawn, then took his carriage back to his office. His plan was to sign his daily paperwork and spend the rest of the day recovering at home, but when he arrived at headquarters, one of his aides was waiting on the steps along with a courier in House Dumarque livery.

As soon as Captain Woermann opened the carriage door, the courier handed him a folded note. Fingers trembling, Woermann broke the wax seal. When he opened the letter, he saw only one line on the page.

Get my daughter back.

That was it. Four words written in the telltale angry strokes of a man who had been pushed too far. The note mentioned no reward, but Woermann had received desperate letters before, and they always worked out in his favor.

"Tell Lord Dumarque I am happy to oblige," he said, placing the note in his pocket.

The courier nodded and hopped onto his horse, riding away as fast as he'd no doubt come in. When he was gone, Captain Woermann waved his aide over. "What was the name of the sergeant who was injured when Miss Dumarque made all that trouble?"

"Markus, I believe, sir," the young man answered. "From the Supply Corps."

"Send him to my office," Woermann ordered. "But sober him up first. He'll need his wits about him."

The aide saluted and hurried inside. Woermann entered more

slowly, climbing the wooden stairs to his corner office at the top to make a last-minute alteration to the weekly cannon report.

Since soldiers who'd been up all night drinking couldn't be expected to perform their jobs well the next day, the military traditionally had the morning after Longest Night off. Even Rosalie knew this, which was why she was surprised when the night watch woke her shortly after sunrise and said that Squad 13 had been ordered to report to the lieutenant's office immediately.

"Sorry to ruin your morning off," Brigitte said when they'd all filed in. "But I just got the cannon report, and one of the big guns on the western wall is down. I'm going to need your squad to go out and do repairs."

Willow arched a bushy eyebrow. "Aren't cannon repairs the Supply Corps' responsibility?"

"Yes," Brigitte said. "But headquarters says there's no one in Supply Corps they can roust to do the job right now. Your squad has a gunnery expert and a decent engineer." She nodded at Rosalie and Emmett. "You should be good for the job. Just be quick about it. There's a storm coming."

"But the weather's lovely, lieutenant," Emmett said.

It really was. The morning after Longest Night had broken beautifully clear and cold, but Lieutenant Brigitte was shaking her head. "I've got enough old wounds to feel the weather twenty miles away. It's coming, so I suggest you get your job done ahead of it."

She finished with a pointed glance at Jax, who looked grimmer than Rosalie had seen him since their very first day as a squad. The whole exchange struck her as extremely odd, but orders were orders, so off they went, Jax glowering all the way.

By the time they'd gotten into their gear, found a cannon repair cart, and hauled it up the lift to the top of the wall, the weather was already changing. Clouds were rolling in from the west, turning the blue sky a dark, seething gray.

The strong wind was growing colder by the second. But Rosalie was more concerned about the patches of ice that had started forming on the top of the wall. She was watching her feet so closely to avoid a slip, she didn't even notice the snow until she looked up and realized she could no longer see Trost through a wall of white.

"Jax—"

"I know," he said right beside her, making her jump. "We need to pick up the pace," he called, raising his voice over the wind. "Everyone keep moving, and stay away from the edges. Especially the Maria side."

They all nodded grimly. A slip off either side of the wall would kill you, but a dead body on the Maria side would bring titans. Though he was the one who'd told them to stay away, Jax kept drifting to the Maria edge, peering off the side like he expected a titan to come leaping out of the snow.

"What are you watching for?" Rosalie asked.

"Nothing," Jax muttered, shaking the snow out of his hair. "I just hate not being able to see is all. Weather like this is dangerous anywhere, but especially up here. If Brigitte hadn't given the order personally, I'd say to hell with the cannon."

Rosalie frowned. She had a feeling he wasn't telling her the entire truth. Before she could press him, though, they reached the cannon they'd been sent to fix.

It was a big twelve-pounder, like the guns mounted above the gates. It was already buried in snow, but when Rosalie brushed it off the barrel looked new and clean. She scraped the snow off the gearbox next, looking for the problem while Emmett unpacked the tools from the cart. The more she cleaned, the less things made sense.

"I don't get it," she said, shaking her frozen fingers. "Everything looks good. Crank, pivot, rotating mechanism, the rail lock—they're all fine."

"Firing pin and barrel check out, too," Emmett called over the howling wind. "I even loaded a shell, just to be sure, but it went in great."

"Well if it ain't broken, why did Brigitte send us?" Willow asked, pinching her nose. "Though what *I* really want to know is what smells so bad."

Rosalie frowned. She hadn't noticed with her head in the cannon—machine oil and gunpowder were pretty overpowering—but now that Willow mentioned it, there *was* an odd, sour smell on the cold air.

"It smells like something died," Willow said, covering her face. "Probably a deer."

"Doesn't smell like a deer," Jax said quietly, peering over the Maria side with his hands on his sword sheaths. "Can't see a bleeding thing, though." He glanced back at Rosalie and Emmett. "You're sure nothing's wrong with the cannon?"

"As sure as we can be without firing it," Rosalie said, pointing at the freshly oiled gears. "I don't know what was in the report, but this is one of the better cannons I've seen on the wall."

"Maybe whoever reported it made a mistake?" Emmett suggested.

"Maybe," Jax said skeptically. "Either way, we're done here."

That was the best news Rosalie had heard all day. But when she went to help Emmett pack up the repair cart, Jax said, "Leave it."

"Out here?" Emmett said, looking in horror at the blowing snow. "But it'll get buried!"

"We'll dig out tomorrow," Jax said. "Right now, our priority is to get back to base before we freeze. The cart will just slow us down."

"But it could be ruined by tomorrow," Emmett said anxiously. "You know how Captain Woermann feels about lost gear."

"I'll take responsibility," Jax promised. "It's not safe to be on the wall in weather like this, and I'd rather lose an equipment cart than a squad. Just tie a tarp over it and let's go."

Emmett obeyed reluctantly, covering the cart with its oiled cloth, but Rosalie's eyes were on Jax. He was talking like a responsible officer, but his face was pale and his blue eyes were wide. If she didn't know better, she'd say he looked terrified, and he still hadn't stopped staring over the wall into titan territory.

"This isn't about the weather, is it?" she said quietly, stepping up beside him. "There's something out there."

Jax's fingers drummed nervously on the handles of his maneuver gear. "You've heard about my first squad?"

Rosalie nodded. The moment anyone in the Garrison learned that Jax was her sergeant, they fell over themselves telling her about how his first team had died horribly.

"Did you . . . " Willow swallowed nervously. "Did you kill them?"

"Of course not! Do I look like a murderer?"

Willow and Rosalie exchanged nervous looks, and Jax winced. "Never mind," he said, pinching the bridge of his nose. "Point is, they did die, but I didn't kill them."

"So why don't you tell everyone that?" Rosalie asked angrily. "The whole Garrison thinks you're a killer!"

"I'm well aware of my reputation, thank you," he said testily. "But there's no point in trying to set the record straight. No one would believe the truth if I told it."

"Why not?" Emmett asked, stepping away from the now tied-down cart to join them. "What happened?"

Jax looked nervously at the snow blowing on the Maria side of the wall. "Have you ever heard of the Gobbler?"

Rosalie vaguely remembered the name. "Isn't that a titan?"

"An aberrant," Jax said, nodding. "Looks like a child with weird, long limbs. But he's a big bastard, and he loves the snow. Blizzards always bring him out."

"What makes him so bad?" Willow asked.

"Because when he's out, soldiers vanish."

"Vanish?" Rosalie repeated skeptically. "You mean they get attacked?"

"If I'd meant that, I would have said it," Jax snapped. "But there's no attack. One minute they're on the wall, the next they're not. They're just gone. Poof."

"Wait, they vanish off the *wall*?" Emmett said. "How does that happen?"

"If we knew that, it wouldn't be a mystery, would it?" Jax snapped, pointing back down the wall. "Let's get moving."

They fell in to single file and started marching, Jax in front and Rosalie at the rear. Happy as she was to be headed back to base, Rosalie wasn't ready to let this go. "How does a titan attack people on top of the wall?" she yelled over the wind.

"No idea," Jax yelled back. "But I lost my whole squad that way last winter. One minute we were all there, the next I was alone."

"If they vanished, how do you know it was the Gobbler?" Willow asked. "Maybe they fell?"

"Because I saw him," Jax said. "That's why I was away from the squad when it happened. I'd caught a glimpse of the Gobbler and went to investigate. When I came back, my team was gone. I thought they'd cut and run, but when I spotted the Gobbler again a few minutes later, his hands and teeth were covered in blood, and he had that stupid smile on his face." Jax clenched his fists. "I couldn't even find parts to send home to their families. That's why they call him the Gobbler. Because he gobbles everything up."

Rosalie looked nervously at the curtain of snow shrouding the Maria side of the wall. "And you think he's out there now?"

"I haven't seen him yet," Jax said, picking up the pace. "But this is his weather, which is why we need to get back to base as fast as possible."

"I just wish that awful smell would go away," Willow said, putting a hand over her mouth. "Where is it coming from?"

It seemed to be getting stronger. By the time they'd lost sight of the cannon, Rosalie could taste decay on her tongue. Desperate for something to block the odor, she bent down to grab a handful of fresh snow and shoved it into her mouth, sighing in bliss as the clean, cold meltwater swept down her throat.

The relief lasted only a moment, so she stopped and reached for an even bigger handful. She'd just finished packing the clean snow into a nice ball when something grabbed her from behind, wrapping around her body and yanking her off her feet before she could scream.

CHAPTER TEN

Jax hadn't realized he'd been listening to the comforting crunch of Rosalie's footsteps until they vanished.

He whirled around, hands reaching automatically for his swords, but saw nothing except his squadmates.

Two of them.

"Where's Rosalie?" His voice sounded panicked even to him. "Where's Rosalie?!" he said again, looking around frantically at the blowing snow. "*Rosalie!*"

When no cry came back over the howling wind, Jax's heart began to pound. "Fan out!" he yelled at the others. "Scan the ground! It can't have gotten far."

And then he jumped off the wall.

Jax fired his hooks halfway down, knowing instinctively where the wall was even with the wind blowing snow into his eyes. When his body jerked to a stop, he planted his feet on the icy stone to hang horizontally and looked around, searching the blizzard for a sign. Then, below and to his left, he spotted a dark gray shape huddled against the base of the wall.

It was roughly the size and profile of a collapsed house. It looked nothing like a titan, but only because it was hunched over, its freakishly out-of-proportion arms and legs folded onto themselves like a frog's. And sticking out from between two thick fingers of its barn-door-sized hands was a familiar blonde braid.

"Got him!" Jax screamed, yanking his hooks out of the wall and sending himself into freefall before he fired them again at the titan's shoulder. "Base of the wall! He's got—"

His jaw snapped shut as his body jerked like a fish on a line. The moment the barbed hooks of his maneuver gear sunk into the titan's flesh, the monster jumped. Just leaped straight up, its disturbingly long legs unfolding to launch the creature right up the side of the wall.

Still hooked into its shoulder, Jax was yanked up as well. By the time he recovered control, the titan had landed on the top of the wall. Right in front of the rest of his squad.

Emmett and Willow froze, staring up at the grinning, childlike face looming over them like a hideous moon. They were still standing motionless when the Gobbler leaned closer, its clasped hands rising over their heads like a hammer.

"Move!" Jax screamed, breaking the spell. He hit his triggers to yank himself up to the titan's shoulder. "I'll get the weak spot, but watch his hands! He's got Rosalie—"

The Gobbler whirled around, its huge head turning like an owl's to lock its gleeful blue eyes on Jax. Then, as though the monster wanted him to see, it whipped its impossibly long arms around and shoved Rosalie into its mouth.

"*NO!*" Jax screamed. As he kicked off the wall to swing around the titan's head and stab its weak point, the Gobbler smacked him out of the air.

For a terrifying second, Jax could see nothing but snow. He was spinning wildly in freefall, his maneuver gear cables whipping around him as the hooks tore out of the titan's unfeeling flesh. He fired again blindly, shooting one cable first and the other in the opposite direction, hoping to double his chances of hitting something useful. When neither caught, he thought at last that his luck had run out. Then his left cable jerked hard, knocking the breath from Jax's body as his descent stopped cold.

The second he stopped falling, instinct kicked in. Jax flipped over, planting his boots on the wall's icy surface and looking around to get his bearings. He was less than a meter from the snow-covered ground. His heart was still stuttering from how close he'd come to death when he spotted a growing shadow on the ground in front of him.

The Gobbler landed a moment later, dropping into the snow with an eerily quiet crash. Jax was about to detach from the wall and fire his cables at the titan when he spotted something new moving in the monster's fist. Legs, he realized with a chill. Emmett's legs were kicking from the base of the Gobbler's gargantuan hand. That was all Jax was able to make out before the titan launched itself forward in an explosion of snow and began sprinting away from the wall at terrifying speed.

"Emmett!"

The scream was Willow's, and it was surprisingly close. Jax hadn't even heard her gear fire, but Willow was suddenly falling right in front of him, her face more determined than Jax had ever seen it. A heartbeat later, he realized this was because she *hadn't* fired her maneuver gear yet. She was just falling, letting herself get as close to the ground as possible so she'd have enough line to shoot her hooks into the fleeing titan.

It was a hell of a shot. The Gobbler was already nearly fifty meters from the wall, the limit of their maneuver gear wires, but Willow's hooks nailed the titan right in the calf. Jax barely had time to grab onto her before the titan's momentum yanked them both forward, dragging them along the snowy ground at insane speed.

"Reel in!" Jax yelled, curling protectively around his soldier as they bounced through the drifts. They were moving across open ground now, but if they hit a rock or tree stump at this velocity, they'd be pulped.

Willow obeyed, hitting her triggers to pull them toward the titan before they were dragged to death. When they were close to the Gobbler's pounding legs, Jax fired his own hooks into its back, yanking the two of them upward.

"We have to slow it down!" he shouted over the titan's pounding footfalls. "Take out the legs, I'll go for the neck!"

Willow nodded, firing her hooks into the back of the titan's knee as she dropped. Again, her shot was good. She might be garbage at balancing, but when it came to aim, Jax realized Willow was a damn sight better than he'd given her credit for. He couldn't wait to see if she pulled the rest off, though. He was already climbing the Gobbler's back, stabbing his swords into its flesh as he scaled up to the vulnerable point on its neck.

But then, just as he was about to strike, Jax heard Rosalie's voice. She was screaming. From inside the Gobbler. In its *throat*, right below where he had to stab.

"Rosalie!"

The last thing Rosalie remembered was being plucked off the wall like a weed. It happened so suddenly, at first she didn't even realize that the crushing pressure was hands. Then the massive fingers had opened, giving her a clear view of the Gobbler's enormous face— which looked disturbingly like a little boy's, complete with apple cheeks, a turned-up nose, and empty blue eyes glittering with delight as it shoved Rosalie into its mouth.

The titan's maw reeked of death and decay, the same smell that had almost made her gag earlier. It *did* make her gag now, her chest heaving as she frantically curled into a protective ball to avoid the Gobbler's teeth as they slammed down behind her. She was still blinking in the dark of its closed mouth when the monster swallowed, its massive tongue lifting up to slide her back toward the tunnel of its throat.

With a defiant scream, Rosalie kicked out her legs, but her boots found no purchase. Saliva dripped from the roof of the Gobbler's mouth, coating her like hot grease. Even her hooks couldn't make contact. They slipped out every time she fired, leaving her with nothing as the giant tongue flexed and moved her inexorably toward the black pit of the titan's throat.

Frantic, Rosalie yanked the hardened steel blades out of their sheaths and plunging them into the titan's thick tongue. The swords struck deep, halting her slide, but she was now dangling down the back of the titan's mouth while burning hot blood poured down her arms. She could feel it blistering her skin through her jacket, but the pain only made her cling tighter to the slimy sword grips through sheer force of will. If she let go, she would fall into the lake of acid in the titan's stomach. She'd read about soldiers fighting their way out of titan mouths before, but she'd never heard of anyone coming back from the belly. Her only chance was to climb back up.

Kicking her feet against the titan's flexing throat, Rosalie heaved with both arms, pulling her body up. When her shoulders were even with her swords, she yanked one out and stabbed it in again farther up, scaling hand over bloody hand until, at last, she reached the tip of the titan's writhing tongue.

Rosalie gasped in relief. She couldn't see in the dark, but she could feel the hard wall of teeth right in front of her. Clinging to her bloody swords, Rosalie swung her legs around and slammed her boots into the back of the incisors. When that did nothing, she yanked her right sword out of the tongue and began bashing the blade against the hard enamel. Again, the teeth didn't budge. Next, she tried stabbing its gums, then cutting the top of its mouth. She attacked wildly, slicing every bit of flesh she could reach, but all she managed was to bring more hot blood raining on top of her as the titan's jaw remained stubbornly locked.

Desperate, Rosalie stabbed the edge of her sword into the gap between the Gobbler's pictured-window-sized front teeth. When she'd wedged it in as far as it would go, she leaned on it with all her weight, using the blade like a crowbar. For a soaring second, she could feel the giant tooth turning in its socket. Bracing her legs against the molars, Rosalie pushed harder, shoving until, with a terrifying crack, the hardened steel blade snapped in half.

The sudden loss of resistance slammed Rosalie into the bloody, meaty wetness of the Gobbler's cheek. She would have fallen right down its throat had her left sword not been lodged deep in its tongue. She had spare blades in the sheaths on her hips, but Rosalie wasn't sure what good they'd be. The titan's teeth were unbreakable, and the shallow cuts she'd made in its mouth had already healed. She wasn't even sure how much longer she could hold on to her sword, which was now so slick, her fingers slipped every time she moved. Rosalie was scrambling to think of what to try next, fighting back the panic and revulsion threatening to overwhelm her, when the Gobbler's head lurched to the side, slamming her across its mouth and yanking the sword out of her hand.

She kicked back up the second she hit, her hand flying out to grab the maneuver gear wire that still connected her to the handle of her lost sword, but it was too late. She was already falling like a ball down a chute. Rosalie screamed as she picked up speed, flailing in a last-ditch search for anything to grab onto. Then, just as her legs slid over the edge of the titan's throat, Rosalie heard someone shouting her name.

She screamed back, digging her feet into the walls of the Gobbler's flexing esophagus. She was still sliding, but bracing with her arms and legs slowed her fall. She wasn't stopping, though, and a few seconds later her boots touched the sphincter that separated the titan's throat from its stomach. The grasping muscle caught her left foot like a bear trap. It was pulling her in when a bolt of light shot through the bloody darkness above her head.

Rosalie looked up just in time to feel the blast of cold air as a sword sliced through the titan's flesh where its neck met its jaw. A man's arm appeared next, shooting through the already closing wound and down the titan's throat after Rosalie. Releasing her death grip on the throat's slick walls, Rosalie grabbed back, stretching as high as she could to wrap her bloody hands around the hands reaching out for her.

The moment she made contact, Jax grabbed and pulled hard, yanking Rosalie up out of the titan's throat, through the gaping hole in its neck. Suddenly she was out, falling into something bright, soft, and cold. Snow, Rosalie realized with a gasp. She was kneeling in snow.

"Rosalie!" Jax's frantic voice was right next to her. "You all right?"

She couldn't answer. Coughing up the blood in her throat, Rosalie plunged headfirst into the beautifully cold, clean snow. She rolled frantically, rubbing it against her face and into her mouth to remove the rotten taste of the Gobbler. Her skin was raw when she finished, both from the rubbing and the burns left by the titan's hot blood, but that didn't matter because she was alive. She was *alive*.

"Thank you," she whispered, finally looking up at Jax. "*Thank you.*"

He brushed the snow out of her bloody hair with a gentle hand.

"We're not in the clear yet."

"Jax!"

The panicked scream was Willow's, and Jax shot to his feet. "Don't move," he ordered Rosalie. "I've got to get Emmett next."

Rosalie couldn't have moved if she'd wanted to, but she did manage to turn her head to see Willow frantically hacking at the Gobbler's clutched hand a few meters away. The monster was down, having suffered two strikes to the back of the knee and the bloody mess Jax had made of its face. When he joined Willow by its clenched fist, the two of them managed to pry the titan's fingers wide enough to free Emmett, who fell gasping to the snow just as Rosalie had. Willow grabbed him at once, sobbing into his chest. Rosalie was just happy they were all alive when her head finally cleared enough to realize where they were.

They were on the ground in a field. An open field, on the Maria side. The air was so full of blowing snow, she couldn't see more than a few meters in any direction, but the wall was nowhere to be seen.

Heart hammering, Rosalie shoved herself to her feet, spinning around as she searched the snow for a familiar glimpse, anything that would tell her where they were, but all she saw was white. No wall, no collapsed buildings, not even a tree. Their team was on foot in a blizzard with nothing to shoot their maneuver gear at, no horses, and no way to see other titans coming until it was too late.

"We have to go," Rosalie said, discharging what was left of her broken sword before plunging the handle into her sheath for a new one. "We have to go!"

Willow and Emmett stood at once, but Jax didn't move. "You all start running," he said, turning back to the downed titan sprawled in the crimson snow. "I'll be right behind you after I finish the Gobbler."

"You didn't finish it?" Rosalie cried. "Why not?!"

"Because I could hear you in its throat," Jax said angrily. "If I'd attacked the weak spot, I might have sliced through you too. But it's fine. All I've got to do is pop 'round to the back of the neck and—"

A crash cut him off. Without warning, one of the Gobbler's arms swept across the snow like a plow, smashing into their group and sending them flying. Jax recovered first, yanking the others to their feet as the wounded titan began to thrash, flinging globs of acidic blood from its wounds as it tried to roll over.

"Run," Jax ordered, eyes wide. "*Run!*"

Rosalie ran, her legs pumping as she threw herself through the snow with the rest of her team. But though they quickly left the Gobbler behind, nothing else came into view.

"Where's the wall?" Willow yelled over the wind. "I can't see anything but snow!"

"North," Jax replied without missing a beat.

"Which way's north?"

Jax opened his mouth, then stopped, looking around with a curse that froze Rosalie's blood. He didn't know. Between the fight and the snow and the fall, they had gotten turned around. If they couldn't see the wall, which way should they go?

Jax knelt and shoved his hand through the snow until he hit the dirt beneath. "The fields in this area slope down from the base," he said, sliding his hand along the ground to feel its incline. "If we head uphill, we should find the wall."

"And the wind's been blowing from the west all day," Emmett added, leaning on Willow. "If we keep the wind on our left, we have to run into the wall eventually."

Rosalie nodded, but she kept her eyes on Jax, whose hand was still pressed into the ground beneath the snow. She knew he wasn't just checking the slope. He was feeling for the vibrations of giant footsteps, and from the grim look on his face . . . As if reading her thoughts, Jax met her eyes and brought a finger to his lips. When she nodded, he stood and started to run silently through the snow, motioning for the others to follow.

They moved as fast as they could without making a racket, hurrying up the gentle hill with the wind on their left in what Rosalie desperately hoped was the right direction. Several times she saw shadows looming in the snow, but it was impossible to tell if they were trees or titans. Either way, all they could do was keep moving.

The Gobbler didn't seem to be coming after them. It had to be healed by now, but Rosalie didn't smell rotting meat. She was using that grim fact to keep her hopes up when the blasting snow suddenly began to die down.

As fast as it had started, the blizzard slacked. The world was still white, but Rosalie could see farther with every step until, amazingly, a giant shadow emerged from the snow.

"There!" Willow cried.

The wall was right in front of them, only half a field away. Jax didn't even have to give the order before the squad broke into a sprint, charging toward safety.

Rosalie reached the wall first, but just as she aimed her maneuvering gear to pull herself up, the ground began to shake. When she looked over her shoulder to see why, the Gobbler was staring straight back at her.

Rosalie hadn't realized just how far Jax and Willow had gone to save her and Emmett until this moment. The titan was almost a kilometer away, stomping its feet in the middle of the snow-crushed fields like a child throwing a tantrum. She'd never heard of a titan showing emotion, but Rosalie swore its face lit up with joy when it spotted them, and then the whole world shook as it began to charge.

"Go!" Jax yelled at her. "Get to the cannon!"

Rosalie fired her hooks as far as they would go, pulling herself to the top of the wall in a single shot. When she landed, she ran for the nearest cannon, the same big twelve-pounder they'd originally been sent out to check. The gun was already prepped thanks to their inspection earlier, and was even still loaded with Emmett's test shell. Yet when she spun the crank to aim the barrel at the Gobbler, her stomach clenched.

"I can't hit it!"

"What do you mean you can't hit it?" Jax yelled, running down the wall at her. "Just shoot the damn thing!"

"It won't do any good!" she yelled back. "Look at it!"

The Gobbler was charging across the snowy fields faster than a galloping horse, but it wasn't moving in a straight line. It ran in a zigzag, swinging unpredictably from left to right like a drunken soldier. Rosalie prided herself on being a good shot, but this was an impossible target, and as fast as the Gobbler was going, she'd only get one chance before it reached the wall.

Jax drew his swords. "I'll go."

"No," Rosalie said, grabbing his arm. "You'll get crushed."

"What else is there to do?" Jax cried, yanking out of her grip. "That thing can jump onto the wall! What's to stop it from jumping down into Trost after it's done with us? We have to kill it now. If you can't take it down with the cannon, then we have to use these."

He held up his swords, but Rosalie wasn't looking at him. She was watching the Gobbler, who was terrifyingly close, charging the wall at breakneck speed . . .

"I think I've got it," she said, spinning the wheel to tilt the cannon straight down. "We just need to get the titan in position."

"How are you going to get a titan into position?"

"By knowing where it's going," Rosalie said, aiming down the cannon sight. "I can't shoot him while he's weaving like that, but we know where he's weaving to." She pointed at her face. "Us. We're his target, which means *that*"—she pointed at the ground directly below them—"is where he'll be."

"Assuming he jumps straight at us," Willow said, looking up from where she was bandaging Emmett. "He could come from the side. That's how he did it before. He landed behind us."

"Then we'll just have to hope he takes the straightest path," Rosalie said. "Because this is the only shot we've got."

"Hope doesn't do much good with titans," Jax said. "But I can do you one better. I'll get him to go where you need him. But Rosalie . . . "

She looked up from the cannon, and he flashed her a grim smile. "You better not miss."

And then he jumped off the wall.

Jax fell a long way. Rosalie was soaked in sweat by the time his line snapped taut, leaving him dangling less than ten meters from the ground, within easy reach of the long-armed titan. "Oy, ugly!" he shouted, clanging his swords. "Come and get it!"

His taunt rang clear through the winter air, and the charging titan changed course. It was no longer zigzagging toward the wall. It was coming straight for Jax, arms extended, ready to snatch him into its mouth.

"Rosalie," Willow said anxiously. "You might want to shoot it now."

"Not yet," she said, keeping her eyes on her target. "I've only got one shot."

"But it's right on top of him!" Emmett cried, his voice panicked.

No, it wasn't. Not yet. There was still a good stretch of space between the titan and the spot on the ground where Rosalie had aimed the cannon, a little stretch of snow exactly fourteen meters from the wall. Only when it reached that point could she fire, so Rosalie waited, holding her breath as the Gobbler got closer and closer and closer.

When the titan's long fingers could almost reach Jax, its feet finally entered the zone Rosalie had marked off in her mind. The moment it crossed the line, she yanked the string, firing the cannon shell not at the Gobbler, but into the ground at its feet.

The explosion was instant and enormous, blowing dirt and snow high into the air. As she'd planned, the charging titan hit the crater at full speed and tripped, falling forward. Since Rosalie had been careful to aim her shot fourteen meters out, the last meter of the fifteen-meter-tall titan's body—its head—hit the wall directly below Jax, caving in its skull with a sickening crunch.

"Now!" Rosalie screamed. "Jax, kill it now!"

She hadn't needed to yell. The moment the titan dropped, Jax landed on top of it. Even with its head smashed open, the Gobbler was still alive, its long limbs flailing in a desperate attempt to push itself up. Jax placed his boot on the back of its neck and sliced both of his blades through the weak spot. The Gobbler went still the moment Jax finished his cuts. Then its huge, distorted body started to steam, melting the snow around it. Rosalie was still staring when Jax hauled himself back up the wall and grabbed her off the cannon.

"You did it!" he cried, spinning her around. "You killed the Gobbler!"

"But I didn't," she protested when he finally set her down. "You were the one who—"

"Only because of your shot," he said, hugging her tight. "You were brilliant, Rosalie! The Gobbler is dead! Do you know long I've wanted to gut that bastard for what it—"

He stopped there, his face right above hers. In his excitement, Jax had gotten very close. Closer than he'd ever been. Closer than anyone had ever been, including her fiancé. The whole situation was wildly inappropriate, but Rosalie didn't want it to stop. Quite the opposite. Her heart was hammering in her chest, urging her to move even closer, to press her lips against his smiling mouth and celebrate the fact that they were still alive. She was teetering on the edge of doing exactly that when Jax suddenly stepped back.

"Sorry," he said, looking at the ground, his gear, the dead Gobbler, pretty much anywhere except her. "Got carried away."

"It's—that's fine," she stuttered, pressing her hands to her burning cheeks. "The Gobbler's not going to gobble anyone else ever again. I think that's cause for getting carried away."

Jax nodded, still looking at his feet. Willow, on the other hand, was looking very smug, wiggling her eyebrows at Emmett, who looked embarrassed by the whole thing. Rosalie was desperately searching for a way to change the subject when she spotted something in the distance.

"What's that?"

Jax squinted through the last of the snow flurries. "I think they're soldiers."

He was right. A large group of men was running down the wall towards them. Their uniforms marked them as Rose Garrison, but they weren't Brigitte's; Rosalie didn't recognize any of them. Also, their gear was far too nice. As the men came to a halt, Rosalie realized that she did in fact recognize two of them: Markus, the drunken Supply Corps sergeant who'd nearly gotten them all killed a few weeks ago, and Captain Woermann, bringing up the rear.

"Miss Dumarque!" the captain called, panting from the exercise he was clearly not used to. "Are you all right?"

He sounded utterly terrified, but considering that her uniform was drenched in titan blood, Rosalie supposed he had reason to be.

"I'm fine," she assured him. "But what are you doing here?" She'd only fired the cannon a minute ago. It was way too soon for any response, much less a personal one from the captain of the Garrison.

"I was doing a routine inspection when we heard the cannon," the captain said. "Naturally, we rushed to—"

"A routine inspection?" Jax scoffed. "On the day after Longest Night? In the middle of a *blizzard*?"

"Sergeant Cunningham," Captain Woermann snapped, "Lieutenant Brigitte tolerates your outbursts. I will not. You will keep any further opinions to yourself."

Jax closed his mouth with a suspicious glower, but before Woermann could continue, one of the soldiers gave a shout.

"Sir! Over here!"

Captain Woermann dragged his glare off Jax and walked to the edge of the wall where the man was pointing. "It's just a titan," he said.

"With respect, sir," the soldier replied, "that's not *just* a titan. That's the Gobbler."

"Come off it," Markus said nervously. "The Gobbler's a myth."

"He's not," the soldier said angrily. "He killed one of my squad two years ago right near here. Our sergeant claimed he went AWOL, but I saw that thing skulking around with blood on its face afterward. There was no one else it could have eaten." He looked at Jax. "*You* killed the Gobbler?"

"It was a team effort," Jax said proudly. "After he swallowed Rosalie, we—"

What little color was left drained from Captain Woermann's face. "Swallowed Rosalie?" he squeaked. "A titan *swallowed* Rosalie Dumarque?!"

"He tried to," Rosalie said, grinning at Jax. "But my sergeant cut me out."

"Only after Willow sliced its knees to stop it from running," Jax said, winking at Willow. "Nice job on that, by the way."

Jax turned back to the captain. "We couldn't finish the Gobbler off in the field, so we escaped and started back to the wall on foot. We made it all the way to the base before it spotted us, but Rosalie kept her head. She let him charge in close and then shot the ground out from under him. After that, all I had to do was swing down and make the final cut."

The moment he finished, all of Woermann's soldiers rushed to congratulate them on taking down a mythical titan. Everyone was asking how Jax and Willow had chased a fifteen-meter titan through an open field with nothing to use grapple gear on, and Rosalie was surrounded by soldiers eager for all the gory details of how she'd avoided getting eaten. It was absolute chaos, with everyone talking over one another in happy, excited voices, but it felt more like a victory than anything Rosalie had experienced since she'd come to the front. It didn't even matter anymore that she exhausted, freezing, and covered in still-drying blood. She could have stood there telling the story of how they beat the Gobbler forever if Captain Woermann hadn't elbowed his way in.

"Enough," he said sternly. "Miss Dumarque has had a very traumatic experience. We will escort her back to the base so that she may rest. And she shall have tomorrow off."

"My team and I will have it off, you mean," Rosalie said, giving the captain her sweetest smile. "With pay."

"Of course," Captain Woermann said after a long pause. "If that would please you."

"It would," Rosalie said, turning to grab the repair cart. "Emmett, I believe we were pushing this cart full of tools back to the storehouse?"

"Yes, we were absolutely doing that," Emmett said, limping over. "Blizzard or no, we would never leave anything this valuable out on the wall."

They both smiled at Woermann, but before they could start pushing, Jax grabbed the cart's handle.

"Hold up," he said, his lips curling into a cruel smile. "We pushed it out here because we were filling in for the Supply Corps, who were too drunk to do their job. But Markus is here now, so I'm sure he wouldn't mind pushing it back. Would you, Markus?"

He turned to Markus, who looked like he'd just swallowed a bug. "I—"

"Surely you're not going to let Miss Dumarque push your cart for you?" Jax said. "That's hardly acceptable behavior for an officer. Don't you agree, captain?"

"Now see here," Markus began, but he stopped when Woermann said, "Do it."

Markus held up a bandaged hand. "But Jax broke my—"

"I said push," Woermann growled, holding out his arm to Rosalie.

Rosalie took it with a forced smile, glancing over her shoulder every few meters as they walked back to the base to make sure Jax was close behind.

By the time they'd changed into uniforms that weren't drenched in titan blood, news of the Gobbler's death had spread through the entire base. Even the combined force of Captain Woermann and Lieutenant Brigitte wasn't enough to rein in the chaos, and Markus used that confusion as an opportunity to slip away. He was shoving the repair cart into the armory when a shadow appeared in the door behind him.

"Nice to see you doing work for once."

Markus kicked the cart and turned to glare at Jax. "You made me push that thing the whole damn way." He held up his bandaged fingers. "On a broken hand! Which is *also* your fault, you bastard."

"I'm sure you'll live," Jax said, stepping closer. "What were you doing out there with the captain?"

"My job," Markus said. "We heard one of the big cannons was broken, so Woermann—"

"Woermann can't be bothered to keep all the cannons stocked with shells," Jax snapped. "You really expect me to buy that he bestirred himself from his cozy office to personally inspect a cannon in the middle of a snowstorm?"

"It was an emergency," Markus said. "The cannon—"

"Was fine," Jax finished. "My people checked it from nose to base. That gun is in perfect condition. So you want to tell me why Brigitte thought it wasn't?"

Markus wiped his brow. "How am I supposed to know what the gate lieutenant is thinking?"

Jax leaned closer, his eyes gleaming with a cold, deadly light. "You knew that cannon wasn't broken."

"I did not! I—"

"Shut up," Jax growled. "I learn every damn secret on this wall eventually. If I discover you had *anything* to do with my squad getting sent on a wild goose chase, I'll tell Brigitte every dirty deed you've ever done, and you'll find yourself getting fitted for a hangman's noose."

The blood drained from Markus's ruddy face. "Since when do you care so much about recruits?"

"Since I had to cut one of them out of the Gobbler's throat," Jax snarled. "You've been here long enough to know what comes out in the snow. You could have gotten her killed!"

"Her?" Markus smirked. "So *that's* it. You ain't mad about the cannon. You're mad because of what happened to the Dumarque girl."

Jax grabbed the Supply Corps sergeant and slammed him into the wall. "I'm mad because whatever stunt you and Woermann were trying to pull nearly got us all killed! And if I find out you had anything to do with it, I swear I'll do the same to you, except *I* won't screw it up."

"All right, all right," Markus said, putting up his hands. "I admit there weren't nothing wrong with the cannon. I was supposed to mess it up a bit, but—"

"*Mess it up?*" Jax repeated. "You do know sabotage is a hanging offense?"

"I was only going to remove the firing line!" Markus protested. "And I didn't even do that! I ain't going up on the wall in Gobbler weather."

"Our squad was sent to fix the cannon you failed to break," Jax went on, ignoring him. "Brigitte said it was orders from above, which can only mean Woermann, but that makes no sense. If Rosalie died, her father would have the captain's head on a platter. Why would Woermann risk that?"

"How should I know?" Markus said angrily. "You're the one who likes secrets. I just wanted the money. I will say this, though. No one knew that storm was coming, or that it'd be so bad."

"Brigitte knew."

"Brigitte's crazy," Markus said. "Always feeling the weather, the batty old—"

He was cut off with a gasp as Jax grabbed his throat. "Say one more word about my lieutenant," Jax said, tightening his fingers. "One more and it will be your last."

Markus nodded rapidly, eyes bulging, and Jax let him drop to the ground. "I want you to keep an eye on Woermann for me."

"You want *me* to work for *you*?" Markus said, rubbing his bruised neck. "After the stunts you've pulled?"

"If you don't want me exposing everything you've done, including attempted sabotage, then you'd better work like your life depends on it."

"But there's nothing to watch," Markus pleaded. "It wasn't no big plan. Woermann just wanted to put her on the spot. I was supposed to sabotage the cannon, then lure in a few normal titans. Not too many, just more than you could handle on your own. Then, when things looked bad, Woermann and his men would ride to her rescue. A simple wag the dog, that's all it was, I swear. No one dreamed the Gobbler'd be there. Most of the guys at HQ think he's a myth."

"Thank you for the information," Jax said. "But you're not getting off the hook."

"Oh, come on!" Markus cried. "I was straight with you!"

"And I'm being straight with you," Jax said, stabbing his finger in Markus's face. "Get back to HQ and keep your big ears open and your big mouth shut. If you catch wind that Woermann's come up with any more brilliant ideas, you make sure I find out first. Got it?"

"Couldn't miss it," Markus grumbled. "But I still don't understand why you're risking both our necks for Rosalie Dumarque. Didn't you say all nobles should be fed to the titans?"

"I'll feed *you* to a titan if you don't watch it," Jax snapped. "And this isn't about Rosalie. Woermann's idiocy put my squad in danger, and I take it personally when people try to kill me."

Markus sighed. "Whatever you need to tell yourself, mate."

Jax gave him another of those murderous looks, and Markus backed away. "No need for additional threats. I'll give you a heads-up the moment I hear anything, like a good little dog. But in the meanwhile, kindly go to hell."

"Feeling's mutual," Jax said, stepping aside so Markus could scuttle away.

CHAPTER ELEVEN

As word of the Gobbler's death spread through the Garrison, everyone conveniently forgot all the grim rumors about Jackson Cunningham.

Instead of nervous looks and whispers when he walked through the courtyard, soldiers greeted him with smiles and salutes. They even invited him to eat with them, which Jax treated as a joke before Rosalie convinced him to give it a try. He looked hunted the whole meal, awkwardly answering questions like he was being interrogated. Clearly, being respected was a new experience for Jax. Rosalie, however, loved every moment of it.

She and her team were the heroes of the base. Wherever she went, people smiled and greeted her—not as Miss Dumarque or Charles's daughter but as Rosalie, one of the soldiers who'd killed the Gobbler.

The blizzard had brought winter to Trost

in earnest. Every morning dawned with new snow and ice, which meant that not only did squads have to patrol the wall, but they had to shovel it too, scraping the rails and walkways so no one would slip to their deaths. It was brutal work in bitter cold, but the fact that they no longer had to fear the Gobbler made everyone breathe easier. Morale only improved when the new equipment arrived.

As promised, Brigitte had spent every cent of Rosalie's bride price on gear for her soldiers. One frigid day, a dozen huge wagons rolled up to the Garrison courtyard packed with hundreds of sets of brand-new vertical maneuvering gear plus new wires, blades, gas canisters. The works.

It was all so shiny that the soldiers were afraid to touch it at first. But once Brigitte started passing out sets, they all fell on the wagons in a gleeful rush, strapping on gear and hauling themselves all over the base just for the joy of flying. But the real treat came the next day.

The soldiers of the Trost Gate had been making do with the same threadbare uniforms for years, sometimes wearing mended clothes that other soldiers had died in. Brigitte used the leftover money to commission new clothing for the entire force, for both summer and winter. Rosalie didn't truly understand the gravity of the decision until she discovered her bunkmate Henrietta crying with joy because she finally had gloves without holes and a coat that kept out the wind.

Between the new gear and new clothes, the Trost Gate Garrison was a new force. Nothing could make life on the wall easy, but the general atmosphere of marching toward death had lifted. People smiled more, laughing even as they griped about pushing cannons in the snow.

The Garrison wasn't the only thing getting better. Squad 13 still trained together every morning. It was brutal work, but they were improving every day. Even Jax said so, which Rosalie, Willow, and Emmett all agreed was like being awarded a medal by Garrison Commander Dot Pixis.

Jax's reading had also improved dramatically. He was capable of devouring Rosalie's books on his own, but neither suggested they stop the lessons. When they'd finished all the books Rosalie had brought with her, they just started over, sitting side by side at the top of the empty gate every night. Not even the winter weather could stop them. When the snow piled up, Jax just scraped it away, making an enclosure in the lee of the cannon where the wind wasn't so strong. It was still bitterly cold, but secretly Rosalie liked the icy nights best. They gave her an excuse to move closer to Jax, who was always warm.

Sometimes—the best times—he put his arm around her shoulders. When he did that, reading the familiar stories in his accented voice, Rosalie could easily forget about her upcoming marriage, about leaving the wall and how impossible it seemed that she'd ever reconcile with her father. All she thought of was her and Jax, reading by the light of the winter moon.

So it went for weeks, the short days blending together until winter finally began to wane. Despite his threat to drag her off the wall, her father never came to Trost, and eventually Rosalie stopped worrying about it. She was far more interested in watching the spring crocuses poking up through the crust of the melting snow on the titan side of the wall. A sight she enjoyed often, because now that they were better, she and her team went off the wall nearly every day, killing titans whenever they could get away with it. The attacks weren't strictly permitted—Garrison rules clearly stated that titans could be engaged only if there was an immediate danger to the wall—but Jax was more than happy to look the other way if it meant one less monster in the world.

One evening, a few days after the last of the year's snow had melted, Rosalie was on the gate with Jax as usual. They had spent a long day pushing cannons in the rain, so she'd made herself comfortable, sitting with her head pillowed on Jax's shoulder. She must have drifted off, because she woke with a start when Jax nudged her arm.

"Sorry," she said drowsily.

"It's all right," he replied, his voice strangely deep. "I don't mind, but someone's coming."

Sure enough, she heard the creak of boots on the stairs. Rosalie had just enough time to scoot to a respectable distance away from Jax before one of Brigitte's personal aides, an elderly veteran with a long scar across his face and neck, stepped onto the gate.

"Private Dumarque?"

When she stood, he handed her a sealed note. "From the gate lieutenant."

Rosalie opened it to find an invitation. A command, technically, since it came from her commanding officer, but the language was polite rather than demanding, requesting Rosalie's presence in her office the next evening.

"That's strange," Jax said after the soldier had left. "I've known Brigitte a long time, and I've never seen her do anything like this."

That sounded ominous. "Should I be worried?"

"You should always be worried," Jax said. "That's just common sense. But I don't think it's bad." His face fell. "I guess this means you'll miss reading tomorrow."

"You could always read without me."

Jax scoffed. "Don't be insulting. I'm not going to sit up here reading out loud to myself."

She laughed. "I meant quietly."

"What's the point in that? Hearing it out loud is way more fun, and you know I do the voices better than you do." He smiled at her. "I'll just wait."

The idea of Jax waiting for her made Rosalie very happy as she headed down the stairs to bed.

❀ ❀ ❀

Immediately after dinner the next day, Rosalie changed into a clean uniform and went into the gate tower to see Brigitte. When she announced herself, the guard at door escorted Rosalie straight to the lieutenant's office, as if she was an officer rather than a private.

"Rosalie," the lieutenant said when she came in. "Right on time."

Rosalie nodded, taking a seat in one of the new chairs someone had crammed into Brigitte's closet-like office. She was still getting comfortable when she noticed the lieutenant had a stack of papers on her desk in front of her. She spotted her own name written on the top document.

"Um, Lieutenant," she said nervously, "what is this about?"

Brigitte chuckled. "Don't worry, you're not in trouble. I called you in because I have an offer for you and your squad. One I trust you'll like more than fixing cannons in a blizzard."

That was a relief, but, "If for me and my squad, why am I the only one here?"

Brigitte's smile widened. "Because you're the one they listen to."

She leaned back in her chair, looking up at the map of the land surrounding the gate pinned to the wall behind her. "You've out-stripped my expectations, Private Dumarque. I have to admit, I had serious reservations about taking you into my division, but despite a few hiccups at the beginning, you've proven yourself both brave and reliable. Your squad is now one of my top units in terms of training and skill. You've even managed to put a veneer of civility on Jackson Cunningham, which I'd always thought was impossible. The four of you are among the bravest, most dedicated, most creative soldiers I've ever had the pleasure to work with, which is why I'm request-ing that your entire squad be transferred to Survey Corps, effective immediately."

Rosalie, who'd been floating on a cloud through all the praise, jerked up in her chair. "What?"

"I want you to go to Survey Corps," Brigitte repeated, folding her hands on her desk. "I say *you* specifically, because I know most of these changes are your doing. Willow and Emmett were already practicing on their own, but it wasn't until you convinced Jax to teach them that they started getting anywhere. You're the one who brought your team together and pushed them to the next level. Now I want you to do it again."

"I'll try," Rosalie said, more confused than before. "But . . . if you're so happy with us, why are you sending us away?"

Brigitte looked her straight in the eye. "Because you don't belong here."

Anger flashed over Rosalie's face before she could stop it. When she tried to argue, though, the lieutenant put up her hand. "This is the Garrison," Brigitte said solemnly. "We're defenders, not attackers, but you wouldn't know it from your squad." She narrowed her eyes. "I know all about your little hunting trips off the wall. I've turned a blind eye so far because your squad's killed more titans than anyone else has managed to all year, but I can't keep doing it."

"Why not?" Rosalie asked. "So long as we're not endangering the wall, where's the harm in killing titans?"

"Because, as I told you the first time you came to my office, *that's not why we're here*," Brigitte said sharply. "Our job is to keep people safe, not to go out and pick fights. That's the Survey Corps' job. They were created to do exactly what your squad can't seem to stop doing. And as your officer, I think you'd be much happier working under Commander Erwin than you would under me."

The mention of Commander Erwin's name made Rosalie's breath hitch. She'd never met him, but even her father admitted he was a genius in his own mad way. Yet even though Brigitte's argument made a great deal of sense, there was one vital flaw the lieutenant had yet to address.

"I appreciate what you're saying," Rosalie said nervously.

"But . . . the Survey Corps is a death sentence. I've seen their record, and it's the worst in the military. It doesn't matter how well we'd fit in there, I can't ask my team to go die."

"You already do," Brigitte said, folding her hands in front of her. "Being in the military means putting your life on the line, Dumarque. You risk your skin for the Garrison every time you climb onto that wall. The only reason Survey Corps has more deaths than the rest of us is because they take the fight to the enemy. Attacking is inherently more dangerous than defending, but if we do not attack the titans, we'll never break free of the corner they've pushed us into."

Rosalie stared at her, speechless. Brigitte's words sounded so much like what she'd said to her father, but she'd never thought she'd hear them aimed at her.

"I've dedicated my life to the Garrison," the lieutenant went on. "But proud as I am of that, I know the Garrison can't win this war. If we want a future without walls, it's not enough to just defend them. Someone has to go beyond and face the enemy. That's what Survey Corps does. They are the vanguard, the ones who are willing to take risks so that everyone might one day be free. That's why they get to wear the Wings of Freedom, and why I think you should too."

She pushed the stack of papers across her desk to Rosalie. "This is a copy of my letter of recommendation as well as a transfer request for each of you," she said. "You don't have to make a decision tonight, but I want you to talk to your squad. The bulk of the Survey Corps is outside the wall right now, but the acting commander has already agreed to take you on, so if you decide to go, I can put in your transfer immediately. If you decide not to join, you're welcome to stay as my soldiers, but I will be much stricter about unauthorized trips off the wall going forward. The Garrison is no place for personal heroics. If you want to be a titan slayer, go join Erwin's circus."

Rosalie nodded, her mind spinning as she took the papers. "I'll relay this to my squad," she promised. "But for myself, I'm afraid I can't accept."

Brigitte frowned. "I'm sorry to hear that. I'd thought you'd be the first in line. You're the one who said she came down here to fight the titans."

"I did," Rosalie said quickly. "And I would, but . . . " Her voice trailed off, and she looked down at the applications clutched in her fingers. "It's not my choice to make. I'm to be married soon. The arrangement is very important to my family. So while I thank you for the honor, I'm afraid my answer has to be no."

Lieutenant Brigitte sat back in her chair with a huff. "It's not my place to say this, but I'm old and I don't care about Charles Dumarque, so I'll say it anyway: You shouldn't do what your family says."

Rosalie's head jerked up in surprise. "But they need me. My engagement secures a vital—"

"The Dumarques are one of the oldest noble houses," Brigitte said. "They'll survive a broken marriage contract, but we're all done for if the titans aren't stopped. This is war, Rosalie, and wars are only won with good soldiers. You've proven yourself again and again to be resourceful, brave under fire, respectful of your team, and a crack shot with a cannon. Those aren't qualities that grow on trees. I try not to stick my nose into my soldiers' private business, but I'll be damned if I let a weapon like you be wasted on whatever rich idiot your father's picked out."

Rosalie was speechless. Everything Brigitte had said matched what she privately thought, but admitting it would mean betraying her duty to her family. Betraying her father.

"Just think about it," Brigitte said gently. "And be sure you give those forms to the rest of the squad. If anyone has questions, I'll be available all day tomorrow. Dismissed."

Rosalie rose on shaking legs, saluting her officer before walking out the door.

@ @ @

On the other side of the city, Jax was sitting on a stool in one of Trost's smaller, dirtier taverns, taking care of some unfinished business.

"So you're telling me there's nothing," he said, glaring daggers at the ruddy-faced man sitting at the bar beside him. "Woermann attacked Rosalie and then decided to what? Sit on his hands for two months?"

"Look, I can only tell you what I've heard, and I haven't heard a peep," Markus said, taking a long drink from his ale. "All Woermann wanted was to suck up to Dumarque, but when you lot killed the Gobbler, you became bloody heroes, and heroes don't run home to daddy." He took another drink. "The whole thing went sour on him. Can't blame the poor bastard for wanting to lie low. Anyhow, word is the lady's leaving the Garrison for marriage soon, right?"

Jax had been trying very hard not to think about that. He still clung to each nightly reading session like a dying soldier to his last breath. A wiser man would have already started to distance himself, spared himself the pain, but Jax couldn't kick the fear that once Rosalie was gone, everything good she'd brought to his life would go with her.

"All right, Markus," he said tiredly. "If you don't have anything, why did you ask me to meet you? It certainly wasn't for the company."

"Absolutely not," Markus said, tipping back his mug to finish his drink. "But I didn't come entirely empty handed. I hear tell that Woermann's about to try a new angle."

"That's more like it," Jax said. "What's he got in mind? Because if it's another titan, I'm not even going to bother. Rosalie can carve those up on her own now."

"No, no," Markus said, getting up from his bar stool. "No more titans."

"What is it, then?" Jax asked, frustrated.

Markus smiled wide, showing the gap in his yellowed teeth. "You."

That was all the warning Jax got before something hard slammed into the back of his head.

He woke up tied to a chair in an office.

Captain Woermann's office, specifically. Jax had been subjected to several unpleasant visits here over the years. But though he knew where he was, the finely dressed man standing in front of the fireplace was not Captain Woermann.

He was tall and broad-shouldered and seemed very fit for a man in his fifth decade. He was in shirtsleeves, no uniform, but he stood with the rod-straight posture that only came from a lifetime in the military. His blond hair was cropped ruthlessly short, but his stern face looked very much like Rosalie's when she was angry, which told Jax all he needed to know about exactly how much trouble he was in.

"Let me guess," he said. "You're Lord Dumarque."

The man looked away from the weak flames in the fireplace just long enough to shoot Jax a deadly glare. "I did not give you permission to speak."

Jax sighed. *Definitely* Lord Dumarque. "Mind telling me why I'm here, then? I don't recall doing anything that would warrant a personal visit from a Military Police general."

"I'm not here as a general," Lord Dumarque said, turning at last to walk across the carpet with slow, deliberate steps. "You are meddling with something that belongs to me. I am here to take it back."

"'Fraid I don't follow," Jax said, wiggling experimentally against the ropes that tied his hands behind his back. "I've touched nothing of yours."

"Haven't you?" Lord Dumarque leaned down until he and Jax

were eye to eye. "Because I have it on good authority that you, Jackson Cunningham, have shamelessly seduced my daughter, a noble lady of House Dumarque." He tilted his head. "Do you know what the king's punishment is for men of your station who trifle with noble ladies?"

Jax's mouth went dry. "I believe it is hanging."

"Father's choice, actually," Lord Dumarque said with a slow smile. "I can be quite imaginative."

"Well, that's lovely," Jax said. "But you won't be getting imaginative with me. I haven't done anything to Rosalie."

The lord's blue eyes narrowed. "So it's 'Rosalie,' is it?"

"She's in my squad," Jax said defensively. "What am I supposed to call her? Lady Dumarque?"

"Dissemble all you want," Lord Dumarque said. "But Woermann has several witnesses who've seen you and my daughter being much closer than officer and subordinate should be."

"Then why don't you talk to her about it?"

"If I could talk Rosalie out of her self-destructive behavior, she wouldn't be on that wall," Lord Dumarque snapped. "You are but the latest in a long line of very bad decisions. If we wouldn't be the laughingstock of Sina, I'd drag her home by her ear. The only dignity we have in this disaster is that at least she's making a name for herself in the military. In killing a famous aberrant titan, she's distinguished herself even more than her brothers. We now have some honor to hide behind, but that shelter does not extend to you."

Lord Dumarque reached down and grabbed Jax's jaw, forcing him to look up at his face. "I don't know how you managed it, but if the rumors are true, it would seem my daughter has developed a very unfortunate attachment to you."

Jax, who'd been struggling, suddenly became still.

"Stop smiling," Lord Dumarque snarled. "You clearly care nothing for my daughter's future, so I can only hope you feel differently about your own."

He released Jax's jaw and reached into his pocket, pulling out a rectangular sheet of paper with the Royal Bank's seal engraved on the corner. "I want Rosalie back, and I am willing to put out a great deal of money to make that happen. Name your price, and I'll give you half right now. The other half will come when you get Rosalie off that wall."

Jax gaped at him. "You want to pay me to make Rosalie go home?"

"Yes," Lord Dumarque said flatly. "That's how transactions work."

It took everything Jax had not to laugh in the general's face. "It doesn't matter how much money you throw at me," he said, grinning. "I can't make Rosalie leave. Believe me, I've tried."

"Then try harder," Lord Dumarque said. "Maybe I didn't make myself clear: I can change your life. With the money I'm offering—"

"I don't want your money."

"Of course you do," he said. "Everyone has a price."

"Not me," Jax said angrily. "I learned my lesson about selling people long ago, and I'm not selling Rosalie. You talk about your daughter like she's a lost dog, but Rosalie is a solider. She's not like you, happy to let good men die and children starve so you can have your parties in peace. She's fighting, and she's going to keep fighting until she wins or she dies."

For a moment, Lord Dumarque looked taken aback. Then he smiled. "Now I see," he said with an infuriatingly condescending smile. "Rosalie's not the victim of seduction here. *You* are." He shook his head. "Poor little peasant, you're in love with her."

He stopped, waiting for Jax to argue. When Jax said nothing, Lord Dumarque's face grew furious. "It'll never happen," he snarled. "You might be the big man on the wall, but you're common as dirt, beneath her in every way. A pig in maneuver gear is still a pig."

"I'd rather be a pig than someone like you," Jax replied, looking the man up and down. "You call yourself a general, but Rosalie's a braver soldier than you'll ever be. That's why you're threatening me instead of talking to her. You already know she won't back down, you're just too cowardly to accept it."

Lord Dumarque's fists clenched, and Jax tensed in expectation of one landing in his face. In the end, though, the general just turned away. "I'm sorry you refuse to be reasonable," he said as he walked to the door. It opened a moment later, and Captain Woermann stepped into the room, his beady eyes smug.

"Did he not cooperate, my Lord?"

"He did not," Lord Dumarque said, putting on his coat. "He's useless, but his death will only make my daughter even more unmanageable."

Woermann looked disappointed. "What should we do, then?"

"Whatever you want," Dumarque said as he stepped out of the room. "As long as he can still walk when it's over."

"Yes, my Lord," Woermann replied, opening the door wider to let in two of the largest men Jax had ever seen. "Cunningham's been a thorn in my side for some time now." He grinned. "I'm going to enjoy this."

His goons chuckled, and Jax cringed in his chair, gritting his teeth as he braced for how much this encounter was going to hurt.

CHAPTER TWELVE

"Morning, Rosalie!"

Willow's cheerful voice cut through Rosalie's churning thoughts. The sun had barely risen, but her teammates were already coming out of the stairwell, suited up and ready for practice.

"We're doing sword drills today, right?" Emmett said excitedly, patting his hands against the sheaths on his legs, which he wore much more confidently now. "I sharpened everything! Where's Jax?"

Rosalie wished she knew. The first thing she'd done last night after leaving Brigitte's office was try to talk to Jax, but she hadn't been able to find him. Not even Cooper knew where he was. She'd gotten here early this morning hoping to find him, but still no sign. He technically hadn't missed work yet, so she supposed it wasn't her business, but that didn't make her voice sound any less panicked when she told her squad the truth.

"He must have stayed out all night," Emmett said, scratching his chin. "I thought something was odd when I didn't see him in the barracks. Maybe he's visiting a girl in town for—OW!"

Emmett jumped away, rubbing his side where Willow had elbowed him. "What was that for?!"

The medic rolled her eyes before looking pointedly at Rosalie, causing Emmett's whole face to redden. "S-sorry, Rosalie," he stammered. "I wasn't thinking."

"It's all right," Rosalie said quickly, trying not to wince at the sudden pain Emmett's speculation had lodged in her chest. "Jax and I aren't . . . that is, he's my officer, so we can't be—"

"What's important is that he's missing," Willow said, taking over before Rosalie could dig herself any deeper. She pointed at the stack of papers Rosalie was clutching. "Those look like orders. Did something happen that could have caused him to need to go somewhere?"

"Oh, no," Rosalie said, holding up the forms Brigitte had given her. "These are for us. They're actually why I was looking for Jax in the first place. Lieutenant Brigitte called me to her office last night. She wants to move our squad to the Survey Corps."

Willow and Emmett's faces went blank in stunned shock.

"Are you serious?" Willow demanded.

"The Survey Corps?" Emmett said at the same time. "As in green cloaks, horses, Wings of Freedom—*that* Survey Corps?"

Rosalie nodded. "The lieutenant thinks we're too aggressive for the Garrison, so she's recommended us for transfer. She wrote a letter explaining her decision—"

The rest of what she'd meant to say was crushed out of her as both of her squadmates grabbed her in a hug.

"I can't believe it!" Willow cried in her ear. "We actually made it to the Survey Corps!"

"We're going to ride outside the walls!" Emmett yelled back, nearly cracking Rosalie's ribs in his happiness. "Think of all the secrets we can learn!"

"We could retake our home," Willow said, releasing Rosalie to grab Emmett by the shoulders. "The Survey Corps is on mission in Maria right now. If we joined them, I bet you could come up with a way to patch that hole in Shiganshina's gate. If we repaired the breach, all we'd need to do is kill the titans left inside, and Maria would be ours again!"

"And when we've done that, we could go beyond Wall Maria!" Emmett added excitedly. "Maybe we can even find where the titans are coming from and build a wall around that instead!"

The two of them were grinning so fiercely that Rosalie was amazed they could still talk. "So I take it you two are a yes, then?"

"Absolutely," Willow said. "I'm signing up right now, before Brigitte changes her mind. Where's my form?"

Rosalie held out the paper with Willow's name at the top. The medic snatched it from her fingers, pulling a nubbin of pencil out of her medical bag to sign her name in a scrawl at the bottom. Emmett was slightly more careful. He actually read his form first, but a few minutes later he signed his name as well, beaming at Willow as he handed his paper back to Rosalie.

"We did it."

"We did it," Willow repeated, wiping tears from her eyes as she turned to Rosalie. "Let's go turn them in now. We'll get Jax later. You've signed yours, right?"

"Wait," Emmett said. "*Can* she sign up?" He looked at Rosalie. "You're getting married in the summer, right?"

"I'm supposed to be getting married," Rosalie said, "but . . . "

She looked down at the form with her name on it. Brigitte had written each one very carefully, noting specifically that their squad was to remain together as part of the transfer. It was a future on a page, an invitation to reach out and grab what Rosalie had wanted since the very first time she'd climbed onto her roof: a chance to break free of her own walls, to live as she wanted.

The paper crinkled in her fingers. From the day her father sat her down when she was eleven, she'd known her future was to marry money and rescue the noble House Dumarque from debt. But every time she tried to feel pride in saving her family, all she could think about was that stupid party.

That's what she was saving. Not lives. Not people. She was giving up her future, marrying herself to a lifetime of Ferdinand's tedious conversation, so her mother could keep wasting food to impress other nobles. That was what she'd been sold to buy. And no matter how hard she tried, Rosalie couldn't make herself believe it was worth it anymore.

"Dumarque is more than a house on a hill."

"Sorry?" Willow said, but Rosalie wasn't talking to her. She was speaking to herself, to the eleven-year-old girl who'd known her role in life, but never quite accepted it.

"We can find other ways to make money, but we can't buy back our honor," she said, reaching for Willow's pencil. "Our family has never failed to answer the call to battle. I won't be the first." Her voice was shaking by the end, but her hand was steady as she signed her name. "I'll make them understand."

They wouldn't. Her father would be furious, and her mother would never speak to her again. But terrifying as that was, Rosalie couldn't feel regret because for the first time ever, she was doing what she wanted to do. Not for a month or half a year—forever. She was going to live as she liked because she was not property. She was a soldier, a person who'd heard her whole life about the bravery and nobility of her Dumarque ancestors. Her father couldn't complain now that she was finally living up to her name, and once she helped the Survey Corps win back their lands in Maria, maybe he'd even forgive her.

"I guess that's that," Willow said with a grin. "Congratulations, beanpole. I know this marriage was a big thing for you, but you've definitely made the right decision. You'd be bored stiff as that fancy idiot's wife, and if your former fiancé *does* get mad that you chose titans over him, well he can't do anything, can he? You'll be out in Maria with the rest of us. Like to see him try to follow you out there."

Even with her heart pounding like a drum, the thought of Ferdinand getting anywhere near a titan was enough to make Rosalie laugh. "There is a bit of built-in security, isn't there?" she said as the three of them started toward the stairs. "Even if my father sends a military police squad, they'll have to wait until we come back inside to pick me up."

"Assuming they're willing to wait," Emmett pointed out. "Commander Erwin's been out there for two years already, and I doubt future missions will be any shorter. They'll probably just give up."

Her father would never give up, but Rosalie liked the idea of the walls working to her advantage for once. "Come on," she said, hurrying down the stairs. "If we're quick, we can get these forms in to Brigitte and get out to the field before anyone knows I'm gone."

The three of them went down at a dead run. As they turned to head for Brigitte's office, Rosalie spotted Jax limping through the base's front gate.

Jax hobbled through with one minute to spare before being counted AWOL. Thanks to Lord Dumarque's orders, Woermann's "lesson" had left no lasting damage aside from a cracked rib on his left side, but his body was still a mass of pain. He wasn't even sure how he'd made it all the way back after they'd dumped him in the alley behind headquarters. His current focus was finding a place where he could flop over unseen, but then he heard Rosalie's voice.

"Jax!"

She sounded terrified. By the time he looked up to see why, his whole squad was on top of him.

"What happened?" Rosalie cried, sliding herself under his right shoulder while Emmett took the left. "Who did this to you?"

"We need to get him to the infirmary," Willow said, her freckled face all business. "And get him off his feet. He should not be walking in that condition." She turned to the gate guards. "Don't just stand there. Help us!"

Under Willow's sharp instructions, the guards picked up Jax like he was a sack of flour. While they hauled him across the yard, Willow sent Emmett and Rosalie ahead to alert the base doctor. On his back and in pain, Jax didn't catch much of what happened after that. There was a lot of swaying and a flurry of chatter followed by the doctor's slurred voice telling Willow she could use one of the rooms in the back, which was a huge relief. The tower doc was fine when sober, but as drunk as he sounded right now, he'd be more likely to choke Jax with bandages than treat his injuries.

"Cut his shirt off," Willow ordered, tossing Rosalie a pair of scissors as the guards set Jax down on the triage cot.

"Don't you dare," Jax groaned. "I just got this uniform." It was one of the new ones Brigitte had bought with Rosalie's money. He'd wear it until he died. "I'll . . . take it . . . off myself."

"You can't raise your arms over your head," Willow snapped, but Jax was already sitting up, gritting his teeth against the pain as he shed his jacket onto the bed. His bloody shirt went next, leaving him bare-chested and blinking spots out of his eyes while Willow shook her head.

"That was very stupid," she chided, leaning over him. "Where does it hurt?"

"Faster to say where it doesn't," Jax muttered. "But the ribs are probably the worst." That was the pain that brought him closest to blacking out, anyway.

Willow nodded and moved in, prodding the deep-purple bruises on Jax's side with her fingers. Meanwhile, Rosalie set to work on his face, using a wet cloth to gently scrub away the clotted blood from the long cut above his eye.

"Who did this to you?" she demanded.

"It's nothing," he said, careful not to look at her. "Just a bar fight."

"*You* came out of a bar fight looking like this?" She scoffed. "Impossible. We'd have heard the battle from here." When he shrugged, Rosalie leaned down so she could glare straight into his face. "What happened, Jax?"

"It was just a fight," he said, angry that the lie sounded so weak. He kept his mouth shut after that, staring mutely at Rosalie until she threw down her bloody cloth in disgust. He could see her trying to think up a new angle when the door opened and Lieutenant Brigitte burst into the room.

"What's this rubbish about Cunningham being down?" she demanded, her eyes widening when she caught sight of Jax. "Good God, what happened to you?"

"The usual," Jax said. "Went somewhere I shouldn't." He winced as Willow rubbed a stinging salve over his ribs. "Got in trouble, paid for it. You know, normal night on the town."

Brigitte snorted. "When you come back from a night on the town looking like that, I feel obligated to notify the Military Police to look for the bodies."

"He says it was a bar fight," Rosalie cut in, moving to stand beside the lieutenant so they could glare at Jax in unison. "I don't believe him."

"I don't either," the lieutenant said, narrowing her eyes. "You want to tell us what really happened, Soldier?"

"I'm sure you'll hear about it soon enough," Jax said stiffly.

Brigitte swore under her breath. "You will be the death of me," she muttered, glancing at Willow. "Fix him up, Private. I want him standing when I drag the truth out of him."

"Yes, Lieutenant," Willow said, her hands flying as she wrapped white gauze around Jax's chest.

Brigitte nodded sharply and marched back out, only to stop in the doorway. "Just so I know if he's still mine to dress down, have you signed your forms yet?"

Jax scowled. "What forms?"

"Three of us have," Rosalie said, pulling a folded stack of papers from her pocket and extracting one before handing the rest to the lieutenant. "But I haven't had a chance to talk to Jax yet."

"Excellent," Brigitte said, her wrinkled face splitting in a warm smile as she looked at the squad, but especially at Rosalie. "I think you've made the right decision. I'll put these in immediately. Good job, Private Dumarque."

"Thank you, Lieutenant," Rosalie said, putting her fist over her heart in salute as Brigitte walked out.

"I realize the irony," Jax said when she was gone. "But would someone please tell me what the hell is going on?"

No one looked eager to tell him anything. Eventually Rosalie gave in. "While you were off having your 'bar fight,' Lieutenant Brigitte offered our squad a transfer to the Survey Corps."

Jax wondered if the beating had affected his hearing. "She's . . . *Brigitte's* kicking us to the death corps?"

Rosalie opened her mouth, but Willow beat her to it. "She's not kicking us, and it's *not* a death corps," the medic said angrily. "She's doing her job as our officer. Everyone in our squad wants to fight titans, but that ain't what the Garrison does, so Brigitte's sending us where our skills will be better applied."

"She's giving us a chance to fight," Emmett added. "Think of it that way, and it's basically a promotion. Say what you want about the Survey Corps, they don't have to push cannons."

Jax stared at them in shock. "So you're going, then?" he asked, his eyes landing on Rosalie. "All of you?"

Rosalie nodded determinedly. "We all signed up this morning. You're the last one."

Now Jax was sure he'd been hit on the head too many times. "What about your fiancé and all that duty to your family?"

Her jaw tightened. "I *am* doing my duty as a Dumarque. The world doesn't need more noble ladies and well-kept homes. It needs soldiers. Any ground I can help the Survey Corps gain will do more good for the Dumarques in the long run than a marriage. My father might not see it that way, but it's not his life. It's mine, and I mean to spend it doing something that matters."

"Then . . . " Jax said slowly, feeling a bit punch-drunk from all this information. "You're not getting married?"

"No," Rosalie said, smiling for the first time since he'd come in. "I'm moving to the front lines. We all are, and we'd very much like it if you came with us."

Jax closed his eyes with deep breath. *Bloody hell. Bloody, bloody hell.*

"The survival rate in Survey Corps is low," Willow said. "But those people aren't us. We survived the Gobbler. Surely we can take this."

"You've gotta come, Jax," Emmett added. "Your training is the reason this happened."

Jax felt a piece of paper slide into his hands, and then Rosalie's voice spoke very close. "I hope you'll come. If anyone can survive out there, it's you, and I can't think of anyone I'd rather have watching my back."

Jax opened his eyes to find the whole squad looking at him hopefully, and he blew out a long sigh. "Would you two mind leaving the room for a moment?" he asked Willow and Emmett. "I'd like a word with Rosalie."

Willow and Emmett exchanged a worried look, but eventually they filed out, leaving him and Rosalie alone.

"Are you all right?" she asked nervously when the door closed. "I didn't mean to pressure you, it's just—"

"I'm fine," Jax said. "It's not that. It's . . . " He looked down at the transfer form she'd placed in his hands. "You've already signed yours, right? That was what you gave to Brigitte?"

"Yes," Rosalie said, sitting down on the cot beside him with a worried frown. "Did you hit your head? You're acting very strange."

"My head is fine, thank you," Jax said irritably. "I just wanted to make sure, because I haven't signed mine yet." He held up his blank transfer application. "Until I sign this, I'm still in the Garrison. But your transfer form is already turned in, so you're technically in Survey Corps, which means I'm no longer your officer."

Rosalie frowned, thinking that over. "I suppose that's right."

"Good," Jax said, leaning in. The sudden movement made him dizzy, but Jax didn't care. He swept his arms round Rosalie, pulling her close to press his lips to hers with all the pent-up emotion he was finally free to act on.

Jax was kissing her.

Rosalie was stiff with shock, her brain a spinning top. She'd never been kissed before. She was still trying to wrap her head around the idea that she was being kissed *right now* when Jax suddenly pulled back, looking down at her with a silent question in his eyes.

Is this all right?

Rosalie had no idea, but life suddenly felt too short and precious to worry about doing the proper thing. Especially since he felt so *right* right now, his body warm and strong against hers. All she wanted was to keep kissing Jax, so she did, wrapping her arms carefully around his bandaged neck as she brought her lips back to his.

It was much better this time. The moment she kissed him, all the anxious tension left Jax's body, leaving only the good behind.

Even through the bandages, Jax's skin was like fire under her fingertips. Touching it made her feel alive, and that feeling only grew when he pulled her closer. Rosalie gladly clutched him back, practically climbing up his chest in her rush to touch more of the strength and warmth she'd felt though his coat during all those cold nights reading on top of the gate. His hands were in her hair now, his mouth sweet and hot against hers. In that moment, it didn't matter that the rest of their squad was waiting just outside or that they'd soon be riding into a battlefield where no one's survival was certain. The entire world had shrunk to the small, sunny infirmary room and the two of them, tangled together on the cot so tight, nothing could pull them apart.

Until someone knocked.

Jax jumped back like he'd been burned. Rosalie was also reeling, shaking her head in a vain attempt to clear it. She was still pulling herself back together when Willow called through the door.

"Sorry," she said sheepishly. "But the doctor says we have to get out of the room."

"We'll be right out," Jax said, his voice oddly husky as he turned to smile at Rosalie. "Was that . . . ?"

"I think it was," Rosalie said, smoothing her rumpled hair back into its braid.

"Was what?"

She shrugged helplessly. "I'm not sure, but it was nice."

"A lot more than nice," Jax said. Grinning, he turned and grabbed his transfer application off the bed where he'd dropped it. Next he picked up a pencil from the table, then wrote his name on the line in careful, neat letters.

"There," he said, showing her when he'd finished. "Brigitte will be impressed. When I signed up for the Garrison, I couldn't even spell my last name."

"Let's go show her, then," Rosalie said, reaching out to take his paper, but Jax caught her hand instead.

"I'll take it to her myself, if you don't mind. If I'm going to get chewed out, I'd rather not have an audience. Gotta say, though, the timing of this is amazing. After last night, a guaranteed transfer to Survey Corps suddenly sounds like a very nice gig."

Rosalie scowled at him. "And what *did* happen last night?"

Jax's answer was an infuriating smile as he reached to open the door, sending Willow—who'd been standing with her ear pressed against it—sprawling onto the floor.

"Do you mind?" Jax said.

"Sorry," the medic replied, her face flaming as she scrambled back to her feet. "I was just, um, worried about your injuries."

"Right," he said, rolling his eyes. "Thank you for your concern, Willow, but I'm doing much better. Now that I'm all patched up, I'm going to hobble down to Brigitte's and give her this."

He showed them his signed transfer form, and Emmett's face lit up. "You're coming with us, then?"

"You wouldn't survive without me," Jax said, limping into the hall.

While Jax went to face Brigitte's wrath, the rest of them went back to work. There was a lot to be done. Now that winter was officially over, the Garrison's spring recruits were pouring in from the Training Corps. Since the Survey Corps was still out on mission, the Trost Garrison was handling their recruits as well, which meant the wall was packed with earnest young teens who had no idea what they were doing. One green-eyed boy was talking loudly about how he was going to kill all the titans while the other recruits laughed at him.

Rosalie chuckled, too, but only because she'd been that way when she arrived at the wall. She understood his anger, though, and hoped he'd find a squad that would teach him as much as hers had.

One morning, so many newcomers arrived that just organizing them took hours. To escape from the crush, Rosalie led a group of recruits to the top of the gate and showed them where to stand while loading a cannon onto the rails so the gun wouldn't roll back and crush their feet.

She heard something crack in the air above her.

The sound was like a thunderbolt, despite the clear sky, and so loud that Rosalie felt it as much as heard it. Had a cannon fired? With the recruits babbling in their confusion, Rosalie scanned the top of the wall for the cause.

The world slowed to a crawl. A titan was staring down at her.

It was standing right beside the gate, a titan that was a full head and shoulders taller than the fifty-meter-high Wall Rose. A titan with no skin, just exposed red muscle, bone, and sinews, like an autopsied cadaver, and steaming in the bright sunlight. A titan that, Rosalie realized with a stab, she recognized. It was the one whose picture was at the front of all her titan-slaying manuals. Humanity's greatest enemy, the monster who'd destroyed Shiganshina.

The Colossal Titan.

The name was still echoing in her mind when the giant pulled back its leg and kicked in the gate.

CHAPTER

THIRTEEN

The blast of wind that followed blew Rosalie off the wall, along with the recruits under her charge and every other solider she could see. For a terrifying second, she spun in free fall high above Trost. Then instinct kicked in. Her hands grabbed the handles of her maneuvering gear from their holsters, squeezing the triggers before her brain realized she needed to fire.

It was a blind shot. Clouds of burning-hot steam rolled off the Colossal Titan, stinging her eyes. But the wall was a big target, and her hooks landed in the stone. Others weren't so lucky. She saw one fast-thinking recruit catch herself and then fire her other cable to spear a falling soldier through the leg before he landed. Others weren't so fortunate. They hit the ground like rotten fruit, their bodies exploding on impact with a wet *thwack*.

It was a sound Rosalie knew she'd never

get out of her head. For several heartbeats, she couldn't do anything except hang there, catching her breath, staring down at the dead. Then the dust cleared, and she spotted something worse.

The massive brick slab of the Trost gate had a tunnel going right through it. The Colossal Titan had kicked a hole in the gate. Rosalie could see the overgrown fields on the other side. Which meant there was now nothing keeping the titans out of the city of Trost.

"They're going to get in!" screamed a panicked voice somewhere above her. "*They're going to get in!*"

The cry knocked Rosalie out of her shock. She was fumbling for her triggers to pull herself back up when one of the recruits flew past her on his cables. It was the green-eyed boy from before, the one the others had laughed at for his boasts about killing titans. He fired his cables again when he reached the top of the gate, shooting his lines into the Colossal Titan from midair as he pulled his swords like he meant to fight the giant all by himself

"*Get to the cannons!*"

The recruit's shout was so far away she barely heard it, but Rosalie was already moving. Crushing the triggers on her cables, she flew up the wall, kicking her feet off the stone to move even faster. She was nearly there when the Colossal Titan swept its arm across the top of the wall right above her head.

With a sound like a tornado ripping through trees, the titan cleared the gate, his massive forearm knocking over the cannon emplacements like toys. Rosalie had to flatten herself against the wall to keep from being crushed as cannon barrels and broken pieces of rail fell past, crashing into the street below.

When it was safe to raise her head again, Rosalie stared in horror at the wreckage. All the cannons on the Trost Gate were now lying scattered in a hundred-meter arc on the ground.

But how was it possible?

Titans were mindless. They didn't plan or use strategy. She'd seen them cheerfully walk straight into cannon fire. Their lack of intelligence was the one edge humanity had over them, but this one had clearly just acted with purpose, using its arm to destroy the weapons pointed at it.

Shaking, Rosalie squeezed her triggers and pulled herself up the wall. The air at the top was thick with dust and pockets of steam. Blinking against the burning in her eyes, Rosalie armed her swords by feel and stepped forward, almost tripping over a shattered cannon emplacement. There were bodies too, the still forms of fallen soldiers like shadows in the dust. She spotted the lone recruit being helped to his feet by some comrades. In the distance, more soldiers were running along the wall toward them, but there was no sign of the monster that had done this.

Rosalie froze, staring uncomprehending at the now empty air in front of the gate. The Colossal Titan was gone. Vanished as fast as he'd appeared. She was still struggling to understand how that was possible when she saw that all the titans in the field below were now walking toward her.

Toward the broken gate.

Rosalie turned and sprinted back to the edge of the wall, yelling at the others to get moving. The attack had just begun.

The base was in absolute chaos when Rosalie arrived. Lieutenant Brigitte was in the center of the maelstrom, shouting orders for all squads to man the ground cannons on the road in front of the breached gate. She grabbed Rosalie the moment she landed. "Did you see it?"

Rosalie nodded rapidly. "It was the Colossal Titan, Lieutenant. It kicked in the gate and knocked all the cannons off the wall, then disappeared."

She expected Brigitte to question the last part, but she'd forgotten the lieutenant had been at Shiganshina. She'd seen this before, and her old face was hard as stone as she released Rosalie. "Get to the cannons in front of the gate," she ordered, turning back to the rushing soldiers. "All of you! I want every person in this base at that gate to hold the line. *The titans do not enter Trost!*"

Her shout was still echoing up the wall when Rosalie felt the deep, familiar boom of titan footfalls.

"Everyone to the cannons!" Brigitte roared, shoving past Rosalie to sprint toward the permanent ring of cannons that had been pointed at the inner side of the Trost Gate for the past five years. "If you're not firing or loading, I want you running ammunition. Empty the damn armory if you have to, but we are holding this gate!"

She was still shouting when Rosalie reached her station. Emmett slid into position a few seconds later. He was helping her open the rusted firing hatch when Willow showed up with a box of shells. "Here!" she said, dropping the ammunition on the ground beside Rosalie. "I'll be back with more."

Rosalie could see two titans through the hole in the gate. They peered through the shattered brick with delighted faces, staring into the city as if they had all the time in the world.

She grabbed a shell as Emmett finally popped the rusty hatch. The moment the breach was open, Rosalie shoved her shell inside and slammed the hatch shut again, taking only enough time to ensure the barrel was pointed in the right direction before she pulled the firing line.

"Fire!"

The shot exploded, rocking the cannon back, and the ten-meter titan that had stepped through breached gate stumbled, its head blasted off its shoulders. Before Rosalie could celebrate her good shot, though, the headless titan's fallen body was pushed aside by two more giants shoving themselves through the tunnel, their idiot faces grinning with glee.

"Reload!" Rosalie cried, scrambling for the next shell as Emmett opened the barrel for her. "Quickly!"

More cannons were active now. The din of their explosive shots drowned out even the thunder of the titan's footsteps. Inside the tunnel the Colossal Titan had kicked through the gate, monsters fell on top of each other, their bodies blown to pieces by the constant explosions. The titans were packed in so tight, no shot could miss, but it didn't seem to matter. Every time one monster went down, two more stepped in to take its place, their sleepwalker faces fixated on the humans behind the cannons as they pressed relentlessly forward.

"There's too many!" Rosalie cried as she fired again. "Even if we kill one with every shot, we just can't fire fast enough."

"But we have to," Emmett said, his face pale. "If they get through . . . "

He looked over his shoulder at the street behind them, packed with panicking civilians. Rosalie swallowed.

"We have to find a way to block that hole," she said as they re-loaded. "Any ideas?"

Emmett bit his lip. Before he could answer, they heard the clatter of hooves. Rosalie took her next shot, blasting a five-meter titan in half. Only then, while Emmett was reloading, did she turn to see Captain Woermann and his guards pulling their horses to a stop.

"Stand down!" the captain yelled, his voice high and shaking with fear. "The gate is lost! Everyone grab whatever you can and fall back through the city to Wall Rose!"

"Ignore that order!"

The roar came from Rosalie's left, and suddenly Brigitte was there, her weathered face scarlet with rage. "All troops stay in position!" she bellowed. "We hold the line!"

"Are you mad, woman?" Captain Woermann cried, barely holding onto his reins as his horse reared in fear from the thunder of constant cannon fire. "You're just wasting shells!"

"The Garrison does not abandon its post!" Brigitte yelled at him. "We will keep the titans back with our lives to buy the rest of Trost time to evacuate."

"How dare you defy an order from your captain!" Woermann shouted. "This is insubordination!"

"This is our job!" Brigitte shouted back. "I failed at Shiganshina. I will not fail here. Until I'm stabbing my way down a titan's throat, I will hold this gate."

For a moment, Woermann was too taken aback to speak, and then rage beat fear as he gestured to one of his guards. "I give the orders here, Lieutenant!" he cried as the guard leveled his rifle at Brigitte's chest. "This is your final warning! Stand down now!"

Brigitte glared down the rifle barrel so hard, the man holding it flinched. "No."

From the corner of her eye, Rosalie saw Woermann jerk back on his horse. His bluff had been called; clearly he didn't have the resolve to follow through on his threat and shoot her. He was looking at the soldier as though he didn't know what to do next when the sudden crack of a gunshot cut through the air.

Rosalie screamed, dropping the shell Emmett had just handed her in the rush to help her lieutenant. But Brigitte was still standing. It was the soldier who'd gone down, his rifle discharging harmlessly into the air as he was knocked off his horse by someone flying in from the left. Someone with gleaming swords who was already on top of the soldier wrenching his arms behind his back.

Jax.

The rest of Woermann's men were frantically pulling their rifles now, taking aim at Jax as the downed soldier screamed. Rosalie was reaching for her swords when Brigitte grabbed her arm.

"You have a job to do, Dumarque," she growled, her eyes fixed on Woermann. "Shoot your cannon. We'll handle this."

Rosalie didn't see how that was possible. Woermann had a whole ten-squad with him. But before she could argue, another soldier dropped off the barracks roof, swinging down to crash into Woermann's men like a pendulum, knocking them off their horses.

"Cooper!" Jax yelled, grabbing a rifle from the soldier closest to him. "Here!"

Cooper caught the gun without looking and swung it like a club, knocking another soldier to the ground.

"Dumarque!"

Rosalie jumped. Lieutenant Brigitte was in her face, grabbing her shoulders with both arms. "Focus, Solider," she growled, shoving Rosalie at her cannon before turning to yell at the entire firing line. "All of you, ignore the force from HQ and focus on my voice! I want three soldiers on each cannon—one loading, one firing, one running ammo. If you are not doing one of those three things, get back to base and help unpack the reserve shells. Go go go!"

The order came not a second too soon. In the half minute she— and apparently everyone else—had been distracted, the titans had made it through the breach and were now walking into the city.

Furious with herself, Rosalie took aim and fired, shooting the head off a crone-faced titan who was reaching with clawed fingers for the cannon squad closest to the gate. The explosion hadn't even finished before Emmett was there, shoving the next shell Willow had brought them into the back of the cannon. He closed the cap and locked it, then jumped out of the way as Rosalie took aim again, cranking the barrel down to shoot the legs out from under the fifteen-meter titan with a barrel chest and a bald head who was currently standing at the mouth of the breach.

As she'd hoped, the shot knocked the monster backward, blocking the hole with its massive body. This bought the other teams time to finish killing off the titans who'd made it through. Rosalie was lining up a kill shot when she heard the crack of a rifle directly behind her.

She smelled the blood before she felt the spray across her neck.

When she looked down, her left arm was covered in bright red.

"Brigitte!"

The scream was so raw and angry, Rosalie didn't recognize it as Jax's voice until he was suddenly there. He caught the lieutenant before she could fall, pressing his free hand down on the blood spreading rapidly across the front of her uniform.

"You," he snarled, turning on Woermann, who was sitting on his horse with a shocked look on his face. "You did this!"

For a moment, Rosalie didn't know what he meant. Captain Woermann didn't even have a rifle. Several of the other soldiers did, though. The shot that had hit Brigitte must have been an accident, but that didn't matter to Jax. Nor did it stop Woermann from pulling the pistol off his belt as Cooper rushed over to back Jax up.

"She got what she deserved!" Woermann shouted, moving his gun frantically between the two deadly-looking soldiers. "She was disobeying orders! You all heard her! It was insubordination! Mutiny! She would have been hung for treason, anyway." His voice cracked. "It wasn't my fault!"

"You're still *dead*," Jax snarled, pressing his hands tighter against Bridgette's wound. "I'll—"

"You can't do anything!" Woermann cried, pointing his pistol at Jax's head. "You attacked my men! That makes you co-conspirators." The gun began to rattle in his shaking hands. "I could shoot you all!"

"Not with just one gun," Cooper said, his normally carefree voice cold and deadly.

Rosalie exhaled slowly, assessing the situation. She could hear all the cannons still firing behind her. Between their roar and the shouts from the city, none of the other teams were close enough to realize what was happening. Woermann's men that Jax and Cooper hadn't knocked out had fled when Brigitte went down, leaving their captain alone. Alone and desperate and holding a gun, which he was almost certainly going to use if Rosalie didn't do something.

"Emmett, Willow," she said quietly. "Take over the cannon for a second."

"What?" Emmett yelped, but Rosalie had already stepped away, walking swiftly past Jax, Cooper, and Brigitte to put herself between them and Woermann.

"Rosalie!" Jax hissed, grabbing her arm with a bloody hand. "What are you doing? Get out of here!"

Rosalie shook him off and focused her attention on Woermann's pistol, which was now pointed at her head.

"Miss Dumarque," the captain said, lowering his gun, though not by much. "This is no place for a lady of your station. Get on my horse, we're leaving."

"No," she said, glaring at him. "We're not done here."

"Are you insane?" he cried, his wild eyes flicking up to the titans barely held back by the cannons. "This fight was lost before it began! Brigitte was leading you all to suicide!"

"Lieutenant Brigitte was upholding the mandate of the Garrison!" Rosalie yelled back. "We swore an oath to protect the people of Trost at any cost!"

Woermann's pale, terrified face turned scarlet. "Enough!" he bellowed, shoving his gun at her face. "I am your captain! You follow *my* orders, and I order you to retreat!"

"We will not retreat!" Rosalie cried, leaning forward until her forehead was touching the barrel of his pistol. "You want a mutiny? I am Rosalie Dumarque, the king's cousin! By my birth and name, I am the highest authority present, and as of this moment, I am taking over the Gate Division of the Trost Garrison."

Woermann jerked back in his saddle. "You can't do that!"

"Too bad!" she yelled. "Because I am. There are tens of thousands of men, women, and children who still need to be evacuated. It's our duty as soldiers of the Garrison to buy those civilians as much time as we can, so that's what we're going to do. If you have a problem with that, go ahead and shoot me."

The gun rattled louder in Woermann's shaking hands, but he didn't lower it. Rosalie stood her ground, staring up the pistol's barrel at the man on the other side, daring him to pull the trigger.

"Rosalie," Jax whispered, his voice terrified. "Rosalie, don't do this."

"I'm the only one who *can* do this," she said calmly, never taking her eyes off Woermann. "I'm noble. If he shoots me, it won't matter if he retreats all the way to Sina. He'll still hang." She smiled coldly. "And he knows it."

Captain Woermann's terrified eyes flickered like he was going to pass out. Then, with a high-pitched curse, he yanked back his pistol and whirled his horse around, galloping as fast as he could down the street full of panicking townsfolk.

Rosalie dropped to her knees, her chest heaving. Jax was at her side at a second later, grabbing her with his bloody hands and hugging her so hard she saw spots. "Don't you ever do anything that bloody stupid again!"

She nodded, still panting. Then she turned to look at Brigitte.

Cooper had taken over holding her wound, but the old lieutenant was terrifyingly still and pale. Her chest rose in tiny, ragged motions beneath her blood-soaked jacket, but that was the only movement she seemed capable of, and not for very much longer.

Jax must have realized it too, because he bolted back to his commanding officer. "Hold on," he said. "I'll get Willow to—"

"No," Brigitte wheezed. "Hold . . . the gate."

"We will," Rosalie promised, kneeling beside Jax. "We'll hold them back, Lieutenant. Until everyone is out."

Brigitte's eyes fluttered open. "What the . . . hell are you doing . . . Dumarque?" she gasped, staring at Rosalie in fury. "Get back . . . to your . . . damn . . . cannon . . . "

Her voice faded, and then Brigitte fell still, her blue eyes staring empty at the sky. Jax closed them a moment later, gently brushing his bloody hands over her face before turning to Rosalie. "I guess you're in command now," he said. "What do we do?"

Under any other circumstances, Rosalie would have taken that as a joke. But Jax's voice was as grim as the blood on his hands, and she already knew the answer to his question.

"We follow Brigitte's last order," she said, turning back to the broken gate where the titans were still pushing through despite the roar of the cannons. "We hold."

"We can't keep this up forever," Jax said.

Rosalie shook her head. "We don't have to. We just need to keep them bottled up in the gate long enough for the civilians to escape. How much ammunition do we have?"

"Not enough," Cooper said, looking over his shoulder at the base where soldiers had formed a chain to transport boxes of shells from the armory to the cannon line. "Brigitte hoarded ammunition like she knew this day was coming, but at the rate we're burning, even her supplies won't last long. If we keep firing all-out like this, we've got enough for ten, maybe fifteen more minutes."

That wasn't good enough. The streets around them were still choked with fleeing people. There was no way everyone could escape through the gate on the other side of the city that quickly.

"We'll just have to figure out a way to use less ammo," Rosalie said, running her hand through her tangled braid. "Any ideas?"

Jax was about to answer when the road fell quiet. Not silent— there were still alarm bells and screaming and the thunder of giant footsteps—but the boom of the cannons had stopped.

"Are we out already?" Jax demanded.

"No," Rosalie said, heart pounding. "It's a gap. When you have multiple teams, sometimes everyone has to reload at once." It was perfectly normal, one of those unavoidable scenarios every cannoneer was trained to just push through, except this time, they couldn't.

"Fire!" Rosalie screamed as titans began pouring through the undefended gate. "*Someone* fire!"

The cannon assault resumed immediately as teams finished reloading, but they'd lost precious ground. The titans were now pushing through the breached gate as fast as the explosions could knock them down. One more gap like that, and the Garrison would be completely overrun. The only solution was constant fire, but how could you keep that up without firing everything you had?

Rosalie's grabbed Jax's arm as the idea finally came to her. "We can do a round!"

Jax arched an eyebrow. "What's that?"

"A tactic I learned at the academy," she said as they ran back to her cannon, where Emmett was still firing with Willow frantically reloading for him. "We fire in a sequence—one cannon, then the next, then the next and the next until we're back at the beginning. Each cannon reloads while the next is firing. That way, we can have a shell landing on the breach every few seconds *and* we'll use less ammunition because no two cannons fire at the same time."

"No wasted shots," Cooper agreed. "I get it. But what about Jax and me? We're ace at killing titans, but we can't shoot to save our lives."

"You'll be back there," Rosalie said, pointing to the city block beyond the cannons. "If we're all firing at the breach, there's no chance to switch targets if something does get through. That's where you come in."

"We'll guard your backs," Jax finished with a grin. "If any titans get past the firing line, we'll move in and take them out."

Rosalie nodded, and Jax turned to Cooper. "Round up our best killers," he ordered. "We'll form a semicircle on top of the apartment buildings. That'll give us the best angle to come in on our wires if any of those bastards go for the cannon teams."

"Yes, sir," Cooper said, gripping his swords with a deadly grin.

"Nothing like going out in a blaze of glory, eh, Jackson?"

"I don't want anyone going out at all," Rosalie said angrily. "Our goal is half an hour. That should be long enough for everyone from this part of the city to reach the Rose Gate. We'll hold until then, and then we'll retreat through town ahead of the titans, protecting civilians along the way. Got it?"

Both men nodded, and she sent them away, lifting her voice over the roar of the cannons to call out the new plan.

CHAPTER FOURTEEN

Relaying Rosalie's orders to all the cannon teams took some yelling, and lots of running. After a few gaps and bursts, the squads found a rhythm and the cannons started going off like clockwork. Each fired as soon as the cannon to its right began to reload, which meant a shell was landing on the breach every five seconds.

The constant explosions hammered the titans backward at first. Because the soldiers had no time to aim, kill shots were rare. But even when they didn't die, the monsters still went down, their twitching bodies and severed limbs serving as a dam against the river of titans pushing in from outside. That should have been enough to turn the tide, but the monsters kept coming.

Rosalie couldn't understand it. Could the dumb creatures somehow signal that there'd been a breach in the wall? How had they known to swarm Trost Gate from every corner of the countryside? When a runner finally came down with a report from the top of the wall, he told Rosalie the titans were piled ten deep, crawling over one another in their eagerness to get inside.

But not a single one made it through. Now that the squads were shooting in a round, the cannon fire never stopped. For twenty glorious minutes, they held the line without a single break. Rosalie was about to relieve Emmett, who'd been firing capably since the round began, when she saw one of the recruits running toward her.

"Ma'am!" the girl called, raising her voice to be heard over the cannon fire. "We just sent out our last round! The stockpile's empty!"

"Empty?" Rosalie cried. "It's only been twenty minutes!"

"We double-checked the whole armory," the recruit said, her voice panicked. "There's nothing left. All we've got is what's out here."

Rosalie scanned the cannon line, doing the math in her head. The neighborhood was empty of civilians, but there was no way everyone had reached the other side of the city. They had to buy more time.

"New orders," she said to the recruit. "Relay this to all firing teams: we're slowing down the round. Ten seconds between shots, starting with my team. Move!"

The recruit took off, and Rosalie turned around to see Emmett and Willow staring at her in horror. "Are you sure about that?" Willow asked, glancing at Emmett, who looked pale. "Ten seconds is a *big* gap between explosions."

"We don't have a choice," Rosalie said, turning back to check that the recruit had made it all the way around the firing arc. "I'll call it out. Fire the next shot on my mark . . . "

The cannon to her right fired, and Rosalie waited, keeping her face calm but feeling the blood drain from her cheeks as she slowly counted down from ten. When she reached one, she turned to Emmett. "Fire!" He yanked the line, and their cannon rocked backward, sending its shell straight into the face of the fifteen-meter titan crawl-ing through the broken gate. The moment the thundering explosion faded, Rosalie turned to the team on her left. "Not yet!" she shouted as they got ready to fire. "Next shot, ten seconds!"

The squad nodded anxiously, their faces ashen as they waited for the go-ahead. As the seconds ticked by, cannon-blasted titans began picking themselves up from the blood-soaked cobbles, their vacant faces turning hungrily toward the humans only a few meters away.

"*Fire!*" Rosalie screamed.

The shot went off before the word was out of her mouth, blasting the titans back again.

But it quickly became obvious that the situation was different now. After every cannon shot, the ten-second silence allowed the monsters to creep a few steps forward. Each shot pushed them back again, but never quite as far as they'd gained. Bit by bit, the grotesque mass was pressing in, closer and closer.

The minutes crawled by. Rosalie wished she could tell every soldier how proud she was of their resolve, their discipline in holding to the round despite the titans advancing after every shot.

And then, in an instant, the delicate balance tipped.

Rosalie's team had just fired a shot when she saw a titan wrig-gling through the mass of broken bodies piled on top of it. Small by titan standards at only three meters, the creature was unbelievably nimble. Like an eel, it wiggled between the bodies, squeezing free just as they fired their shot. It jumped straight at Rosalie's cannon.

She didn't even have time to reach for her swords. The titan was already on top of them, its mouth hinging open like a snake's. Rosalie was rearing back to throw the shell into its gaping throat when Jax sailed down on his maneuver gear cables and cut its head off.

"You all right?" he asked, shaking the blood off his swords.

Rosalie was fine, but . . . the titan's decapitated body had fallen directly on top of their cannon, knocking it sideways and blocking the barrel.

"Help me move it!"

Jax was at her side at once, shoving his still-bandaged shoulder under the titan's bloated stomach. Although the monster wasn't much bigger than a man, it was impossibly heavy and bulky. Even with the help of Willow and Emmett, rolling the steaming body out of the way took far too long. The other cannons kept firing, but when their place in the rotation came up again, Squad 13's gun was still pointing in the wrong direction.

A terrible silence ensued. When she realized they weren't going to make their shot, Rosalie turned to the next cannon team to order them to fire, but she was too late. During the delay, the titans had surged forward.

The blasted ones in front reached all the way into the street. Not completely regenerated, they stumbled on their broken limbs toward the circle of cannon emplacements. Terrified, the squads began firing wildly at the titans coming toward them. This knocked down the ones in front, but with no shots landing at the gate, new titans surged through like rats.

"Focus fire!!" Rosalie screamed as they shoved their cannon back into position. "The maneuvering gear teams will take care of the runners! Keep your guns on the breach!"

The other teams tried to obey, training their cannons on the broken gate once more, but it was too little too late. In the thirty seconds the barrage had stalled, the titans' front line had pushed out of the bottleneck and into the street. The moment they got through the hole, the titans fanned out, each heading for a separate cannon squad. The maneuvering gear kill-teams moved in, swinging down from the roofs, but they couldn't keep up with the flood.

"Fall back!" Rosalie yelled. "We're overrun! Get to the roofs!"

"Wait!" Willow cried, closing the hatch on the shell she'd just finished loading. "We just got pointed the right way again! One more shot—"

Behind Willow, a ten-meter titan shoved itself forward. Its blank, dreaming face split in a huge grin as it spotted the soldiers desperately shooting their maneuvering gear at the nearby rooftops. It charged forward, reaching out with greedy hands big enough to grasp a horse. But the ground was littered with fragments of the monsters that had fallen, and it slipped, its shadow swallowing Willow seconds before its giant body landed on her with a fleshy *thunk*.

"No!" Emmett screamed, jumping on the collapsed titan. "Willow!"

With more strength and speed than Rosalie had ever seen him use, Emmett drew his swords and slashed the back of the titan's neck, cutting into its vulnerable spot like he was slicing open a fish's belly. The blood was still flying when Emmett rolled to the ground and dove under the titan.

"Help me!"

Rosalie and Jax grabbed the steaming corpse, with Jax doing most of the work to lift its dead weight enough for Emmett to pull Willow free.

The moment she emerged, Rosalie knew it was bad. Willow's body looked intact, but her torso was soaked with blood. More was oozing from her mouth, her lips turning blue as she struggled to breathe.

"I've got you," Emmett said, frantically brushing the blood off her face. "I'll save you, Willow, don't worry. Just tell me what to do."

"Not much . . . to do," Willow gasped, pointing at her bloody chest, which Rosalie could now see was caved in. "Crushed ribs . . . into my lungs."

"It's all right," Emmett said, his voice weirdly calm. "We can fix this."

Even blue and gasping for breath, Willow still managed to roll her eyes. "You can't fix . . . a punctured lung, Emmett."

"Then tell me what I can do!" he cried, bowing his head over her. "I can't lose you."

"And I can't lose you," she said, smiling at him. "That's why you need to go. They're coming, and I don't want them to get you, too."

Emmett shook his head frantically. "I'm not leaving you."

"You have to," she wheezed. "You have to go out there and find answers to all our questions."

He bent lower with a sob, pressing his forehead against hers.

"See the world for me," Willow whispered, closing her eyes. "Jax, would you please . . ."

Jax nodded and grabbed Emmett around the waist.

"No!" the boy screamed as Jax lifted him. "*Willow!*"

But Willow had gone still and the titans were everywhere. They lifted their heads when Emmett screamed, their faces lighting up at the prospect of an easy meal. With a bitter curse, Jax turned his back on Willow and fired his lines, pulling himself and a still-screaming Emmett off the bloody street. Rosalie was right behind them, shooting the steel hooks of her cables into the tile roof of the shabby apartment building beside the Garrison base. When she landed, she forced herself to turn and assess the situation.

From the rooftop, she had a clear view of the countless titans pouring through the breach like hungry vermin into a larder. She must have called the retreat in time, however, because all the cannon teams seemed to have escaped.

Except for Willow.

Rosalie clamped her jaw against the sob rising in her throat. Not yet. She needed to stay calm. Be a solider. Be—

"Rosalie?"

She turned to see Jax watching her. Beside him, Emmett had finally stopped screaming and was now staring blankly at the titans filling the street below.

"We need to get moving," Jax said, placing his hand on the spare silver cylinder strapped to the top of his blade sheath. "We've got two gas canisters each. That's not enough to get us across the city, but if we hustle, we can get ahead of the titans and refill at the headquarters building in the center of town. Sound good?"

When Rosalie nodded, Jax turned to grab Emmett, but the thin boy yanked his arm away.

"I can make it myself," he said. "Willow was always worrying that we didn't pull our weight. She'd never forgive me if I dragged you down. You'd do better to check on the reserves at the base. I don't know if they heard the call for retreat."

"If they're not out yet, they're not coming," Jax said grimly, nodding behind them.

Rosalie turned to look, clutching her mouth. The base she'd come to think of as home was completely overrun. Titans crawled over the stone buildings like roaches, breaking down doors and shoving their arms to grab the soldiers trapped inside. One popped two recruits into its mouth at once, sucking their bodies between its lips before Rosalie could look away. She was fighting the urge to be sick when the building beneath them started to shake.

A giant hand grasped the edge of the roof they were standing on. Next appeared a head, an old wrinkled face the size of a small cottage rising above the building like a hideous grinning moon. Rosalie pulled her swords instinctively, but before she could take a step toward the titan, Jax shoved her in the other direction.

"Run!" he yelled.

"But—"

"There's nothing left to fight for here!" he cried. "*Run!*"

Rosalie shoved her swords back into their sheaths as she, Emmett, and Jax scrambled across the tiles, jumped, and kept going, using their maneuvering gear to move from rooftop to rooftop while the narrow streets below them quickly filled with monsters.

Titans were everywhere. Every time Rosalie looked down, there seemed to be more, walking between the tall brick buildings and poking their arms into the shops and houses. But as she and her squadmates fled across the city, Rosalie could see that all the buildings they passed were empty. They'd done it. Thanks to their fight to hold the line, everyone in the southern half of the city was able to evacuate.

Unfortunately, this also meant that she, Emmett, and Jax were the titans' only meal.

"They're onto us," Emmett said nervously as they landed on the slanted roof of a furniture shop. "There's a herd of them following us. At this rate, we'll be bringing a stampede to HQ."

"Don't worry about that now," Jax said. "Just focus on making the jumps. We've got a lot of ground to cover and not much gas to waste doing it."

"We'll be fine," Rosalie said. "Another few blocks and we should be able to see the building, right?" She turned to Jax for confirmation, but when he nodded and moved to the edge of the roof, she noticed that the strap on top of his blade sheath was empty.

"Jax," she said, her voice alarmed. "Where's your spare canister?"

"I'm already using it," he said without looking back.

"What?" she cried. "When did that happen?"

"Just after we left the cannons. I was already low when I saw Woermann riding up and charged out to help. With everything going to hell, I didn't have time to nip back into the base for a refill."

Rosalie paled. "Are you going to make it?"

"I'm damn well going to try," he said, jumping to the next roof. "I've coasted on low gas before. If I get stuck, I'll just give you my canisters to fill and hide out on a roof until you get back."

"Absolutely not," Rosalie said angrily as she jumped after him. "They've got eyes on us. If you stop, they'll climb up and get you, and without gas, you'll be a sitting duck."

"If you've got a better idea, I'm all ears," Jax snapped. "But right now, our only choice is to keep moving. It's not that much farther to HQ. We just need to . . . "

He trailed off as he landed, squinting at something in the distance. Rosalie skidded to a halt as well. "What is it?" she asked as Emmett landed behind her.

Jax pointed at the city in front of them. Rosalie lifted her hand to shield her eyes, squinting through the bright afternoon sun. Then she saw it.

Directly ahead, at the heart of the city center, was the towering block of the Trost Garrison Headquarters, the building they'd been desperately racing toward. And it was swarmed with titans. The monsters were poking their arms through the doorways and windows and sticking their heads through the elevated gates. They were inside as well. From this high, Rosalie could see smaller titans walking around in the big equipment area, right next to the compressors they needed to refill their gas canisters.

"Damn," Jax breathed. "Damn, damn, *damn*. There goes our resupply."

"Why are there so many titans?" Emmett demanded. "What are they looking for?"

Rosalie's stomach sank. "People. All the other buildings were evacuated, but the Supply Corps would have stayed back to protect supply lines for the front. They must have attracted the titans' attention and gotten overwhelmed."

"But there are recruits in there," Emmett said, his voice shaking. "We have to do something!"

"What can we do?" Jax said. "Assuming I can make it on the gas I've got left, that place is crawling with titans, and there's only three of us. We're good, but we're not *that* good."

Rosalie nodded gravely. "He's right."

"Not you too, Rosalie!" Emmett cried. "We can't just leave them!"

"If we go in as we are, we're just throwing our lives away," she pointed out. "That doesn't help anyone. Our best bet is to get across the city as quickly as we can and report the situation to the Garrison at the Rose Gate so they can send a rescue unit that can do some good."

"Good thinking," Jax said. "Meanwhile, we find somewhere else to resupply."

Emmett swallowed. "But there is nowhere else."

"I know," Jax said, tightening his hands on his maneuver gear handles. "But we'd better think of something, because I'm down to my last few jumps, and you two will be on your spare canisters soon."

Emmett crouched, drew a line in the dust of the roof, and made an *x* in the middle. "There's the inner gate." He drew an arc from one end of the line to the other, creating a tall semicircle. "There's the city's outer wall, and we're"—he marked a spot close to the middle of the shape—"about here, more or less . . . which means we've got at least as far to go as we've already covered. If Rosalie and I trade out our canisters now and give you the ones we're currently using, what's left *might* be enough to get you across."

"Except I'm heavier than either of you," Jax pointed out. "I'll go through gas faster than you."

While Jax and Emmett argued over the exact ratio of gas usage to weight, Rosalie scanned the nearby streets. They'd pulled ahead of the mob following them, but their lead wouldn't last long. She turned to tell Jax and Emmett to run while strategizing, and her eyes drifted across the rooftops to Wall Rose, the same arc that Emmett had just drawn . . . "We can use the wall," she said.

"We're trying to get to the wall," Jax reminded her.

"Not the wall where the inner gate is," Rosalie said. "Our wall!"

She pointed across the roofs at the wide sweep of white that encircled the city. The arc Emmett had just drawn. The petal of Wall Rose that shielded Trost. "The outer wall! We can run along the top of it, all the way to the inner gate," she said excitedly. "We won't even need our maneuvering gear!"

"That's a damn good idea," Jax said.

"And we're closer to the wall than we are to the inner gate," Emmett said, drawing a line from their spot in the diagram to the encircling arc. "If we alternate canisters, we should have just enough gas!"

"We *all* should have retreated to the wall when the cannons fell," Rosalie said, pressing her hands to her head. "Why didn't I think of that earlier? I sent everyone into the city. I might have gotten them all killed!"

"Don't count the Garrison out yet," Jax said. "We're a tough lot. You don't last long on the wall if you're not a survivor."

"We'd better get going, then," Emmett said. "If we talk here much longer, survival won't be an option."

He nodded down at the street. Rosalie turned to see that the crowd of titans following them had caught up. Some were tall enough to reach the roof, their fingers plowing up the tiles as they felt blindly for their prey.

Jax signaled silently for the squad to move down the eastern edge, but just as they were about to jump, Jax stopped short. When Rosalie looked at him questioningly, he held up the handles of his maneuver gear, squeezing the triggers to show the nothing that followed.

"Looks like that's it for me," he whispered. "No time to switch gas, so you two go ahead. I'll stay and hold them off."

"No," Rosalie said, grabbing the spare canister off her belt.

"We are *not* leaving you," Emmett echoed, unscrewing his canister as well. "Take what's left of mine. I'll switch to my spare and—"

The tiles beneath them exploded, flinging the three soldiers into the air as a titan's giant hand burst through the roof they'd been standing on. Rosalie and Jax managed to land on their feet, but Emmett was thrown several meters away. He landed on his left leg, which made a sickening crack.

Emmett screamed in pain, a horrible sound that ripped out of him before he managed to clap a hand over his mouth. But it was too late. The sound of wounded prey drove the titans mad. They clawed at the building in a frenzy to reach the top.

"Sorry," Emmett gasped as Rosalie ran to his side.

"It's okay," she said, fixing her eyes on his face to keep him from looking at his leg, which was bent entirely the wrong way. "Everything's fine. We'll just carry you."

Jax was already stepping in to pick up Emmett, but the moment he shifted his body, Emmett screamed again.

"Sorry again," he whispered, tears streaming down his face. "Willow always said big-bone breaks were the worst."

"You'll have to bear it," Jax said. "If we don't move now, we're all going to get eaten."

Something had changed on Emmett's pained face. "Not all of us," he said.

The calm in his voice made Rosalie's blood run cold. "Emmett—"

"Let's be . . . smart," he said, panting with shallow breaths. "I'll just slow you down, and I think I'm probably bleeding internally." He closed his eyes as another wave of pain wracked his body. "Certainly feels like it, so—"

"No," Jax growled through clenched teeth. "I see where you're going, and the answer is no. We're not leaving you."

"You wanted us to leave you," Emmett reminded him.

"That's different," Jax snapped. "I could defend myself. You can't even move."

"And we're not leaving anyone," Rosalie said firmly, glancing over her shoulder at the titan who'd broken through the roof. The ten-meter creature resembled a gargoyle, with a hunched torso and short, thick limbs. "Come on. We have to go."

She reached to help Jax hoist their injured squadmate, but Emmett smacked their hands away. "I won't be the reason you die," he said desperately. His breathing was even shallower, and his eyes were losing their ability to focus, but his pale face was more determined than ever.

"Willow was my other half," he said. "Without her, I'm just a fraction. Take my canister, get away."

"No!" Rosalie cried, at last losing her composure as she fell to her knees. "I won't lose you, too." She reached to touch his face, feeling his terrifyingly cold, clammy skin before he shoved her hand away.

"Rosalie . . . go . . . "

"No!" she cried. "We're not leaving anyone!"

"Rosalie!" Jax shouted, but it was too late. The titans had heard her voice, and they were coming, their smiling faces hungry and excited as they pulled themselves over the edge of the roof. Jax whirled and drew his swords to face six titans. Four were over ten meters tall.

Rosalie was about to jump up to join the fight when Emmett grabbed her wrist.

"Sorry," he said, smiling sadly as he reached with his other hand to shove his spare canister into the clip on her blade sheath.

"Stop," she ordered. "What are you—"

But Emmett had already slid his hand down her wrist to the handle of her maneuvering gear. He squeezed the trigger, firing Rosalie's hooks into the roof of the building across the street. A second later she was yanked off her feet, hauled up by her wires as they reeled in.

It was only thanks to months of training that she landed on her feet. Yanking her hooks out as fast as she could, Rosalie spun around to leap back across the street. But just as she was about to fire, Emmett began waving his arms.

"Here!" he screamed, grabbing a sword from his holster and drawing it across his shoulder. "Over here, you bastards! Eat me!"

The wound was a deep one, and the titans all froze. The metallic reek of Emmett's blood in the air called to them like a promise. They turned as one, pivoting from Jax to close in on Emmett, whose uniform was now bright red.

"What the hell are you doing?" Jax screamed.

Just before the monsters engulfed him, Emmett yanked his gas canister off his maneuvering gear and threw it. The metal cylinder bounced over the clay roof tiles, bumping to a stop against Jax's boot. But Jax didn't pick it up. He stood and stared in horror as the titans formed a circle around his squad member, their greedy hands reaching down.

"NO!" Rosalie screamed, firing her maneuvering gear. Now that the titans were grouped together, she had a clear spot to land, but it was miles too late. Emmett was already buried inside the circle of flesh-crazed monsters, the smell of blood so overpowering, it made her eyes water.

Rosalie equipped her swords and charged forward anyway, intending to hack through whatever the cost, but Jax grabbed her shoulder. She was sobbing and fighting him when the biggest of the titans, a fat, hairless eleven-meter nightmare with eyes bugging out of his head like a goldfish, raised his sausage-fingered hand to shove something bloody and broken into his mouth. The hunk of red meat didn't even look human anymore, but Rosalie forced herself to watch.

"Rosalie!"

Jax's voice sounded so far away, as if she was underwater. But his face was close, his blue eyes desperate. He hooked the gas canister Emmett had tossed him into place. The moment it clicked, he grabbed Rosalie and then they were in the air. Where to, Rosalie couldn't see. The whole building was sliding sideways as even more titans climbed up following the scent of blood. Under all that weight, the supports couldn't hold, and the two of them swung away just as the structure collapsed with an echoing boom. She was watching the titans wiggle out of the rubble when she felt someone gently shaking her.

"Come on, Rosalie," Jax said. "Don't you dare check out on me."

Checking out sounded like a marvelous idea. They were on a roof across the street, hidden between chimney stacks. It was quiet and safe, and her body felt numb. Nothing hurt. Why should she leave? She was so tired. Why not just rest . . .

"No," Jax said sharply, grabbing her shoulders when she started to slump. "Dammit, Rosalie. Don't quit on me now. Don't let the titans win!"

"But they did win," she whispered. "I couldn't save him."

"It's all right," Jax whispered back.

"It's not," she said, pushing him away so she could curl herself into a ball. "I couldn't save him or Willow. I couldn't do any—"

"Stop," Jax said angrily. "Before you say another word of that nonsense, look down at the street and tell me what you see."

A confused Rosalie looked, but all she saw were titans. There were more of them than ever, big ones and small ones ambling side by side between the empty buildings, their vacant faces stupid and terrifying as they searched for new prey.

"I don't understand," she said, turning back. "It's just titans."

"Exactly," Jax said, smiling. "There's nothing in the streets but titans because *you* bought the people who lived here time to escape. You stopped Woermann from letting the breach fold, and then you came up with the plan that held it. You're the reason Trost isn't becoming another Shiganshina, and because of that, we might be able to take it back. But we can't do anything until we rejoin the rest of the Garrison, and that means *getting to the wall*."

He put his hands on either side of her head and gently turned it toward the white line sparkling like snow in the sunlight across the river, less than a kilometer away.

"Come on," he said, putting his hand in hers. "Let's get out of here so we can start fighting back."

Rosalie squeezed his hand so tight, she heard something crack.

Jax just grinned and squeezed back, reaching down with his other hand to replace her nearly empty canister with the spare from her blade sheath. When she was all hooked up, he said, "Ready?"

Rosalie nodded, letting go of Jax's hand to wipe her eyes before grabbing her maneuvering gear handles. "Let's go."

The river made the rest of their flight easier. Where Rosalie and Jax could hop across the abandoned boats using their maneuvering gear, the titans pursuing them sank into the mud. This slowed them significantly, giving Jax and Rosalie a clear run to the wall and enough gas to get to the top.

After everything that had happened, being back in familiar surroundings felt unspeakably strange. Even the cannons were still in place, though useless now—they were all facing the wrong way, locked on the tracks with their barrels pointed beyond Wall Rose into Maria territory.

But they didn't need cannons. There were no titans up here to get in their way. All they had left to do was jog along the curve of the wall until they reached the point where the arc that encircled Trost met up with the main circle of Wall Rose. It was a trip Rosalie had made a hundred times during patrols, but she'd never before been this tired. All she wanted was to lie down and rest, but she forced herself to keep moving, focusing on the back of Jax's head to keep from falling off the wall.

As they ran, she caught glimpses of the devastation in her peripheral vision. Pillars of smoke and dust; wrecked, tumbled, burned, and smashed buildings; the unmistakable shambling forms that wandered the empty streets, pushing over houses and shouldering aside trees and bridges. There were sounds too. Barking dogs, the avalanche of collapsing walls, and the relentless thunder of hundreds of giant footsteps. Rosalie was trying to take comfort in the fact that she heard no screams when their goal finally came into view.

"There's the gate," Jax said, jogging to a stop. "And still standing!" He grinned across the rooftops at the giant wall of moveable brick—which looked exactly like their own Trost Gate, complete with the cameo of Saint Rose—before turning his smile on Rosalie. "Let's catch our breath here a moment, just in case there's a problem when we get to the—"

A large crash interrupted him. They both spun around, searching below for the source of the noise. "There!" Rosalie said, pointing toward the city center.

Nearly all the way back where they'd come from, in the streets near the Garrison HQ, a fresh plume of dust was rising from a building on the other side of the river. A building with a titan crashed into its side, almost as though it had been thrown into it.

"What the hell is that?" Jax said, lifting his hand to shield his eyes from the sun.

A few blocks away from the building, another titan was stalking down the road. Fifteen meters tall, it towered over the shops and warehouses. Even from this distance, Rosalie could clearly see it was a strange one. Its body had the normal proportions of a human being, with a more muscular physique than most of its kind. Its prominent jaw was square and wide, with flat teeth exposed on the sides as if it had no flesh on its cheeks. Steam curled from its mouth as though it was breathing smoke. But the strangest thing of all was the way it moved. It didn't shamble or charge wildly like other titans. It walked with purpose, striding directly toward the titan who'd just pulled itself out of the collapsed building.

"It's gotta be an aberrant like the Gobbler," Jax muttered. "Strange physique, weird behavior—"

His voice dropped away as Rosalie gasped, and together they watched the strange creature pull back its boulder-sized fist, lining up its shot like a boxer before slamming into the other titan's stupidly leering face.

"Did you see that?!" Rosalie cried, grabbing Jax's arm as the other titan was sent flying, its head dangling from its shoulders. "The aberrant just attacked another titan!"

"I saw it," Jax said, "but I don't believe it. I've never see a titan go after one of its own like that. Never even heard of it."

Rosalie scowled. "Why would he—"

She was cut off by a horrible sound. The aberrant was *roaring.* She'd never heard a titan make a sound before. They were always voiceless, even when you shot their legs off, even when they were giddily squeezing their victims into pulp.

Not this one. It screamed with a furious, haunting cry that echoed through the city. A sound of triumph, madness, death, battle. A sound Rosalie feared would shake loose all the emotions she'd been desperately keeping down for the last hour if they didn't get away.

"Come on," she said, grabbing Jax's arm. "Let's get out of here."

He nodded and they started running again without another word. Behind them, Rosalie could still hear the echoes of the scream, along with more sounds of destruction that she guessed were the doings of the strange new monster. Another time and she would have watched, learned its weaknesses, but she'd seen too many monsters today. She could already feel her earlier numbness from the roof returning, but she couldn't break down yet, so she focused on Jax and forced herself to keep going. One foot in front of the other until, at last, they reached the junction with Wall Rose.

Rosalie almost cried in relief when her feet crossed the line where the Trost Wall met the larger circle of Wall Rose. She was fighting not to flop down right there when Jax pulled her forward.

"We're in luck," he said excitedly, pointing at the top of the inner gate, the same gate Rosalie's carriage had passed through in her mad rush to report to the Garrison, what felt like a lifetime ago. "Looks like most of the Garrison made it through."

Just seeing the soldiers up there lifted the weight on Rosalie's chest. But as she started to run forward, a rifle shot rang out clear and sharp in the afternoon air, and Jax went down like a stone.

CHAPTER FIFTEEN

The gunshot was still echoing when Jax hit the ground, leaving a streak of crimson on the white stone. Rosalie dropped to his side, turning his body over as he gasped in pain. The bullet had landed in his right thigh, and the wound was bleeding like a fountain. As she was ripping off her jacket to bind it, someone grabbed her from behind.

"No!" she screamed, kicking and fighting as a soldier lifted her into the air. "Let me go! He's going to die!"

"Of course he's going to die," said a sneering voice. "That's why we shot him."

Rosalie's head snapped up. While she'd been working to save Jax, a ten-squad of soldiers in Military Police uniforms had surrounded them. The biggest of the men was carrying a rifle, and behind him was Captain Woermann.

"Sir," the officer holding the gun said with a cruel smile, "we got him."

224 · RACHEL AARON

"Excellent," Woermann replied, looking down at Jax with terrifying hate. "Sergeant Cunningham is a traitor. He attacked his fellow Garrison soldiers and threatened his superior officer."

"That was me!" Rosalie said frantically, struggling against the soldier holding her fast while the pool of blood beneath Jax's leg grew. "Punish me, not him!"

"I would," Woermann said. "But as you were so quick to point out back at the gate, you're noble. That means your fate lies in the hands of the king. This filth, though . . . "

His voice trailed off as he lifted his leg to place his boot on Jax's heaving chest. Jax wheezed under the weight, but his glare was pure murder as he grabbed the captain's foot. "I can still throw you off the wall before you kill me," he said through clenched teeth.

"Don't be ridiculous," Woermann replied, his eyes shining cruelly. "We're not going to kill you here." He leaned closer, putting more weight on Jax's chest. "A quick death is too good for a traitor like you. In situations such as these, examples need to be made. As soon as the Trost situation stabilizes, we're going to hang you in front of the entire Garrison."

Woermann removed his boot. "Patch him up so he doesn't bleed out and throw him in the brig," he ordered. "We'll hang him as soon as approval comes back from high command."

"Yes, sir," the Military Police officer said, glancing at Rosalie. "And the private?"

"Throw her in as well," Woermann said. "I'll inform her father."

The soldiers saluted, and the man holding Rosalie began to drag her away. She fought him as hard as she could, digging her nails into his and kicking her heels against his legs until, with a curse, he struck her over the head, sending the whole world dark.

❧ ❧ ❧

Rosalie bolted upright, wincing as the motion sent a wave of pain through her aching head. She was in a shadowed room on a stone floor. Woermann must have made good on his threat to put them in the brig, because she saw iron bars as well. She was looking for a door when she spotted Jax sitting against the wall in the adjacent cell. His leg was bandaged, which was a relief, but his face was terrifyingly pale. She was about to ask if he was all right when Jax tilted his head at the corridor beyond the bars.

Confused, Rosalie turned to see a standing figure silhouetted in front of the jail's only torch. Between his Military Police uniform and the terrible light, she assumed he was a guard. Then he stepped forward, the flickering light shifting to reveal the familiar face of Charles Dumarque.

"Father!" Rosalie gasped, standing up. "What are you—how did—"

General Dumarque pushed a key into the lock of her cell door and swung it open. "Come," he ordered. Then, to Rosalie's shock, he turned and unlocked Jax's cell as well.

"Can you walk?" he asked Jax, his voice devoid of emotion.

"I can hobble if someone helps me," Jax replied, casting a nervous look at Rosalie. "Why?"

Instead of answering, Lord Dumarque snapped his fingers, and a guard who'd been lurking in the hallway entered and hoisted Jax to his feet.

"Father, what's going on?" Rosalie asked as the guard shuffled Jax out of the cell.

"The consequences of your actions," Lord Dumarque replied, his voice deadly. "Come with me and don't say a word. Not one word, Rosalie, do you understand?"

She nodded, following him silently out of the brig. Other soldiers were waiting in the hall outside. Her father's men, Rosalie realized. They escorted the prisoners up and out of the small jail and

226 · RACHEL AARON

into the chaos of the Garrison at war.

It was still daylight. They were in the base on the other side of the Rose Gate from Trost. All around, soldiers scrambled past them, hauling supplies, marching off in small squads, helping injured comrades. Lord Dumarque ignored all of it, letting his guards clear their path toward the base of Wall Rose, which loomed like a cliff over their heads.

When they arrived at one of the lift stations, Rosalie watched as a giant platform was slowly lowered down the wall. When it reached the ground, a dozen wounded soldiers staggered off. Some were missing limbs, the stumps of their arms and legs tied off with crude field dressings. Many had so much blood on their uniforms, it was impossible to tell what Garrison unit they were from. But all of them had the same distant look, their blank eyes moving over Rosalie without seeing her as they shuffled past.

When the wounded had cleared the platform, the soldiers manning the lift saluted, and Charles Dumarque, his escort, and the prisoners stepped aboard. At least Rosalie stepped aboard. Jax had to be carried, his body slumping between the two soldiers holding him up. The scrape of his pained breaths was like a knife in her ears, causing Rosalie to shake as she moved closer to her father. "Why are you taking us to the top of Wall Rose?"

"Because I have no other choice," Lord Dumarque said, keeping his eyes straight ahead as the lift began to rise. "Congratulations, Rosalie. You've finally gotten yourself into more trouble than even I can get you out of. Now we're both going to have to play it by ear. Just let me do the talking, and we'll see if I can't save the life you seem so determined to throw away."

His tone was coldly furious, but Rosalie didn't even flinch. Now that the shock of seeing him had faded, all she wanted to do was wrap her arms around him and tell him how much it meant that he'd rushed from Wall Sina into a city besieged by titans for her sake.

"Thank you," she whispered as the lift creaked to a stop.

Lord Dumarque dismissed her words with an angry jab of his hand and walked onto the top of the wall. Captain Woermann was already there, and next to him, looking out over the smoking city of Trost like he owned it, was a bald old man with a neatly trimmed mustache and sly eyes. His uniform was identical to every other Rose Garrison officer, but Rosalie knew him immediately, and she stopped with a gasp.

"What?" Jax whispered nervously, struggling to stand on his own as Dumarque's guards positioned him beside her. "Who is that?"

"That's Dot Pixis!" Rosalie whispered back, her voice frantic. "He's the Garrison's High Commander for the entire Southern Defense!"

Jax's pale face turned even paler. "What's he doing here?"

Considering what was happening, the High Commander's presence at Trost was practically mandatory, but Rosalie understood what Jax meant. Why would the High Commander be *here*, with them? She was wondering the same thing when Woermann stepped forward.

"That's them, High Commander!" he cried, flinging out his hand to point at Rosalie and Jax. "Cunningham attacked my soldiers on Brigitte Morris's order, and Rosalie Dumarque led a mutiny against me to seize command of the Trost Gate for herself. I demand they be punished to the fullest extent!"

"So you have said many times," Dot Pixis replied, sipping from the flask he carried before turning to face Rosalie and Jax.

"With respect, High Commander," Lord Dumarque said stiffly, "this man is a fool. Rosalie Dumarque is noble. Her fate is the king's alone to decide."

Rosalie blinked in surprise. She'd never heard such genuine deference in her father's voice when speaking to another military officer. Woermann, however, seemed to be finding new shades of red for his face.

"She's a traitor!" he yelled in Lord Dumarque's face. "The king will say the same!"

"She's my daughter!" Lord Dumarque yelled back.

"Gentlemen," the High Commander said, raising his hand, "I've heard both of your arguments already. I don't have time to hear them again. The plans to retake Trost will be back from my strategist any moment."

"Retake Trost?" Rosalie said, eyes wide. "You're going to retake the city?!"

"We're going to try," Pixis said, looking her up and down. "You're Private Dumarque?"

"Yes, sir," Rosalie said, cringing as she remembered to whom she was speaking. "Forgive me for speaking out of turn, sir."

"That's the least of your worries right now," the High Commander said with a chuckle. Then his face grew serious. "Do you understand the charges against you?"

When both Jax and Rosalie nodded, Commander Pixis stepped closer. "Tell me what happened at the Trost Gate."

With a deep breath and a glance at Jax, Rosalie told him. She told him about the Colossal Titan's attack and the desperate gambit to keep the titans from coming through the gate. About Captain Woermann's arrival and the order to retreat, about Brigitte's refusal and death. She told him about the cannon round and how the Trost Garrison soldiers had bravely held the gate until the bitter end. She told him about running through the city, about losing Willow and Emmett.

She told Pixis the whole story, but it was her father she was truly speaking to. She wanted him to hear what had happened so he'd understand why she'd done what she'd done. She would have looked straight at him if she could, but she didn't dare take her eyes off the High Commander. So she continued, reciting everything exactly as it happened until she reached the present moment.

When at last she fell silent, Commander Pixis turned to Jax. "Is this your account as well?"

"Yes, sir," Jax replied.

"You see?" Woermann said, shooting a victorious sneer at Lord Dumarque, who looked shell-shocked. "They both admit it was mutiny!"

"It was," Commander Pixis agreed. "Private Dumarque's story matches what I've heard from other survivors of the Vanguard." He looked sadly at Rosalie and Jax. "They are traitors."

"The *boy* is a traitor," Lord Dumarque said desperately. "Hang him, but give my daughter back to me!"

"She may have been born yours," Commander Pixis said. "But the moment she signed her enlistment, she became a solider of the Garrison, and soldiers must answer to military law."

"But she—"

Pixis stopped Lord Dumarque's argument with a wave of his hand, stepping forward until he was standing face-to-face with Jax and Rosalie.

"Brigitte Morris was an old friend of mine," he said, reaching out to steady Jax, who was listing to the side. "She wrote to me just the other day asking for permission to recommend that a particularly troublesome squad be transferred to the Survey Corps." He smiled. "That was you?"

There was no way he didn't already know the answer, but Jax and Rosalie dutifully nodded.

"The Survey Corps," Lord Dumarque whispered, his face horrified. "Rosalie, you *didn't*."

"Did you accept?" Commander Pixis asked, speaking over the general.

"Yes, sir," Rosalie said, doing her best not to look at her panicking father. "We all signed up together. We were going to transfer as a squad, but then . . . "

She couldn't finish. Telling the story of Willow and Emmett's deaths once already had almost been too much. Fortunately, Commander Pixis seemed to understand.

"The loss of comrades is always hard," he said gently. "But to die in battle protecting your home and your comrades is a soldier's greatest honor. Why did you agree to join the Survey Corps? Most who seek out the Scouts do so because they have nothing else left, but you have a good home and a loving family. Why would you leave that world for such dangerous work? Is this just a way to escape your safe, dull life in Sina?"

Rosalie's cheeks began to burn. "There was a bit of that at first, sir," she admitted. "I joined the Garrison because I wanted to prove myself. I used to look at Wall Rose on the horizon and hate the fact that it was there. I thought I knew better, that I could beat the titans and show everyone, but that was before I served in the Garrison. I understand now how important it is to shield the people so we can hold on to what we have. Brigitte taught me that, and Jax, and Emmett and Willow and everyone else. So many Garrison soldiers gave everything to protect us today, and I deeply respect that, but . . . "

"But?" Pixis said, arching an eyebrow.

"But by itself, holding on to what we have left is not enough," Rosalie finished, clenching her fists. "Important as the Garrison's work is, we can't defend forever. If we're ever going to beat the titans, somebody has to go beyond the walls and take back what we've lost. Lieutenant Brigitte said that being in the military means putting your life on the line, but if I'm going to stake my life on something, I want it to count. I want to put the titan-killing skills I've learned to the best possible use;. And for me, that's the Survey Corps."

"The lure of the Wings of Freedom is strong indeed," Pixis said wistfully as he turned to Jax. "What about you, Sergeant Cunningham? Did you feel the same?"

"Not exactly, sir," Jax said, glancing nervously at Rosalie. "Rosalie had high ideals from the start, but I joined the Garrison because it was a job that kept me fed and let me kill titans. I've seen a lot of good soldiers die in the years since, but there never seemed to be a point. No matter how good we did our jobs, life never got better. Food was still scarce. The city was still crowded with refugees. Titans kept coming. I thought that was how it would always be, but then—"

He coughed several times, then caught his breath and continued. "But Rosalie and Willow and Emmett . . . they took everything I could throw at them. I came to trust them with my life. So when they told me about the transfer, I figured I ought to listen. I've always known that being a soldier meant risking my life, but I'm no more dead outside the walls than I'd be on top of them. If I was in the Survey Corps, though, there's a chance my death might actually change something for the better. That seemed like a good trade, so I took it."

Rosalie swallowed. Jax's eyes had stayed on her the entire time. Pixis must have seen that as well, because his smile warmed.

"Those are good answers," he said, turning to walk back to the edge of the wall. "You both seem to be good soldiers. I just wish you'd been wiser ones."

"Sir?" Rosalie said, confused.

"Treason is not something we can take lightly," Pixis replied solemnly, his arms folded tight behind his back as he stared down at the titan-filled city. He turned to Captain Woermann and General Dumarque. "By their own admission, Rosalie Dumarque and Jackson Cunningham are guilty of mutiny against a superior officer, the punishment for which is death, traditionally by public hanging. However . . ."

He glanced down the wall at the gate, where the Garrison was still evacuating stragglers from the city. "These are extraordinary times. Morale is very low, and the troops are afraid. A public execution would only make that worse. Therefore"—he turned to Rosalie and Jax—"as High Commander, I will accept the burden and execute your sentence myself."

He pulled his pistol from his belt.

"No!" Lord Dumarque cried, lunging forward to place himself between Pixis and Rosalie. "High Commander, *please*, this is my daughter. My little girl."

"That doesn't matter to the law," Pixis said.

"What about the lives she saved?" he cried, his voice closer to tears than Rosalie had ever heard. "Is this how the military recognizes heroism? What will the soldiers think?"

"They'll think nothing's more important than obeying orders," Woermann replied, contempt dripping from his voice. "Which is the only way a military can function."

"You coward, Woermann!" Dumarque shouted. "You can hide behind the law, but *nothing* will save you from my retaliation if you go through with this!"

Woermann staggered back as though struck. "How—how dare you threaten me! I'm a captain of the Garrison!"

Lord Dumarque proceeded to tell Woermann exactly what he thought he was, but Rosalie wasn't listening anymore. Instead, she reached for Jax's hand. He met her halfway, his eyes so full of sadness and pride that there was no need for words. He knew as well as she did that this was the end. They'd done the right thing. They'd held the gate, protected hundreds of thousands of lives. If they had to die for that, she'd count it a cheap price for what they'd saved that day.

"It's all right, Father," she said, reaching out to touch his shoulder. "I'm ready to accept—"

"No!" he shouted, whirling around and grabbing her so fast, he nearly knocked her over. "Don't be stupid, Rosalie! You're a noble, and you're still engaged to the Smythes! They already paid for you. If you die, they lose their investment. That gives us a suit for damages against the Garrison. We can petition the king for your life!"

"What about Jax's life?"

"He's common," Lord Dumarque said dismissively. "Nothing can save him. But you—"

Rosalie set her jaw. "If Jax gets shot, I get shot."

"Now hold on a moment," Jax said, his eyes wide. "I didn't know we could bring the king into this. Rosalie, maybe you should—"

"No," she said stubbornly. "There's no point in dragging this out. We committed the same crime, we'll face the same fate."

"Do you not understand what's going to happen, Rosalie?" her father said, his voice truly frantic. I can still get you out of this if you'll just stop—"

"I won't stop," she said, stepping around her father to face Pixis, who'd been watching silently. "The commander has already handed down our sentence, and I don't dispute it. We *did* commit mutiny at the Trost Gate, and I would do it again. Because if we'd followed Woermann's orders and retreated, half the city would have died to-day. If being shot is the price for that, then I'll pay it gladly."

Lord Dumarque began to sputter, but Pixis silenced him with a look. "Is this your final word?" he asked, turning back to Rosalie. When she and Jax nodded together, the High Commander smiled and holstered his pistol.

"What are you doing?" Woermann demanded.

"You're sparing her," Lord Dumarque said, his body slumping in relief. Rosalie wobbled as well, her knees nearly giving out as her body realized it wasn't going to die. But though the Commander had put away his weapon, he was still shaking his head.

"I'm not sparing anyone," Pixis said firmly. "The law must be enforced equally if we are to have order. But while the punishment for mutiny is death, Garrison regulation doesn't specify *how* they must die." He touched the pistol at his hip. "I don't feel this is an appropriate time to waste good bullets or good soldiers, so I'm sentencing Rosalie Dumarque and Jackson Cunningham to the Survey Corps instead, effective immediately."

Woermann looked at the High Commander like a child whose favorite toy had just been snatched away. "You can't do that! They *wanted* to go to Survey Corps! You're supposed to sentence them to death!"

Pixis shrugged. "Given the mortality rate of the average Survey Corps soldier, no one can argue it's not a death sentence. *And* it puts two brave and proven effective soldiers back on the field at a time when we need them most. Personally, I think it's quite an elegant solution. My only regret is that I'm losing them to Erwin." He smiled at Rosalie. "You would have made an excellent Garrison officer, Private Dumarque."

Rosalie dropped her eyes. "Thank you, sir," she whispered, her voice thick.

"You're most welcome," Dot Pixis said, turning to his aide, who'd just come running down the wall.

"Sir," the adjutant said, barely stopping to salute before she blurted out her message. "We have the Yeager plan ready for your review."

"Excellent," the commander replied, pulling out his flask again. "I'll be right down. You're dismissed, Woermann."

The captain gaped for another good ten seconds before turning on his heel and stomping down the wall, his soldiers trailing behind him like frightened mice.

"Get Sergeant Cunningham to the infirmary and patch him up," Pixis ordered. As the soldiers ran to fetch the medical squad, he turned back to Lord Dumarque. "Charles, please escort your daughter to the infirmary as well. When they're both well and rested, the Survey Corps will deal with them."

Lord Dumarque nodded sharply, keeping his hand firmly on Rosalie's arm as the medical team arrived.

Jax went down the moment the medics touched him. Rosalie held his hand until they laid him on the stretcher, and then the medics carted him off, leaving her alone with her father.

"Father," she said, clutching her hands together. "I—"

Lord Dumarque grabbed her by the shoulders. Rosalie thought he was going to shake her, but instead he wrapped his arms around her, pulling his daughter into the biggest hug she could ever remember receiving from him.

"I'm so happy you're alive," he whispered into her hair. "When I heard about Trost, I was sure you were dead. Even learning you'd been charged with treason was a relief because it meant you were alive. But then Pixis pulled that gun and I . . . " He hugged her tighter. "I'm so glad you're alive, Rosalie."

Rosalie squeezed her eyes shut. "I'm happy I'm alive, too," she said in a small voice. "So many died today and I . . . " Her voice faded as she hugged him back tighter than she'd known she could.

"It's all right," he said. "You made it. The titans came, but you survived." His voice warmed. "You took command, as a Dumarque should. They can call it treason all they want, but you honored the family when you rebuked that idiot Woermann and held the line. I hate that you had to do it, I hate that you were there at all, but I'm proud of you, Rosalie." His voice cracked. "I'm so proud."

Rosalie took a deep breath. This wasn't the first time he'd told her he was proud, but he'd never sounded so sincere. "Does this mean you'll support me in the Survey Corps?"

Lord Dumarque stepped back as though stung. "Absolutely not."

"But you just said—"

"Did you not hear the High Commander?" he snapped. "Erwin's crusade is a death sentence! Just because I'm proud of what you did at the breach doesn't mean I want you to do it again! What kind of father lets his daughter walk into titans?"

"One who trusts her to beat them," Rosalie said fiercely. "The war isn't lost, Father. We can fight back, just as we did today. We can win."

"Nothing in Trost was won today," Lord Dumarque said. "I

don't know what insanity Pixis is planning, but—"

"At least he's trying!" Rosalie cried. "If we don't do that, then we've already lost!"

"You're the one I don't want to lose," her father said, his voice thick with hurt and anger. "Let someone else try. You belong at home!"

"No, I don't," Rosalie replied. "I'm a Dumarque. A solider, just like you. I know you need me to get married for the money, but—"

"Forget the money!" he cried, clutching her shoulders. "You're my child! I love you and I don't want you to die. Why is this so hard for you to understand?"

"I do understand," she whispered, reaching up to touch his face. "I love you too, but I have to do this. If you're truly proud of me, you'll understand."

Lord Dumarque clutched her hand to his cheek. "I won't stop trying to bring you home," he said angrily. "I'll ride with the Survey Corps all the way to Maria myself if I must, but I'll find some way to bring you back."

"I know you'll try," Rosalie said, patting her father's hand.

ONE WEEK LATER

"I knew you'd be here."

Rosalie looked over her shoulder with a smile. She was sitting on top of the gate. *Their* gate, at the southern tip of Trost. High above, wispy clouds were dispersing to reveal a brilliant blue sky, bathing the repaired cannons and rails in sunlight as Jax hobbled toward her, as dexterous on his crutches as he was with his maneuvering gear.

"And I'm surprised you weren't up here already," Rosalie said with a grin as he lowered himself beside her, settling into their old spot.

"I'm a bit slow on account of this." He patted his bandaged leg. "But the doctor says I'll be up again in no time. In the meanwhile, you'll just have to put up with me lagging."

"After how you were when we first met, I can put up with anything," Rosalie said, leaning in to brush a kiss against his lips.

She'd meant it to be brief, but Jax caught her head with his hand, holding her gently as he deepened the kiss until she was breathless.

"So," she said shakily when he finally released her, "only an hour before we ship out to Survey Corps headquarters. Last chance to enjoy the view."

"Can't say I've ever enjoyed it," Jax said, looking down at the abandoned fields dotted with spring wildflowers. "But I have to admit, it feels different now. When I looked out there before, all I could think about was what the titans had taken from me. My family, my sister, my home, it was all just . . . pain, you know?" He rubbed his chest. "I don't think that'll ever go away completely. But when I look out there now, there's more to it. I feel like I can see beyond what happened. Beyond the titans." His cheeks colored. "That doesn't make any sense."

"It makes perfect sense," Rosalie said, swinging her legs over the edge of the wall. "The whole reason I wanted to come here was because, when I looked off my roof, this was what I saw." She rapped her knuckles on the stone. "I thought Wall Rose was the end of the world, but I know now that's wrong. It's the beginning."

She looked down at the fields splashed with new green. No titans were visible today. Just flocks of geese arrowing across the last delicate clouds, flying in for summer.

"We're going to make the world bigger," she promised. "We're going to push back so hard, the titans will be the ones who run. When that happens, this wall will be nothing but a line between one part of our world and the next."

"There will always be walls," Jax said.

"Will there?" Rosalie turned to him. "When I was little, my grandmother used to tell me stories about a time when there were no walls. Just a big open world where people could come and go wherever they pleased. I always thought it was a fairy tale, but if we beat the titans, why couldn't it be possible?"

"You're asking the wrong guy," Jax said uncomfortably. "I'm still coming to grips with the idea of willingly going beyond this wall. But if you believe it, I'll believe it."

"Okay then," she said, putting out her hand. "You and me, we'll do it."

"Do what?"

"Fight for the end," she said proudly. "The end of the end of the world."

Jax looked confused for a moment, and then a smile spread over his face as he grabbed her palm in his. "To the end of the end of the world," he promised, squeezing her hand. "Or die trying."

Rosalie nodded and turned back to the horizon, resting her head on his shoulder as they stared together at the world that would someday be theirs once again.